THE FIFTH DOOR

By

Roy M. Burgess

ROY M. BURGESS

Yorkshire born and bred; Roy was once an IT manager. This involved sitting in a cubicle and making stuff up. Having retired from this high-octane lifestyle, he now sits in his home office and makes stuff up.

Roy spends a lot of time staring out of the window from his tower – yes, he lives in the tower of a converted mill – at the Leeds-Liverpool canal. Music is a constant companion to his writing.

THE FIFTH DOOR

First published in Great Britain by Mill Tower Books 2025. This paperback edition published by Mill Tower Books in 2025.

A CIP catalogue record for this book is available from the British Library.

ISBN: 978-1-7394807-4-5

Ebook: 978-1-739480-7-6

PRAISE FOR ROY M. BURGESS

The Price We Pay

An excellent first for an author whose other series got me hooked with my preferred fictional theme of escapism and humour. Now I find myself enjoying detective thrillers, something I thought I'd left behind a couple of decades ago.'

CK01 on Amazon ☆☆☆☆☆

The Fifth Series

Have read all three books in five days. Please let there be more!! Addictive, funny, enjoyable, and beautifully written. Please keep them coming.

P. Wells on Amazon ☆☆☆☆☆

The Fifth Series

These tales are genuinely refreshing and beautifully crafted reads. The characters are immensely likeable and utterly relatable and I enjoyed every page with them.

George McCarron on Amazon ☆☆☆☆☆

ALSO BY ROY M. BURGESS

The Fifth Series

The Misadventures of Frankie Dale:

The Fifth Tweet

The Fifth Thunderbolt

The Fifth Man

The Fifth Door

DI Carrie Taylor

The Price We Pay

Coming Soon:

Fair Play

For Ruth,

Who encouraged me to write and inspires me every day.

Ruth Burgess 1969-2018

1

2019

Had Jen fallen asleep? Her breathing was slowing. This had been the perfect Saturday evening. The monkfish masala was a masterpiece, if I say so myself. My newly found culinary skills were just another facet of my life that had changed so much over the last couple of years. Who'd have thought that the pathetic, recently dumped me who'd sat alone in The Crown that night would now have a loving family and a killer recipe for fish curry? It was all down to Ambrose. He challenged me to change my life based on the next five tweets in my timeline. As a result, I met and ended up engaged to Robbie. I had a successful online business from writing a silly little story. That was thanks to meeting Jen at a writing workshop. I thought life was good, right up until Robbie scarpered with all my money. Turns out her dad was a criminal mastermind. Well, maybe not a mastermind. He got caught. Both he and Robbie are in prison for what they did.

Jen changed everything. We decided to write together. Since then, we've made a successful, small-budget film, and I've written a series of children's books. Oh, and we solved a murder, and turned that into a hit TV show. Did I mention that I fell arse over apex in love with Jen? For reasons known only to her, she fell in love with me, too. At the risk of tempting fate, life was good again. In fact, my main problem now was the aftereffects of the fish masala. If Jen was asleep, that was easily solved. I shifted my hips a little and relaxed. That was better.

'Why did you never do that before we were married?'

Not asleep then.

'Lack of confidence, I suppose.'

'There'll be a lack of something else if you do it again. Now open a window.'

Jen was laughing, but I knew not to push it. Instead, I topped up both glasses. This was nice. I was comfortable, relaxed and, yes, happy. Then she said something that struck fear and panic into my heart.

'Happy anniversary, darling,' said Jen.

Panic. I pictured my brain exploding. What's today's date? Who the hell knew that? Certainly not me since I'd started working for myself. March somethingth, surely? We got married in September. First time we, you know…No. That was May – cup final weekend. Eden Hazard scored because I remember thinking – not important now. Think. What anniversary is it? I must've squeaked slightly as Jen had shifted in her seat and was staring at me. I was about to squeak again when she put me out of my misery.

'Six months. It's our half anniversary. Don't tell me you'd forgotten?'

'No, of course, half anniversary, I knew that.'

Who is this creature I've been married to for the last six months (apparently)? How did I not know that she's the kind of woman who celebrates half anniversaries? More to the point, what the hell should I do now?

'So, have you got me an extravagant gift, my sweet?'

How could I have got myself into this?

'I…that is, it's…'

Squeak.

Jen burst into what I can only describe as a cackle.

'Got you. Who gets gifts for half-versaries? Plonker.'

Sometimes I think I'm too nice. I joined in the laughter, relieved that my heart looked like it was going to survive the major panic. I held out my arm and Jen took the hint, snuggling closer. She curled her legs up onto the sofa.

'Six months, eh? Where does the time go?'

'We've achieved quite a lot in that time,' said Jen.

'Have we?'

'Apart from finishing *Burning Down the House* and getting nominated for an award, let me see. We moved all your records in here, for one thing. Maybe you could build those units you mentioned, rather than just having them piled up in the corner.'

'Nicely done. I can take a hint.'

'Really? You haven't taken it for the last three months.'

I was being got at. It's not like I'd been totally inactive on the DIY front. I'd hung two frames in the hall. Admittedly, the one with Charley's picture of Ziggy Stardust was a second attempt after the first fell down. I think the nail was defective. The second one was the mysterious envelope in a frame. A wedding present from Joe and Rupert. The lettering just said, *In case of relationship emergency – break glass*. We had no clue what was inside and, I suspected, we never would.

'Time just seems to pass so quickly these days. They say time flies when you're happy.'

'If my dad's right, it's going to fly a lot faster now. He reckons it speeds up once you hit forty. And you, my slightly whiffy husband, hit that milestone months ago.'

'What? That can't be right. I'm still the young and virile red-carpet newcomer I was when we met.'

'How's the clicky knee?'

'Fair point. Actually, the other one's started as well.'

I tried to stretch for my glass but couldn't reach. Jen lifted slightly, and I tried again, making the kind of noise I'd heard my dad make whenever he got out of a chair. When did that happen?

'Relax, old man. I'll get it for you. Any idea what you'd like for your team birthday?'

The team birthday was a new concept, dreamt up by Jen. I'd been moaning in the pub about having to remember so many birthdays when she suggested we all celebrate on one day to make it easier. Everyone around the table agreed and the team birthday was born. Secretly, I was looking forward to a big party without looking too excited. I was trying to be cool, pretending to forget the details.

'I usually get socks. Have done since I left school.'

'But I'm not your mother. Surely we can do better than that?'

'What do you get the man who has everything?'

'So you don't want anything?'

'Let me think about it,' I said, not wanting the chance of presents to disappear. 'Actually, maybe a beard trimmer,' I said, running a hand over the luxuriant recent addition.

'That scraggly thing needs trimming?'

'It's not scraggly. OK, maybe a bit. It'll grow on you.'

'I'll have you know a lot of time and money is spent making sure I don't grow a beard.' She took a sip of wine. 'A trimmer would be a good idea. You'd probably look quite distinguished with it trimmed.'

'That's better. Thank you.'

Just then, there was a shout from upstairs. Charley was awake.

'I'll go,' said Jen. I listened carefully, but neither of her knees clicked. OK, I suppose she's younger than me. Watching Jen head for the stairs, I took a sip of wine.

Charley had adapted well to Uncle Frankie becoming her mum's new husband. Uncle Frankie had adapted well to moving into this small, welcoming house. I was happy, apart from the prospect of a trip to IKEA for some units to house the records. The boxes in the corner were mounting at an alarming rate. Thanks to a combination of earning decent money and having best mates who owned a record shop, the collection was growing. Joe was like a pusher. He knew exactly what I wouldn't be able to resist and, more often than not, just seemed to have a copy in the storeroom.

Certainly, life had changed over the last three years. Just after Cheryl dumped me and made off with my business partner, Ambrose had come up with the Five Tweet Challenge. It certainly changed everything, although there have been a few bumps in the road. Being robbed and jilted by my then fiancée was a big bump. But it worked out well. I wouldn't have been with Jen if things had gone according to that plan. I wouldn't swap Jen for anything or anybody.

Rupert was Robbie's brother and had served time for his role in the fiasco. Since his release, we'd become even better friends, and he's now married to another good friend, Joe. It's all a bit complicated. Rupert had mentioned Robbie would be released from prison at some point in the next few months. Hopefully, she'll have the good sense to move away from the area and start her life again.

Jen was back.

'Apparently, madam has decided she wants to join the next school strike and had to let me know she was going to stop the sea from getting higher,' said Jen as she snuggled under my arm again.

'That's nice. Hang on, she's six. How does she know about the student strike and global warming?'

'She's taken to watching the news with Grandad when she stays over. Think I need to have a word with him.'

'Sounds like she's better informed than me.'

'She's certainly more focussed when it comes to what she wants for birthdays. Unlike somebody else...'

'But it was my birthday months ago.'

'And you insisted on being a grump and not having a party. Team birthday is non-negotiable.'

'When is it again?'

'First Saturday in June every year. It's genius. Come on. Instead of having to remember all the different birthdays we all celebrate on the same day – our team birthday. Big party. Everybody happy. And just for you, grumpy bollocks, nobody has to stand around while the rest of us sing *Happy Birthday*.'

'And that covers everyone?'

'Except me and Charley, obviously. Forget those and your history, pal.'

Looks like I had no choice. Being forty had made me wise.

'Actually, I've thought of something that would make my life complete.'

'Is it the twelve-inch single of 'Contact' by Edwin Starr on white vinyl?'

'No. Although that would be kind of cool. Where on Earth did you get that idea from?'

'Something Joe mentioned in the pub last night when you were talking to Ambrose. Well?'

'Well, what?'

'What would make your life complete?'

I took a deep breath.

'How about a brother or sister for Charley?'

'But I've told Joe we'll have the white vinyl now.'

Was she avoiding an answer? The pause stretched a lot longer than I'd hoped. Eventually, she sat up and turned to face me.

'Are you serious?'

'Of course.'

'It's just such a big step. I thought the idea was to get the writing career established properly. Then there's my dad. He's in remission just now, but who knows…?'

'Even more reason not to wait. Look, if we hang about five years, you'd still be a youngish mum.'

'Youngish? If you want to retain the ability to father a child, be very careful what you say next.'

'OK. Young. You'd still only be mid-thirties. But by the time he started school, I'd be fifty. I'd be in my mid-sixties when he left.'

'So, it's a boy, then?'

'That one is. I figured maybe one of each.'

'Why stop at two? Why not go for the whole football team?'

'I'm up for it, if you are.'

'Over my dead body. I love Charley dearly, but the thought of another ten of her. Not a chance. Suppose I could cope with the idea of one, though.'

'Really?'

'Yes. Why not? Let's do it.' I looked at my watch. Jen punched my thigh. 'I didn't mean right this minute.'

'Why not? *Match of the Day's* not on for another hour.'

'Thin ice, pal. Very thin ice.' Jen giggled as she put her hand on mine. Then I did that thing that I do.

'Tell you what. Do that again and you might be in with a shout. Lineker might have to wait a bit.'

2

With work on the TV series finished, I found myself in the unusual position of having nothing to do on Monday afternoon. The world-class husband in me was heading to IKEA to get the units. All too soon, the lazy-arse husband in me was taking over. I parked outside the record shop/music venue owned by Joe and Ambrose. As I walked through the door, the speakers boomed out Jean Knight's 'Mr Big Stuff'.

Joe shouted above the music.

'Ladies and gentlemen, please welcome the award-winning writer of *Burning Down the House*, mister big bollocks himself, Frankie Dale.'

Joe and Ambrose applauded wildly as I waved regally, picking my way down the stairs.

'Too kind. Too kind. Would you like me to sign something for you?'

'No. But I'll make you a cup of tea. Kettle's on,' said Joe, shaking my hand. Ambrose turned the volume down and joined us.

'Anyway, it's only a SCRIPTY, not the BAFTA we wanted,' I said. 'But a cuppa would go down nicely, especially if you've got biscuits too.'

The three of us trooped into the back room. A plush, red chaise longue was the latest addition to the once tatty office.

'Very classy,' I said, taking a seat.

'Bit of an indulgence,' said Joe. 'It's not really for work, just storing it until the house is ready.'

'House? What house?'

Ambrose rolled his eyes.

'You've started him now. Here, have a couple of Hob-nobs. You could be a while.'

'He's only jealous,' said Joe.

'Fair enough. It does look spectacular, but there's so much work to do.'

Ambrose ferried two mugs of tea across, and Joe unfolded a piece of paper from his pocket.

'What do you think of this beauty?'

'It's a carpet shop,' I said.

'Is that all you see?'

I looked again.

'It's a carpet shop with a scruffy garage falling down at the side of it.'

'Peasant,' said Joe. 'What you see is a beautiful art déco cinema with many original features, tastefully converted to a residential palace, set in landscaped gardens.'

'It's a carpet shop.'

Ambrose could see I was winding Joe up and tried to suppress his laughter.

'I thought you were the one with the imagination. This philistine, I expect to take the piss.' He jerked a thumb at Ambrose. 'But you. You should be able to visualise the possibilities.'

'I can see you selling a lot of carpets.'

'Like I said. Peasant.' Joe folded the paper. I stopped him and looked again.

'I'm just winding you up. It looks amazing. Can you really get planning permission to convert it?'

'Apparently so. It will cost an absolute fortune, but my Rupert is worth it. Well, I am at any rate. Sometimes, you have to make the big gesture to keep the fizz in a marriage.'

'You see, that's where I disagree,' said Ambrose. 'Don't get me wrong. I think it's a beautiful old building and will make a spectacular home. I just don't think you need the grand gesture. It's the hundred and one small gestures that really makes a marriage work. Remembering birthdays. Taking the bins out. Wearing the odd costume. Don't ask. Just do the things that'll make your partner happy.'

'But converting a cinema into a house seems a lot easier than going to IKEA and putting cupboards together,' I said with a shudder.

They both agreed that I had a point. We all took a slurp of tea before a loud beep signified the entry of a customer.

'I'll go,' said Ambrose.

Joe offered me another biscuit.

'How's married life treating you?'

'It's great. Couldn't be better. Six months and still going strong. Actually, we might be in the market for a new house, too.'

'Really? Tell me more.'

'It's just…' I hesitated. Joe was a good mate, but should I really be sharing this?

'Is she up the duff?'

'What a quaint turn of phrase. No. She's not up the duff. Not yet, anyway.'

'But you're trying? That's fabulous. I'm thrilled for you. Have you started yet?'

'Bit of a personal question.'

'Looking for a house. Not – you know. I assumed you were already doing that.'

I grinned again.

'No, not yet. To be honest, it hadn't occurred to me before today. Jen's house is lovely, but it's a bit small. Adding me and all my stuff in is a bit of a squeeze. Another child would be too much.'

'I'll give you the number of Tania. Dreadful gossip, but a magician when it comes to finding the right property. Trust me. She'll find you something spectacular. Just wait till I tell Rupert. He'll be so excited for you.'

'Slow down. I think I should at least mention it to Jen first. It is quite a big step. That house means so much to her.'

'Of course. I'm getting carried away. Any idea what you'd be looking for?'

'I've no clue. Something with plenty of built in storage so I don't have to go near IKEA would be perfect.'

'Call Tania. May as well get the ball rolling. She'll find the perfect home and you can present it as a token of your eternal devotion.'

'Sounds expensive.'

'You're making good money now. At least, I hope you are?'

I shrugged and nodded.

'Can't complain.'

'What's your next project?'

'No idea. We decided to take some time out to rest before we start again.'

'That must be great, to have the time to do exactly what you want. How's it going?'

'I was supposed to be at IKEA this afternoon. That suggests it's going a bit shit, really. I'm a bit bored.'

'Find a house. Let that be your project. Once you get moved in, you can come up with the next great film script.'

'It would get me out of going to IKEA. You're on.'

Joe produced his phone in an instant.

'Tania, darling. I need you to find something special for my dear friend Frankie.' Whatever she said made Joe howl with laughter. Had he even blushed? 'Here he is.'

He passed the phone across. Two minutes later, Tania was hunting for the perfect home.

3

I could've walked on air as I left the record shop. Jen would be thrilled if I could find our dream home. Then it dawned on me that I'd no idea how long it would take to complete the purchase, even if Tania worked her magic immediately. I'd bought two properties in my life. Robbie, my ex, had organised the purchase of the barn conversion. The less said about that, the better. Then, when I was getting back on my feet, I bought my little house opposite the pub. It had been brand new and ready to move in. I suspected the next one may be more complicated.

Thinking of the house gave me an idea to kill some time. When I moved in with Jen, Angel had rented my house from me. I sent her a text.

You in the office?

No. Day off. At home. Coffee?

Perfect. There was no way I'd have time to go to IKEA if Angel needed to see me. It felt strange knocking on my old front door. At least I already knew that the bell didn't work. I put it on my mental list of stuff to do.

'It's open.'

Angel was in the kitchen. I could've convinced myself I was dreaming. Everything was so familiar, but the wrong way round. Familiar cups and furniture, but it was Angel making coffee, and telling me to take a seat.

13

She gestured towards the living room. I was about to sit in my beloved armchair, then realised I was a guest, and made for the sofa. Before I could lower myself to the seat, Angel was laughing.

'You can have the armchair. I know it's your pride and joy.'

I tried for a graceful swerve but sort of ended up sprawled, half on the seat, and half on the arm of the sofa. I tried to style it out.

'I wouldn't dream of it. I'll be fine here.'

We both knew I wouldn't. In truth, I'd always found it a bit low. Now I was like an overturned tortoise, struggling to move. Angel hauled me up by one arm and guided me to the chair. So this was what it would be like in the old people's home. Seconds later, Angel was back with coffee and a plate of biscuits. A plate? Now things were getting strange.

'I didn't realise you were posh,' I said, pointing at the plate.

'I'm trying to impress.'

'Oh yeah. What are you after?'

'Well,' said Angel, flopping onto the seat I'd recently vacated so elegantly. 'Funny you should ask. How would you feel about me having somebody staying here for a bit?'

'Not a problem.'

'I just worried that you might not be keen.'

'I think I'm fairly broad minded. How long are we talking about?' Angel looked shifty. 'So it's more moving in than staying over?'

'Only on trial. If he gets on my tits, he's history, no messing.'

'Bit of a dark horse on the quiet. I didn't even realise you'd met somebody.'

'More of bumping into somebody, sort of.'

Angel was actually squirming now. Then the penny dropped.

'Hang on. It's not your ex, is it? It is. You've got to be joking. Is this the bloke you firebombed?'

'No.'

'Thank God for that.'

'He lived next door but one. I got the wrong house, if you remember.'

'You know full well that's a technicality.'

'It was dark. I was pissed and angry. He'd been irresponsible and lost our house in a scam. But he's changed.'

'Changed from being a treacherous, lowlife arsehole?'

'Dipshit.'

'Pardon?'

'I always referred to him as a treacherous, lowlife dipshit.'

'Sorry. My mistake. And what happens when he reverts to his erstwhile dipshit status, and you firebomb him again? What happens to my house then?'

'Hang on. I did my time, and I've learnt my lesson,' Angel said, folding her arms. 'I've got contacts these days. They'd dispose of him on the moors somewhere.'

I realised, just in time, that she was winding me up.

'How can you be sure he's changed?'

'That's why he's on a trial. We're having fun. I want you to meet him. He's quite sweet, really. Why don't we sort out a night and the four of us can go for a drink?'

Before I could answer, an ice-cream van pulled up right outside the open window, and treated us to a blast of the *Match of the Day* theme. I struggled with two options. Explain to my friend why she was making a mistake or get an ice cream. Besides, with the windows open, the noise from the engine made conversation difficult. When Angel stood up, I assumed she was going to placate me with a 99.

'Here. I'll get them,' I shouted over the din, only for the engine to cut out while I was mid-sentence. Now I was just sitting in an armchair and shouting. Then the front door opened, and a very loud voice announced its approach.

'Brace yourself, babe. I'm home and horny and we're all bound for Mu Mu Land.'

As he burst through the door, Angel was quick to shout back.

'We've got company. Justin. This is Fran—'

'Fuckwit Firth.'

Angel looked at me, open-mouthed.

'Frankie? Bloody hell. Not seen you since…forever.'

'Barney's eighteenth. You went off to some poncey university, never to be seen again.'

'Oxford is not poncey. Actually, it is. How the hell have you been?'

I was on my feet now and briefly considered hugging my long-lost mate, but settled for a handshake.

'I take it you two have met,' said Angel.

'We go way back,' said Fuckwit. I suppose I was going to have to get used to calling him Justin now. Angel's Dipshit appeared to be my Fuckwit. There was a pattern. At least Fuckwit was better than his previous nickname. For years, he was known as Mary. It was our PE teacher that came up with Mary – as in Virgin Firth.

'How come you lost touch?'

It hit both of us at the same time. Shit. The bloody key! I looked down at the floor to avoid eye contact. There's a faint wine stain, just visible on the carpet by the chair arm. I should get that cleaned again now I had a tenant. I risked a glance out of the corner of my eye. Justin was picking intently at his thumbnail. Silence.

'You know what? I don't want to know,' said Angel. 'Not yet anyway. Now play nicely or there'll be no tea for either of you. Agreed?' She made a show of slapping Justin's hand to stop him from picking. 'Agreed?'

Without looking up, he replied, 'Agreed.'

I was about to protest but realised it would be childish. So I grunted agreement instead.

'Justin. Would you like a coffee?'

'Please, babe.'

'Very well. I'll get you one as long as I can trust you both not to regress to being children.'

Angel disappeared into the kitchen. The silence stretched out for what seemed like ages. I cracked first.

'So, what went wrong at Oxford?'

'What do you mean?'

'Well, you're driving an ice-cream van for a living.'

'I own a retail business, if that's what you mean. And nothing went wrong. I got a first, then a doctorate.'

'You're a doctor?'

'Of philosophy, not medicine.'

'So, I don't call you Doctor Firth?'

'No. Technically, it probably should be Professor Firth. Or, at least, it was.'

'Don't tell me. You couldn't keep it in your trousers.'

'Safe to say, at the crucial point, there weren't any trousers. Just the freezer aisle of Morrisons.'

'The freezer aisle? How on Earth—'

'Very carefully. Just not carefully enough as it turned out. And in my defence, I had no idea she was a member of parliament.'

'That was you? I remember something in the papers. Dickhead.'

I shook my head, and we both got the giggles, just like we'd usually done all those years ago.

'What are you two laughing at?'

Angel was back and handed over a mug to Justin.

'Just getting acquainted again, dear. We're playing nicely, as requested,' said Justin.

I took another biscuit and asked the burning question.

'What have you been up to for the last twenty years, then?'

'This and that. A bit of this and quite a lot of that. I admit, I've made the odd poor investment decision along the way.'

'Like losing the house we were supposed to be living in after we got married.'

This, from Angel, sounded remarkably good natured, given that she'd attempted to avenge the poor decision with a Molotov cocktail.

'I can only apologise again, my love. Sometimes, I'm too easily led into poor financial choices.'

'Get rich quick schemes,' she said.

'So what's with the ice-cream van?'

'Apart from it being justified and ancient? It's a pilot scheme,' said Justin. 'A proof of concept, if you will. All part of my market research. When the university invited me to find other career opportunities, I upped sticks and moved to Italy.'

'Italy?'

'It was the love of ice cream what done it gov. One of my former students was working in the family firm, making top-notch desserts. They supplied restaurants and high-end delis, that sort of thing. They took me in as a kind of apprentice. We began our quest to raise gelato to an art form.'

I expected a sarcastic comment from Angel, but I was wrong.

'Actually, the ice cream is fantastic,' she said, patting his hand affectionately.

Justin warmed to his subject.

'I've always loved ice cream. It turns out, having a PHD in chemistry from the world's top university gives you a unique insight into what makes the perfect ice cream. When the old man died, things went a bit pear shaped for the business. Long story short, I ended up in Budapest with my own small operation. Been there for years. I would've still been there now if it wasn't for bumping into this vision of loveliness again.'

Angel rolled her eyes.

'That's a story for another time, over a few pints. Tell him about the ice cream,' she said.

Justin smiled at Angel. These two had got it bad.

'So far, I believe I've perfected three flavours. A superb vanilla is essential if often under-rated. I added strawberry and chocolate chip to prove myself in the children's market. They're the staples and I use the van to try out new flavours. I'm booked in to spend the summer touring festivals and the like testing stuff out. The minute the government legalises cannabis, I'll make a million overnight. My latest creation is also for the adult market. Would you like to try some?'

'I thought you'd never ask.'

Angel's eyes followed Justin as he stood and made for the door. Once he was through it, she turned to me.

'I can't believe you two know each other. What a small world.'

'Who would've thought that the ex-fiancé you tried to firebomb would be an old mate of mine? Then you end up in a cell with my ex.'

'It's just like a fairy tale.'

Justin was back from the van and handed me a small tub and a wooden spoon.

'Try this. I'm quite proud of it.'

'What flavour is it?'

'You tell me. It may be a bit hard at first. Just let it soften a moment.'

I peeled away the paper cover on top of the small pot. Sure enough, the centre was solid. There was no clue to the flavour from the colour. I tried the sniff test but failed miserably. The edge of the pot was softening, and I ran the spoon around the side until I had a good dollop.

'Here goes,' I said.

The sensation was remarkable. It was thick and creamy. Luxurious was the word that came to mind. Then the flavour burst into life in my mouth. The ice cream was cold (as you would expect) but warming.

'Whisky?'

'And?'

'Ginger. You've made whisky and ginger ice cream. Bloody hell. This is good.'

'And all natural. Not one for the kiddies, but the adult market is huge.'

'This is fantastic. And you make it yourself? Where?'

'Ah…'

Angel sounded worried.

'Here? You've set up a mini factory here?'

'It's not like it's a factory. Just a bit of home baking. Once I get the money through from selling the business in Hungary, I'll look for premises here.'

'Don't get me wrong. I'm just amazed that you can do this in my old kitchen. I thought beans on toast was complicated when I lived here. What else are you working on?'

'I've got another three at various stages of development. Struggling to crack the tikka masala at the moment.'

'He's not joking,' said Angel in response to the look I gave her.

'It's so close. When I get it right, it will be unbelievable.'

'So, what's holding you back?'

'Well, I'm not exactly a great risk for the banks. Like I said, a few poor investments over the years.'

'So, you might need an investor?'

'If it would get us up and running, maybe.'

'Leave it with me. I might have an idea. When you got home, it sounded like you had a plan, so I'll get off now.'

'Sorry about that.' He actually blushed.

'But it's been fantastic to see you again, Fuckwit.'

'Cheers, matey. Here, I'll come out with you and get you some samples to take home.'

'In that case, you have my blessing to move in. But no upsetting her, OK? I only just decorated, and firebombs tend to affect the value of the properties around here. Just one small thing.'

'Name it.'

'You need to move the van.'

'You think it lowers the tone of the neighbourhood?'

'Hardly. I think it'll probably get nicked once word gets round.'

4

Feeling pleased with myself, I stashed the ice-cream samples in the freezer just as I heard Jen's key in the lock. A six-year-old bundle of energy flung itself into my arms. Her mother was slightly less frenetic, but just as affectionate.

'Hello, you. Great timing, I just got in,' I said, simultaneously admiring Charley's latest painting and kissing my wife.

'I come bearing gifts. This was lurking outside waiting to ask if you could play out.' It was only then that I saw Rupert hovering just behind Jen. 'Trouble is, I was hoping you'd watch Charley for an hour while I pop over to make sure my parents are OK.'

'No problem. We can have a beer here. That OK with you?'

Rupert nodded and grabbed a seat at the kitchen table. Jen produced two beers from the fridge.

'Right. Love you and leave you. Don't worry about food, I'll bring pizza. You staying, Rupert?'

'Sorry. Can't tonight. Joe's got a night off and he's doing Nigella's *Coq au Riesling*.'

Jen instinctively knew I was about to be smutty and raised a finger to me.

'Behave, you. Sounds lovely, Rupert. If you're not here when I get back, give my love to Joe.'

She kissed Charley and headed back out of the door.

'Can I watch a DVD?'

'Of course.'

Charley wriggled free and headed to the other room, pausing only to fist bump Rupert. I knew it would be seconds before *Frozen* would be off and running.

'I remember having that much energy,' said Rupert.

'No way I'd have kept up with her, even at that age. Good to see you. Cheers.'

We clinked bottles. I grabbed a bag of nuts from the cupboard before sitting opposite Rupert.

'How's things with you? Keeping busy?'

'Not really,' I said. 'We're between projects at the moment. Jen's almost finished the biography she's working on. She's due in London in two weeks for a couple of days doing pre-release press interviews and stuff. Once that's done, we agreed we'd start something.'

'Anything in mind?'

'I think Flic and Demus have been cooking up something or other. I should find out, really.'

'Still can't believe you're big buddies with Demus Wolf. You know Joe's got a crush on him, don't you?'

'Hey, I'm straight and married, and I've got a crush on him.' For once in my life, when I tossed a cashew nut in the air, I caught it in my mouth. Rupert tried the same. As he bent to pick it up off the floor, I tried to hide my pleasure.

'Must be nice to spend time playing happy families, surely?'

'It is. I love being married,' I said.

'Bloody hell, thought I was the soppy one around here.'

'You must be the same. Joe seems to make you very happy still.'

'He does. We have such a laugh. But there's more to it than that.' He took a long drink, draining the bottle. I nodded towards the fridge and he got up to get two more. 'I've never told anybody before. That apartment we live in is the first place I've ever felt truly happy.'

'You mean just getting away from your dad?'

'Partly. But there's more to it than that. I love the light from the big windows. There's nothing better than sitting with a coffee and watching the sun rise. Having said that, we've often still been sitting there with a glass of wine at that time. It's magical. Then there's the next-door neighbour's cat. It seems to know when Joe's not there and walks along the balcony wall and comes to sit with me.'

'Never when Joe's there?'

'No. Not anymore. They don't get on.' Rupert took another drink. He was deep in thought. 'I suppose I feel safe. After all the crap with Dad, prison, and everything. He controlled so much of my life. Made all the decisions, even down to the colour of my bedroom walls. When I moved into the apartment with Joe, I felt safe. The first thing he did was get the whole place repainted, so it didn't just feel like me moving into his place. It just became ours. Nothing bad can happen in that apartment. I can see us getting old there.'

Shit. I couldn't tell him what Joe had planned. That was way above my pay grade. Instead, I made sure Charley was engrossed in the other room, then changed the subject.

'Talking of moving, I can trust you to keep a secret. I'm planning a big surprise for Jen. We're having a baby, and we'll need a bigger house. I'm going to find the perfect place. She won't have to lift a finger.'

'Jen's pregnant?'

'Keep your voice down. And no, she's not pregnant, not yet anyway. But with these bad boys, it's only a matter of time now that we've decided.'

'I'm pleased for you. At least I will be – when you've completed the mission, so to speak. Where will you move to? Not too far away, I hope.'

'Don't know yet. I'm picturing a big garden, maybe a pony for Charley. Certainly lots of bedrooms for mates to come and stay.'

'Sounds perfect.'

'But remember, not a word to Jen. She doesn't suspect anything. She'll be so chuffed if I can pull it off.'

'Mum's the word.' Rupert sat back, reading the label on the beer bottle. He took a deep breath, as if he'd decided something.

'What's up?'

He tapped his fingers on the table before answering.

'I need to tell you something.'

'You're not pregnant, are you?'

'No. Dickhead. It's my sister.'

'Robbie? What about her?'

'She's getting out on Friday.'

'This Friday? As in three days' time?'

'Yes.'

'But that's early, surely?' I'd always thought my ex was going to be in prison for several more months yet.

'She did some sort of deal. Think she gave them more on Dad to get out earlier. Anyway, I just wanted to let you know, in case you bump into her.'

'Where's she going to live?'

'She's moving in with Mum, at least to start with. Thing is, she wants to see you.'

'Not a chance. Why would I want to do that?'

'Look. She knows you're happily married, and she blew it with you, big time. I think she just wants to be friends. Would that be such a disaster?'

'Yes, it would. Look, I bear her no ill will, despite what she did. But I don't feel in any way responsible for her or what she thinks. She needs to get on with her life, just like I'm getting on with mine. Me and Jen are very happy. She's all that matters to me. Besides, they were hardly best buddies before all the trouble kicked off.' Did I really want to open up that can of worms again? No. Definitely not. Then again, doesn't everyone deserve the chance to rebuild their lives if they've paid their dues? No. This was decidedly an SEP (Somebody Else's Problem). 'Sorry, buddy. Not going to happen.'

Rupert shrugged.

'I said I'd ask. We still good?'

'Course we are, idiot.'

'Good. Now, my *Coq au Riesling* awaits.'

'I can't compete with that. See you soon.'

Once Rupert had gone, I dropped the empty bottles into the recycling bin. I was confident that they went in there. Everything else was a bit of a gamble. At least the cashews had stopped my stomach rumbling. I wasn't sure why, but Robbie's imminent release had rattled me.

The sound of Charley singing along made me smile. She saw me slip into the chair and left her spot on the rug to join me. This was nice. Cosy. Jen would be back soon and the three of us would settle down for pizza. An evening with my new family. Could it get any better than this?

My phone snapped me from my reverie.

'Hello, Mum. Everything all right?'

'What was that woman called?'

'Which woman?'

'You know which woman. Lived next door. Big woman. Drank pints of Guinness at the club.'

'Mrs Rafferty?'

'That's it. Eileen Rafferty. Been bugging me all day. Could see her face, clear as day, but couldn't put a name to it.'

'Why were you thinking about her?'

'No reason. Just bugged me when I couldn't remember her name. Anyway, so glad you rang, but I need to go now. My programme's just about to start.'

The line went dead. Odd. She'd normally want to speak to Charley, who was now looking at me as if I'd done something wrong.

'Granny sends her love. She couldn't stay on the phone, though. You can speak to her next time.'

She shrugged and went back to the film. Five minutes later, Jen arrived with the pizza, and Charley abandoned Elsa for the day.

5

I'd just dropped Charley at school when my phone rang. It was Tania, Joe's estate agent superstar. She gushed about the perfect property. It was in a village I'd never heard of.

'It's about ten miles southeast of York. Lovely place. Super neighbourhood and a primary school to die for. But you need to move quickly. I could set up a viewing for this morning. How does eleven o'clock sound? Brilliant. I'll email the details and see you there. Ciao.'

I'd said less than a dozen words to her, but it appeared I was meeting Tania this morning. I was concerned that my stipulation of within five miles of where we lived now had gone out of the window. Still, a primary school to die for was a plus. Then I panicked. Which email address had I given her? If it was the business one, Jen might see it, and my surprise would be blown. Then I realised it was unlikely. She was very strict about distractions. When she was writing, she blocked all emails and internet alerts. I recognised this was good for productivity, but I was always terrified of missing out on something. As a result, distractions came every five minutes.

As it turned out, I needn't have worried. The email pinged into my personal account. As soon as I arrived back home, I opened the attachment. The house was certainly impressive. Five bedrooms, a large garden, and even a paddock for a pony. I was excited. Then I saw the price and was horrified. Even if we sold both our houses and took out a mortgage for the rest, it would be a stretch. I'd have to turf Angel out onto the street. But this could be our dream home. At least I should have a look.

So, at two minutes to eleven, I pulled up outside an imposing house in a village I'd never heard of before. I gathered the woman, who immediately embraced me, and proffered her cheek, was Tania. She took my arm and guided me up the garden path. To say I found her intimidating wouldn't do it justice. I was terrified.

For twenty minutes, I toured the house open-mouthed. It was certainly impressive. As we inspected the paddock, I couldn't help seeing Charley proudly posing for photos on her pony.

'What do you think? Wonderful, isn't it?'

'It's a beautiful house.'

'Would you like me to make them an offer? I know there's another couple interested. What do you say? Twenty grand below asking price? Just to get a conversation going.'

'I...'

'Or we could just cut the games and offer the full amount.'

'I...' For fuck's sake, Frankie. Get a grip. You could end up buying the thing just because you can't give her a coherent answer. I panicked. 'I don't like the wallpaper in the living room. Sorry.'

'OK. We can change that. I happen to know one of the designers from *Changing Rooms*. He would do a first ra—'

'Sorry. Let me think about it. I'll get back to you.'

After a brief but firm handshake, I strode off to the car. Well done. What an idiot. I could see in the rear-view mirror that Tania was standing in the road, hands on hips, and shaking her head. Maybe I needed a different plan. My heart was pounding. I pulled over into the first lay-by and realised I didn't have a clue where I was. I tried to zoom out on the satnav map but got a screen I didn't recognise. Which button had I pressed? I began pressing random buttons before the machine got bored with me and asked where I wanted to go. I was about to press the icon for home when I saw my parents' address below it. I couldn't be that far away. Let's have a trip to the seaside and see what they're up to.

The satnav cheered up markedly and announced I was only half an hour from my destination. Just in time for lunch. I was about to pull out when a Porsche roared past at near supersonic speed. Call me cynical, but I suspected Tania was not happy. I sent a text to Mum and had a *kettle on* reply within seconds and set off for the coast.

My mum had some kind of sixth sense that could detect my presence within a mile of their house. It was unusual not to be greeted at the door. I found her engrossed in the TV.

'Hello, love. I didn't know you were coming. You should've let me know. I'd have had the kettle on. Still, while you're on your feet, you might as well do it.'

I was about to remind her that she's just sent me a text but remembered the advice not to correct her. I was soon back with tea, expecting the programme to be zapped as soon as I sat down.

'You made me jump. I didn't know you were coming,' she said, raising her voice above the deafening TV.

'Just a spur-of-the-moment thing.'

'A what?' I pointed at the TV, then my ears. Thankfully, the music suggested the programme had finished. 'Hang on, I'll turn this down. I can't hear a word. You mumble sometimes.'

There was the usual delay while she located the remote. I tried to hide a snigger as her chair began to recline.

'Bloody thing. Why does it do that?'

'I think you've got the wrong remote. That one's for the chair.'

She looked at me as if I was crackers, then found the other remote. The volume reduced to next to nothing, but I could see her eyes still following the pictures.

'Your dad's in the kitchen, I think.'

'He must be out. His coat's not on the hook,' I said. 'Why don't you switch the telly off and tell me what you've been up to?'

'Not a lot happens here, love. Besides, I don't want to miss my programme.'

I heard the back door open, and Dad poked his head through from the kitchen. Mum gave me a *told you he was in the kitchen* look.

'Hello, son. Didn't know you were coming today.'

'Last minute decision.'

'Just been out to pick up our prescriptions. They actually gave me a carrier bag today. I swear there's more stuff every time I go.'

Some kind of hidden signal passed between my parents, and Mum switched off the TV.

'Don't let me miss my programme,' she said with a sigh.

'What programme's that Mum?'

'You know. I watch it every week. Got that man in it we met at the Imperial in Blackpool.'

Luckily, Dad stepped in.

'It's called *Johnny Doc's Treasure Trove*. Don't worry, love. We won't miss it. It's not on until Saturday.'

'It's Saturday today.'

'No, love, it's Tuesday.'

'Are you sure?'

'Yes. All day.'

'So why is Frankie here?'

She had a point. A midweek visit was rare, if not unique. I took the chance to distract her.

'You say you met Johnny Doc in Blackpool?'

'We did. He was still Johnny Docherty then. He had the same Paisley shirt as Len was wearing. That's what got us chatting. He bought me a gin and bitter lemon and a pint for your dad. He even gave me a ten pence piece to put David Essex on the jukebox, said he was his favourite.'

Given that she couldn't remember the text from twenty minutes before I arrived, I was dubious about this tale until Dad confirmed it.

'She's right. I hadn't thought about that for years.'

How was it possible that she remembered a conversation in a bar fifty years ago, but not whether her husband was in the kitchen?

'What's the show about, Mum?'

'What show?'

'*Johnny Doc's Treasure Trove*.'

'That's my favourite. Don't want to miss it.'

She began rummaging for the remote again.

'It's not on yet, love. Don't worry, we won't miss it. Why don't you tell Frankie why you like it so much?'

Mum frowned, as if I should already know the answer.

'It's a bit like that other one. You know…'

'*Antiques Roadshow*,' said Dad.

'That's it. Except you have to pick a door to see if you win. You must've seen it. It's my favourite show all week.'

Again, she fumbled for the remote. When the chair started to recline, Dad calmly leant forward and returned the chair to upright. He looked at me and picked up the explanation.

'It's a combination of *Antiques Roadshow* and *Deal or No Deal*, I suppose. People take their antiques for valuation. You get some right tat but some good stuff as well. Then the valuers each take an envelope from a table and go into the treasure house. There's five doors, and the person has to pick a door. Each one has a valuer inside. They open the envelope and that decides how much they pay for the antique. It can be the valuation they just came up with or it can be a multiple of it. They might get double, treble, or even half of it. One door just has a cabbage, and that's all you get, but one can be worth up to a thousand times the valuation.'

'It's funny if they get the cabbage,' said Mum with an evil chuckle.

'So why would they accept the cabbage?'

'They have to. That's the gamble if they want the stuff valued.'

It didn't sound like my cup of tea, but Mum obviously loved it.

'We're taking those paintings,' she said.

'What paintings?'

Dad stepped in again.

'Your grandad gave us two paintings just after we got married. Said they'd be worth something one day.'

'And are they?'

'I doubt it. He also had a signed photo of Ken Dodd that he thought was worth a fortune. Can't see it somehow.'

'Where are the pictures now?'

'They're in the loft. I'll get the ladder down and get them.'

'Don't be daft. I don't want you climbing ladders. I'll go.'

I wasn't keen on ladders myself, but knew he shouldn't be climbing anything at his age. The loft had probably been unvisited since they moved over here, years ago. The strange thing was, I recognised most of the stuff as having come from the loft at the old house. You had to question why they'd brought it. In truth, there wasn't that much, and the search of a Safeway carrier bag revealed two framed paintings, both square and about eighteen inches wide. The carrier bag was probably a collectable these days and worth more than the pictures.

I stashed the bag by the top of the ladder and did a quick scan of the room. There was a pile of stuff that looked like mine. It struck me again that as far as the collected tat was concerned, mine all stemmed from after the fire. A whole childhood of toys and books up in flames. This lot was from when I was older. A whole season of Bradford Bulls programmes from 1997 that I was convinced would be worth a fortune one day. Dream on. Then I spotted it. The metal money box. I hadn't even thought about it for years until the reunion with Justin. Was this really the reason we fell out, all those years ago?

Of course, it wasn't so much that the box caused us to fall out, it was a lack of access to its contents at a critical time due to Justin being a fuckwit. He'd stolen the key. The box was useless without the key. I wondered if he still had it. Doubtful. I picked up the box and the paintings and headed for the ladder.

Back in the cosy living room, I laid the pictures on the coffee table. They looked familiar. A series of matchstick figures walking towards a butcher's shop. The window display housed every cut of meat you could think of. Behind the shop was a canal bridge. The scale of the bridge made me think it was the Manchester Ship

Canal. My heart started to beat just a little faster as I scanned for a signature. Nothing.

'Where did Grandad get them, do you know?'

Mum was now scanning the *Radio Times* and not remotely engaged with what we were talking about.

'Not sure,' said Dad. 'I seem to remember some tale about his brother passing them on. He could just as easily have won them at dominoes. He played dominoes against half of Salford in his time. Do you think they're worth anything?'

'Not a clue. Maybe getting them valued would be a good idea.'

'Like I say, we applied to be on the show ages ago. At least then we'll know if they're worth owt. Tell you what. Why don't you come and help me make some sandwiches? You must be starving.'

I followed Dad into the kitchen. He made a point of closing the door behind us and whispered as he fussed with the loaf of bread.

'I'm worried about your mum. Hell, I'm worried about both of us, to be honest.'

'Her short-term memory seems to be getting worse.'

'It is. The last few months it's been getting worse every week.'

'Is she getting any help?'

'Refuses point blank. Says I'm the one with dementia. And I know that's true. I go to the dementia group every week. They've helped me understand what's going on. I can be fine for days, then I have an episode where I remember bugger all. But at least I can cope with that. But your mum. You've seen how she is.'

'But she remembers every word of a conversation in a bar from fifty years ago.'

'That's how it works. I hate to say this, because we've loved living here. I think we need to move to a care home.'

'Really? Isn't it a bit soon for that?'

'I'm not sure I can cope. She keeps leaving pans on like she did at Christmas.'

'Have you thought about sheltered housing? You could have people coming in to cook, that sort of thing.'

'Nay, lad, I don't understand that sort of thing.'

'Do you want me to look into it?'

'Would you?'

'Of course. Leave it with me.'

'And I think we need to be closer to you as well. Don't want you having to trail all this way, just to see us. Pickle?'

'What.'

'On your sandwich. Do you want pickle?'

'Yes, please.'

'I'm assuming you'll stay for *Countdown*?'

'Of course. Just go easy on me. I'm out of practice.'

We took the plates and teapot through to the living room. Mum's chair was reclined again, the TV blaring, and she was fast asleep. Dad dragged a blanket over her, and we ate our sandwiches in silence.

6

'Hi, Frankie. It's Flic. You OK to talk?'

'Yeah. I'm in the car on hands-free so fine.'

'Are you alone?'

'Sounds ominous but, yes.'

'Not ominous. Just got burnt once when I launched into a tirade about a certain actress, only to find she was in the passenger seat with my colleague.'

'Ouch. That must have caused a stink.'

'Could've been worse, to be fair. Turned out they were having a mucky weekend away. He was trying to keep her quiet, but she couldn't resist having a row. They say information is king. I had the upper hand when it came to negotiating her next deal. Anyway, how are you? Still enjoying your break?'

'I'm great, thanks. It's really good to be able to do lots of those minor jobs around the house you don't normally have time for.'

'You're bored.'

Was I that obvious?

'A bit. Don't get me wrong. Married life with Jen is wonderful, but I'm used to having a project. She's busy finishing the biography and I'm contemplating IKEA.'

'In that case, I have good news. Demus has been working on an idea for his next TV project. Looks like we may have a green light to produce it, and we want you and Jen to write it.'

'Sounds interesting. What's the big idea?'

'He wants to remake *The Sting* and set it in Yorkshire as a six-part series. Can you make a meeting tomorrow to discuss it? He's over here for a couple of days, so we can do it face to face.'

'That sounds good. I'll check with Jen and confirm later.'

'No need. I spoke to Jen ten minutes ago. She said you'd be up for it.' She laughed. 'Sorry. My blow against the patriarchy to call her first. I'll see you tomorrow at the office.'

'That's great. I'll start doing my homework tonight.'

With the call finished, I was free to panic. I'd never seen *The Sting*. My devotion to *Top of the Pops* reruns meant I had a vague idea that it was Robert Redford and Paul Newman. They always showed the clip of the bizarre Pan's People routine with captions about the film. At least the start of my research was easy enough. I could download the film, sit with a bottle of wine, and call it work. Result.

It would be good to have a new project and get back to working with Jen again. I was suddenly going to be busy if I was to work out a solution to Dad's problem, too. Before all that, I had a tricky conversation coming up. For the second day running, I pulled up outside the record shop.

Ambrose was serving a small queue of customers. He waved to me and pointed to the entrance to El Sotano, the supper club that formed the other leg of their business empire. There was a nice steady hum of conversation from the half dozen tables that were taken even now, around four o'clock. Joe occupied a booth, hunched over a laptop.

'Frankie. Two days running. Good to see you. Drink?'

'Better not, Joe. Got jobs to do. Just picked up a new project and need to start my research tonight.'

I told him all about the conversation with Flic.

'Sounds great. I love that film.'

'That's where my research starts. I've never seen it.'

The look Joe gave me was one of absolute pity. I ignored him and cleared my throat.

'I need a quiet word.'

'Who've you slept with?'

'No. Nothing like that.'

'Because I hope you realise I would personally cut off your bits and feed them to the dog if you messed Jen about.'

'I promise. I would never do anything like that. No. It's you.'

'Me? Who have I slept with?'

'You're obsessed. Nobody has slept with anybody they shouldn't have. OK? Look, this is difficult, but I need to say something.' I shuffled on the bench seat and Joe closed the laptop lid. 'I was speaking to Rupert last night. He was talking about how happy he was with you.'

'Why's that a problem? I'm very happy too.'

'He's also very happy where you live. He loves that apartment. Says it's his first proper home and wouldn't want to live anywhere else. Obviously, I didn't tell him what you were planning. Just thought I'd better warn you before you make your grand gesture.'

'Shit.'

'Sorry.'

'Not your fault. I'm glad you warned me. Trouble is, I've just signed the contract. The cinema's mine.'

'Shit.' I gave it some thought. 'Think we need that drink now?'

The Sting would have to wait. Joe needed some company. He signalled to the young man working behind the bar and a bottle of red arrived with two glasses. I warned him I could only have one glass.

'That won't be a problem. What the hell am I going to do?'

'Could you cancel?'

'Not without losing a very substantial deposit.'

'Looks like you own a cinema.'

'You're good at this comforting business.'

'Ta.' I took a drink. 'Actually, would it be that bad to restore the building and open it as a cinema? I can think of one highly successful production company that would hold its premieres there.'

Joe looked at me with his head on one side.

'You're not as daft as you look, are you?'

'Thanks again. You say the nicest things.'

'I loved that cinema your mate built in his house. What was he called?'

'Bernard. Lovely bloke.'

'Bernard. That's right. Are you still in touch with him?'

'Christmas cards, that sort of thing.'

'Do you think he'd be interested in a bit of consultancy?'

'You serious about this?'

'What else am I going to do? I like the idea of a classy art déco boutique cinema and live music venue. Some of the acts I want to book for here are too big, suit a bigger venue. That could be it. Frankie, you are a genius.'

'I try. Cheers.'

As ever with Joe, conversation was entertaining, and wide ranging. As the glass of wine reduced, I was regretting having the car with me. That changed when I got the phone call.

'Where are you?'

'Hi, Jen. I'm at Joe's. Why don't you leave Charley with your parents and come round?'

'No. I can't.'

I sat bolt upright at the tone of Jen's voice. Joe looked concerned.

'What is it? What's wrong?'

'It's Dad. He's had some kind of seizure. They're on their way to hospital. Can you come home to look after Charley? I need to be with them.'

'I'm on my way. Ten minutes.'

I was there in less than eight. Jen was already on the doorstep when I parked up.

'Thanks for coming so quickly,' she said.

'Are you sure you're OK to drive? We could take Charley, and I could drop you off.'

'No. I'll be fine. Charley's having her tea. She doesn't even know there's anything wrong.'

'Don't worry about her. Call me as soon as you know what's happening.'

Jen was shaking when I hugged her. She waved from her car and was gone. More than anything, I wanted to be with her, to protect her from what may lie ahead. Her father, Ben, had been diagnosed with stage four cancer last year. He'd had a couple of periods when the chemotherapy seemed to be winning, only to have the disease get the upper hand again.

Ben had lived the last few months to the full. The coast-to-coast walk with Jen was a major triumph. Even more remarkable was the two months touring Spain on Harley's. His oncologist had warned him not to do anything too strenuous, but said he wouldn't try to dissuade him. They'd set off while he was still suffering the side effects of the last chemo session. Geraldine had presented him with a T-shirt with the legend 'Queasy Rider' on it.

I closed the door. In the kitchen, Charley seemed to be covered in spaghetti hoops.

'Hi, Charley. What you up to?'

'Chillin' innit.'

She was six going on sixteen and collapsed in a fit of giggles.

'Chillin' is it? And where did you pick up that quaint phrase?'

'What does quaint mean?'

'Quaint is…' What the hell was the definition of quaint? 'Quaint is like your mum would say.'

'Cool.' Again, the giggles. I loved these conversations with my new daughter. She pushed the empty bowl away. Before she could leave the table, I swooped with a wet wipe and cleaned her face.

'There, perfect once more. You're lucky. My mum used to do that with her handkerchief.'

She screwed her face up and said something about bogies that got drowned in more giggles. Then she suddenly looked serious.

'Is Grandad all right? I know he's at the hospital.'

I sat at the table, and she climbed onto my knee.

'You remember we told you that Grandad was poorly, and the doctors are trying to make him better?'

She nodded.

'Will they make him better this time?'

'I hope so. They're very clever.'

'What's do not resusticate?'

I didn't see that one coming. My introduction to parenting seemed to be gathering pace.

'Resuscitate. Where did you hear that word?'

'At Grandad's house when he was talking to Mummy. I was doing the jigsaw with Gran. He wants one. Can we get him one?'

My mind went into overdrive trying to find a way to answer her. What was the right thing to do? She was only six. She shouldn't have to deal with this. The high-pitched tone from Jen's iPad rescued me. It was a FaceTime call. Charley was on it in a flash and recognised the face of Issy – Stella and Ambrose's daughter. The two of them had become close friends and somehow found more to talk about before bed after spending all day together at school. At least I was off the hook. I would need to talk to Jen about how we tackle that particular conversation.

With Charley distracted, I filled the dishwasher and wiped the table clean. Jen and I had had our own conversation about Ben's wish. Predictably, she was against any idea that her father could have a cardiac arrest and nobody would do anything about it. Eventually, I admitted that I kind of agreed with him. If it was me, would I really want my last minutes on Earth to feature somebody pounding on my chest and zapping me like Frankenstein's Monster? Surely better to go peacefully, surrounded by the people I loved? Something in what I'd said obviously resonated with Jen and she'd given her blessing. Ben had grinned at me when he admitted he'd already signed the document.

Would it come to that tonight? Was this really it for Ben? What would that do to Jen, having lost Sean, her first husband, to the same horrible disease? Maybe she'd welcome a fresh start. A project to distract her. Moving to a dream home might be a good plan, after all. I would continue the search and show Jen how much I loved her by finding the perfect home.

7

When I arrived on Wednesday, I reflected on the bomb that had destroyed our old office last summer. The whole team moved to identical premises on the opposite side of the business park. From upstairs, I could see the work to rebuild was in full swing. I pushed open the door to the boardroom. Demus was already there. I was still freaked out that this bloke was my mate. He was a star. Films, TV, even narrating my audiobooks – this guy did it all. He secured his place in my affections when he handed me a coffee and the packet of extremely posh biscuits.

'White chocolate and lemon. They'll blow your mind.'

He was right.

'Instant favourite. Bloody hell, these are good.'

Flic cleared her throat, making a point.

'If you two have finished the biscuit love-in, maybe I could ask about Jen? How is she?'

'Sorry, Flic. Jen's knackered, to be honest. She's been at the hospital all night. Ben's stable, whatever that means. I got her to agree to sleep for a few hours before we visit this afternoon. She's sorry she has to miss the meeting.'

'Family comes first. We could reschedule this if you need to,' said Demus.

'No. Let's do it. Once we finish, I'll go home, make lunch, and make sure she's OK. No Jason today?'

'He's in London, meeting potential investors for his latest project. In fact, he's suggested we may need a second office down there, given the amount of work coming in. I'll make sure that's on the agenda for the board meeting next month. As it's only the three of us, why don't we get started, then you can get off to Jen. Demus, why don't you outline your idea?'

The great man stood and walked to the front of the room. He tapped at a laptop, and I killed the lights. The big screen displayed a simple slide. It just said, *The Yorkshire Sting*.

'I'm assuming you've both seen the Robert Redford and Paul Newman film?' Flic and I both nodded. This was a bit of an exaggeration on my part. I'd read a synopsis on the internet twenty minutes ago. A smug smile crept onto my face. So glad I'd done my homework. Demus continues. 'I've certainly always loved it, and I love *The Hubberholme Syndrome*. What if we merged the two? Bring *The Sting* to the Yorkshire Dales? An intriguing con and the gentle humour and set it against the stunning backdrop of our favourite countryside?'

'From what I remember, Robert Redford wore a flat cap most of the time. Can't get much more Yorkshire than that,' I said, remembering some of the online photos. 'What about the actual sting? I take it you're proposing to set this in the present?'

'I think so. That would mean we'd need a whole new premise, but that's where you and Jen are brilliant.'

'You mean we make stuff up?'

'And you would make up some great dialogue for the star actor.'

Demus smiled and took a deep bow. Flic was enthusiastic.

'Am I right in thinking you want to play the Redford character? What was he called?'

'Johnny Hooker. And yes, as we would produce, I get first dibs on the best part. Frankie, what do you think?'

'I think it's a great idea. Like you say, we'd need a whole new story, really. But we can take the premise of the grifter taking revenge against the bad guy for killing his partner. We could even make it a very obvious homage to the original. If you remember, the film almost divides into chapters, labelled as the stages of the con. Each episode could be one of those chapters. I'm up for this. Let's do it.'

'And you have potential investors lined up, Demus?' As always, Flic had an eye on the finances.

'Yes. They want a joint-production credit, but in principle, they would want us to take the lead.'

Flic turned to me.

'Is it realistic to start this when Jen is so vulnerable?'

'Obviously, we don't know how things are going to pan out with Ben, but she's already said that we can't put everything on hold. I think she'll be in favour.'

'Great. Demus, why don't you set up a meeting for me with the backers and we'll go from there.' Demus nodded as Flic stood.

'If you'll excuse me, I have another call. Frankie, give my love to Jen, and tell her we'll meet up soon.'

As Flic left, Demus slid into the seat next to me.

'So, how long to knock up an outline?'

'No idea. How about we get together in a couple of weeks to see how far we've got? You in a rush?'

'To be honest, I've got a couple of months off, and I'm already getting twitchy. I need to work.'

'I know what you mean. It's been driving me up the wall. Somehow, putting together flat-pack furniture isn't as exciting as writing TV scripts.'

Demus laughed.

'Those things scared me so much I bought a house once just because it had wardrobes built in. Did it all in secret. First my wife knew of it was when the for-sale sign went up on our old place.'

'Wasn't that a bit of a shock?'

'She threatened to kill me. Then she saw the place I'd picked and fell in love with it. Said it was the most romantic thing she'd ever heard of. We moved in almost straight away and we've been there ever since. Sometimes, grand gestures pay off big time.'

'I admit, I looked at a place the other day. Just not sure that I'm built for grand gestures. You know Jen. Do you really think she'd be happy if I made that kind of move?'

'I think she'd love it. Might take her mind off things. What have you got to lose?'

Well, if Demus thought it was a good idea…

JEN WAS ALREADY up and about when I got home. I could tell she was tired, but she still made my stomach do a little flip every time I saw her. She was making sandwiches in the kitchen.

'Here, let me do that.'

'No, it's fine. I need to keep busy.'

'How do you feel?' Jen didn't have to say anything. 'Sorry. Stupid question.'

'Actually, I feel better now. I just called Mum. The doctors are happy that the treatment had the desired effect. Apparently, he's sitting up and asking about going home.'

'That's great news.'

'It is. But this is how his life is going to be now. The slightest infection could put him in hospital.' I hugged her close and felt hot tears on my neck. 'Then one day, they won't be able to fix him.'

It took a full minute for the sobbing to subside. When it did, Jen squeezed me extra-tight and returned to sandwich making.

'How did the meeting go? Do we have a new project?'

'We do, assuming you're up for it,' I said, checking the pickle content of my sandwich.

I told her about the pitch from Demus.

'That sounds like fun. I need another couple of days to finish the final chapter of the biography, then I'm all yours.' Jen's phone vibrated. 'It's Mum. Says Dad's being discharged. They'll be home within the hour.'

'In that case, eat up, and we'll go see him.'

'I don't mind going by myself if you're wanting to get started on a story?'

'No. I want to come. Nothing to stop us swapping ideas on the drive over.'

WE ARRIVED AT Jen's parents' house just after two. The sound of birds in their garden always struck me. It took me a while to realise it was because there was no traffic noise. We crunched over the gravel, but instead of going through the front door, Jen walked down the side of the house. Sure enough, the patio doors were open, and Ben was in the conservatory, being swallowed by cushions. He looked pale but smiled when he saw us approach.

'Clever way to get past the guards,' he said. Jen bent to kiss him. 'She's in the kitchen. You never know, I might get a cup of tea now you're here.'

'Behave,' said Jen. 'Back in a minute.'

I shook Ben's hand. The usual firm handshake felt weak, just a bag of bones.

'Good to see you, Frankie.'

'It's good to see you back home. You had us going for a bit there.'

'Had myself going, to be honest. When they took me in, I was annoyed I wouldn't get chance to prune the bloody roses.'

'Have they said how soon you'll be up to gardening?'

'Doctor reckoned a week or two, but Gerry's warned me to be on my best behaviour.'

'You got enough cushions?'

Ben laughed and patted the small mountain on the seat next to him.

'Didn't know we owned this many. Watch where you sit, or she'll be piling 'em on you next.' The laugh that followed seemed to sap whatever strength he had left.

'Do you want me to do the garden for you?'

'That's a kind offer, but I saw what you did to that geranium. Not exactly green fingered, are you?' I was about to protest, but decided he was right. 'If it comes to it, I'll get somebody in. We all have our skills. It's your other skills I want to take advantage of.'

'Oh yes? What skills are they?'

'Writing. I want you to write something for me. Not a word to Jen and Gerry. I want it to be a surprise for them.' He looked at the door, reassuring himself that we were still alone. 'When I was diagnosed, I started a diary, journal sort of thing. I kept it through doing the coast-to-coast walk. Still at it now, when I get a chance. Would you work your magic on it? Turn my scribbles into something for Gerry and Jen to read after I…'

It was as if he didn't have the strength to finish the sentence.

'It'll be an honour to have a look for you, Ben.'

'You might feel different when you see how scruffy the thing is. But it comes from the heart. I thought you could include some photos, that sort of thing.'

'When do you want me to start?'

'Whenever you can fit it in. I know you two are always busy.'

'It sounds like it's important to you. I'll make time.'

Ben pointed to the door to the dining room.

'In there. Top drawer of the sideboard. Large envelope with your name on it. And not a word to the guards.'

I left my seat and headed for the sideboard. The sealed envelope was heavy.

'Blimey, Ben. How much have you written?'

'There's three books there and I've almost finished another one upstairs. See what you can do.'

He held a finger to his lips as Jen returned with a tray.

'What are you two whispering about?'

'Man secrets,' said Ben. 'Not for your delicate ears, love. What have you two been up to?'

'Apart from tea making, Mum's been showing me her haul of books from the charity shop.'

'If she gets any more, we'll have to build an extension just to house them.'

'Nonsense. Plenty of room in the library yet.'

'I still can't get over you having a library,' I said.

'It's what most people call a cellar. We just happened to put some shelves in there and a couple of comfy chairs.' Ben laughed.

'It's much more than that,' said Jen. 'My earliest memories are sitting down there, with you reading stories to me. It was a lovely way to fall asleep, knowing you'd carry me up to bed. I wish we had space for that kind of room.'

Interesting. I made a mental note of the requirement for the new house. I was getting better at picking up hints.

I SUSPECTED WE'D just been outplayed by two six-year-olds. Charley and Issy cooked up a plan that each other's mother had said it was OK to have a sleepover. When Jen had called Stella, it was obvious she knew nothing about it. Now the joke was on them because it meant we got to have a rare midweek night *out being grown ups* at Joe's bar. Jen was glad of the chance to let off a little steam. In fact, she was well on her way to being steaming by eight o'clock.

Ambrose had taken the night off to help at home, leaving Joe to manage the bar. This seemed to consist largely of testing an endless supply of cocktails and talking about his plans for the cinema.

'Things seem to be moving quickly,' I said.

'You know me. Never put off till tomorrow what you can do today. That way, if you like it, you can do it again tomorrow.'

He laughed hard at his own joke and called for another martini. It arrived within seconds, along with another bottle of red for the rest of us. Rupert topped up our glasses.

'Has Joe told you about his new project?'

At this point, I squirmed a bit, not knowing how much I was supposed to know. Jen saved me, as always.

'Tell us more, Joe.'

Joe loved having an audience for an announcement.

'Well, I am delighted to announce this wonderful venue' – he waved his arms to illustrate his point – 'will shortly have a sister. Ambrose has agreed to become the co-owner of The Roxy, a delightful art-déco cinema and live music venue.'

'He should be here to celebrate,' said Rupert.

'It came as a shock to his wallet, and he had to go home for a lie down.' Again, Joe was delighted with his own joke.

We all drank a toast to the new venture, just as Angel and Justin arrived. She introduced the group to her new significant other.

'So, you're the one who—' said Rupert.

Even I winced at the not-too-subtle kick under the table from Joe that connected with Rupert's shin.

'Yes. I'm that one,' said Justin with a grin. 'Pleased to meet you all. What are we celebrating?'

Rupert rubbed his leg but answered cheerfully.

'Joe and Ambrose have just bought a dilapidated carpet shop.'

Joe rose to the occasion.

'It may be a carpet shop at the moment. Give it six months and it'll be a sparkling entertainment destination, restored to its 1920s glory. A cinema and live music venue.'

'Sounds wonderful,' said Justin. This earnt him a huge new fan in Joe, who insisted on ordering champagne for the group.

'And in the meantime, it will provide secure parking for your ice-cream van,' Joe said. 'Angel mentioned you were looking for somewhere.'

Now everybody wanted to know about the ice cream. Justin was an instant hit, and we were soon laughing like we always did at school. At least we did until....

I was snapped out of my reverie as Angel was standing and needed to pass me to get out. She was about to start her set and made for the backstage area. All of us loved Angel's voice. I'd become very proud of how she's turned her life around. After being released from prison, she'd proved herself to be an invaluable member of the production company team. A sort of researcher cum fixer. On top of that, she was a regular on stage at El Sotano.

'Any idea when you start work on the building, Joe?' said Justin.

'As soon as possible. I've narrowed it down to a couple of architects. My builder is keen and says he can start more or less anytime.'

'Do you mind me asking which architects?'

'Not at all.' Joe fiddled with his phone. 'Rawdon Architects, they're local, and Samantha Crow. Don't tell me you're an architect, as well as an ice-cream baron?'

'No. But I have some experience of Ms Crow.'

'Any good?'

Justin hesitated, weighing his words.

'She had some good ideas.'

'But?'

This time, the pause was much longer.

'She was the one that put me in touch with the TV people. That's how we ended up on *Johnny's House Builders*.'

At that point, Angel walked on stage, and we all clapped, and cheered. It was halfway through Angel's second song that Joe nudged me, holding his phone out. He was showing me an email from Samantha Crow. The title was: *Would you be interested in appearing on TV?*

I pointed at Justin and leant in to speak to Joe.

'Just be careful. Talk to Justin about what happened to him.'

Joe nodded, but I could tell he was delighted at the prospect of appearing on the programme. What could possibly go wrong?

8

'**W**e'll be on telly.'

'Morning, Mum. How are you?'

'Never mind all that. Didn't you hear what I said?'

'You're going to be on telly?'

'Yes. How did you know? It's meant to be a secret,' she said.

'You just told me.'

'I bet it was your father, wasn't it? Never could keep a secret. Anyway, make sure you tape it. Don't want you to miss it. Would you like new video tapes for your birthday?'

'That's OK, Mum. I've got Sky Q.'

'Is it serious?'

'Is what serious?'

'That thing you've got. What did the doctor say?'

'Mum, it's Sky Q. It's a way of recording stuff without tapes.'

'Don't worry, we'll get you tapes for your birthday. Wouldn't want you to miss it.'

Mum's voice was muffled, and I could hear a discussion at the other end. Predictably, it was my dad who spoke next.

'Mum's gone off to make a cup of tea. I take it she's told you our news?'

'I think so. She says you're going to be on telly?'

'That's right. Got the tickets through this morning. With a bit of luck, they'll give us one of the valuation slots. I sent the forms in ages ago.'

'You're taking the paintings?'

'That's the idea. Might as well see if they're worth owt.'

'Will you sell them?'

'I don't see why not. They've been sitting in the loft for the last thirty years.'

'I suppose so. Remind me. What's the programme called?'

'*Johnny Doc's Treasure Trove*. It's at Wetwang Hall next month. Your mother's so excited.'

'I could tell. She seemed a bit…confused.'

'Par for the course, son. Just how it is these days.'

'And what about you?'

'The pills help, as far as I know. From what they tell me, I sort of *switch off* sometimes, so I wouldn't know.'

'I haven't forgotten what we talked about. I've started pulling together a list of the options and I'll be working through it today.'

When we finished the call, I thought about how quickly things changed. It seemed like only yesterday that they were sticking a plaster on my knee or teaching me to ride my bike. Now, it was my turn to step up and care for them. I didn't feel adult enough for that. I'd just spent an hour reading Ben's diary. It was a sharp reminder of what was coming down the line for me and Jen to cope with.

I checked my watch. Another hour before I had to set off to the cottage to meet Jen. The cottage was what we called our little office, where we based our writing business. Jen was at the optician, then we were going to start planning the new project. I picked up the remote and searched the on-demand section of the Sky box. Sure enough, the previous series of *Treasure Trove* was online. I grabbed my coffee and settled in to see what all the fuss was about.

From what I could see online, there were two shows each week, dominating the Saturday evening schedule. Quite how some shows passed me by was shocking to a lot of people. I suppose Saturday night had always revolved around the pub. More recently, settling in with Jen and a film had become the routine. Anyway, part one was a fairly faithful rip-off of *Antiques Roadshow*. Nice weather, impressive grounds of a big house, and flamboyant experts valuing a range of items. Each show seemed to have one star item that was more valuable than the rest, eagerly introduced by the owner. I fast forwarded a lot of the chat. After a break for the news and a dreadful show that cobbled together clips from other dreadful shows, part two of *Treasure Trove* saw a tremendous change of gear. If the early show was quaint English country fare, post-news was brash, an American-style game show with a screaming audience, and loud music. It was a stretch to see my mum enjoying this, but…

Each segment followed the same pattern. A quick recap of the valuation, a chat with Johnny Doc, then the catchphrase, 'Are we going for the doors?' Invariably, the answer was yes. I suppose there wasn't much point if the answer was no. Anyway, this translated as the contestants agreeing to sell the items to Johnny. A couple of celebs (I had to google one to find out what she did) joined the valuers. Each took an envelope and trooped through the main entrance to *Johnny's Treasure House*. Cut to a band lip synching their latest hit (again, I had to look them up) then back for the big moment. Johnny and the guests agonising over which of the doors to open to reveal their fate.

The excitement reached fever pitch as a collection of scruffy teddy bears got the treatment. The valuation was £150. In theory, the sale price ranged from a cabbage up to £150,000. They won £150, but the audience reacted with the kind of celebration that revealed what would happen if football ever came home. I decided it was harmless fun. If it made Mum happy, I was pleased. I was also late, so I grabbed my phone and set off to work.

WHEN I GOT to the cottage, there was no sign of Jen. At least it gave me a chance to do the routine tasks that gave me enormous pleasure. A new project meant creating all the new files we needed. Something in the depths of my psyche loved this bit. We'd come to rely on Scrivener as our software of choice for writing, whether it was books or screenplays. I set up the project with sections for the six episodes we were targeting. Post-its were still crucial and the excitement of opening a new pack set the pulse racing. Maybe I needed to get out more. Before I could make a start on entering headings for the project, my phone rang. It was Angel.

'What were you two drinking last night?'

It was difficult to tell from her tone whether I was in the bad books or not.

'Nothing drastic. You were there. Why, what's up?'

'He's feeling very sorry for himself this morning.'

'He always was a bit of a lightweight.'

'I can see you being a bad influence.'

'Says the Bradford firebomber,' I said. I realised this may be a bit over the top. It was meant affectionately.

'Retired firebomber, if you don't mind. It was a one-off, and I wasn't very good at it. Bloody thing glanced off the wall of the house and hit the shed. Went up in seconds. Four years for a shed. Apparently, it's the thought that counts. Actually, that's partly why I'm calling.'

'Not thinking of a comeback, are you?'

'Maybe, if you don't behave and listen.' I behaved and listened. 'We were talking about it this morning. Justin got another email out of the blue.'

'How do you mean?'

'Sorry. I'll rewind. Last month, he got a message from this bloke in Ipswich. He was asking all kinds of questions about losing the house on *Johnny's House Builders*. Seems he was in the same boat. Lost everything. He was trying to set up some kind of group to see how many had the same story when he had a heart attack. Justin agreed to help but ended up taking over. Progress ground to a halt until this morning.'

'When he got another email.'

'Exactly. This guy was in Edinburgh. Same story. Pushed towards taking on extra finance, problems with the build, and losing the house at the end of it.'

'It must happen all the time with projects like that. People get over ambitious, not organised, unrealistic project plan. I know when we were doing the barn conversion, we overran the budget, even with Robbie being a control freak.'

'I suspect you're right. It's understandable that Justin wants there to be something dodgy going on.'

'Suppose it would mean it was somebody else's fault? But you've moved on from it now. You're back together, new business. You enjoy your work with us. Things look good, surely?'

'Just seemed like a strange coincidence that he was contacted. You're right. I'll tell him to forget it and get back to mastering the Blue Stilton and Cherry ice cream.'

'That sounds…interesting.'

'That's the word I used, at first. He's tried two batches so far. The first tasted like a weightlifter's foot, but the second was much better. He's trying to have it perfect for Easter.'

'That's ages yet. Plenty of time.'

'Next month, apparently. He's really looking forward to the festival season,' she said.

'Are you planning to be his assistant?'

'No way. I might go to the odd one, but standing in an ice-cream van for fourteen hours a day after a night in a tent isn't my idea of fun. Besides, I'm hoping you and Flic are going to keep me busy.'

'What do you know about betting scams?'

'Why? Who said something?'

That was an odd reaction.

'Nobody said anything. The next project is a remake of *The Sting*. We may need some ideas for updating the premise of the con, that's all.'

'Oh. Right. I'll give it some thought. Got to go. Flic's on the other line. Bye.'

I thought again about Angel's odd reaction. Was she hiding something or was I just overthinking things? With impeccable timing, Jen arrived with coffees.

'Hello, love. No donuts?'

'Not today. They're a once a flood treats, not one of your five a day.'

'Shame. That regime would be a lot more popular if they were.'

Jen gave me a withering look and patted my stomach. Ouch. I sat more upright and changed the subject.

'May I present our brand new and completely empty file for our new project? We have the proverbial blank canvas on which to paint our next masterpiece.'

'Wonderful. It'll be nice to get lost in a fictional world for a while.'

I looked across the desk at her.

'I know it's tough at the moment, love. It goes without saying…'

Jen nodded.

'You're doing all the right things. Don't worry. I'll soon shout if you're not. Right. How are we going to structure this thing?'

'Well. I'm hoping you've seen the film.'

'Nope.'

'That could make it more difficult. I winged the meeting by reading a synopsis online.'

'That settles it. Finish the coffees, then home to watch the film. May as well be comfortable on the sofa.'

'Can we have popcorn?'

'You can have popcorn.'

'Maltesers?'

'Don't push it.'

Sometimes there were unexpected benefits of having your own business. And I could sneak a box of Maltesers if I went to buy the popcorn.

'BUGGER. LOOK AT the time. Got to go. Make sure you write up a summary,' said Jen.

'Was I that good you want it writing up?'

'I meant the film, plonker. The rest was pretty good, granted.'

She kissed me, grabbed her keys from the coffee table, and set off towards the car. I took another two Maltesers and sat back, pleased with myself.

We'd spent the first part of the afternoon watching *The Sting* as planned. When the film finished, one thing led to another and…Well, we're still technically classed as newlyweds, and we had the house to ourselves. I made myself presentable and resumed my place on the sofa. Jen was right. I should write up a few notes on the film. It wasn't like we were going to use the actual story in our project. It was more the feel and style we wanted to acknowledge.

After scribbling a couple of pages of notes on my iPad, I checked my watch. Maybe an hour before Jen and Charley got back. Some of the online experts would say you could achieve a lot in an hour. Then again, you could have the rest of the Maltesers and surf the internet. Anyway, I started by looking up the name of Robert Redford's character. Johnny Hooker was a perfect name, and I knew we needed something as strong for our hero. Of course, we could use the same name as a tribute to the original. Was that just lazy? Sounded like me. I typed *Johnny* into the search bar. The name Johnny Docherty popped up, based on my search the other day. The words rabbit and hole came to mind, but I started scanning the entries for my mum's latest obsession.

Johnny Doc was one of those faces that was a regular on TV but had never really registered with me. Then something caught my eye. It was a chat show clip from last year. The description referred to my dear old friend Roddy Lightning. I switched on the TV and started streaming the clip. I had no idea who the host was, but I recognised his guest. The host looked serious as he spoke.

'Johnny, a sad moment this week with the passing of a friend of yours, Roddy Lightning.'

'Yeah, dear old Roddy,' said Docherty. 'Seems like the past caught up with him. You can't do that many drugs over the years and get away with it forever.'

Docherty actually thought this was hilarious. A few in the audience laughed nervously. The host ploughed on.

'You'd known each other a long time?'

'Yeah. I got to know him when I was working in the States. I was a production assistant on the show he did out there.'

'That would be *Black Gold*.'

'That's right. Of course, he was the big star at the time. I was just running around getting stuff for him. You do what you're told at that age.'

'Are we talking drugs here, Johnny?' The host winked at the camera to underline the scandal.

'Let's just say I had contacts. You had to in those days if you were trying to make a career in Hollywood.'

Again, he found this hilarious. I was getting angry. Docherty seemed to say that he was the one who introduced Roddy to the thing that almost destroyed his life. And there he was, laughing about it. What a bastard.

'In fact, you got your big break in front of the camera because of Roddy's – how shall we put it – love of the exotic?' said the idiot host.

'He was up for the role fronting *House Builders*. I was working for the production company. We went for a night out, part celebration and part catch-up. I left after a few drinks, but Roddy stayed. Went on such a bender, the company dropped him. To my amazement, they offered me the role. Never looked back. So, yeah, in a way, I owe him a lot. Cheers, Roddy.'

The rest of the interview continued with the host fawning over how wonderful Docherty was. I thought he was a twat. He seemed to celebrate Roddy's weakness. Had he taken Roddy out intending to get him into trouble and take his job? I knew that was a stretch, but I really didn't like the bloke. I didn't particularly want my parents getting involved in his show.

I heard the car pull up outside and switched off the TV. Ten seconds later, Charley burst into the room, and I was in dad mode.

'Ooof.'

Until recently, I'd never uttered that sound in my life. It was now a regular part of my vocabulary as Charley launched herself to land on top of me. She thought it was the funniest thing she'd ever heard. I dabbed at my eyes and asked her how her day had been. She'd inherited her enthusiasm for storytelling from her mother and I nodded at all the right places.

'Right, madam, leave your dad alone, and go wash your hands. I'll make you a snack.'

Charley flung herself up the stairs, and I struggled to my feet.

'I'll do that, love. You sit down,' I said, knowing that she'd turn down my offer.

'It's OK. I've got it. Besides, you're about to volunteer for something that I'll be very grateful for.'

'I am? That's nice. What is it?'

'Beer?'

'Yes, please. Hang on. How big is the favour?'

'A one beer favour. All right, maybe two.' Now I was worried. 'I just called in to see Mum and Dad.'

'How are they?'

'Fine. Dad's looking much better. Actually, it was him who asked the favour.'

'What is it?'

'Well, apparently, he's been going to the hospice for the last few weeks.'

'Hospice? But that's where people go—'

'Yes – but they do a lot more than that. His doctor referred him. They run a daycare centre for people like Dad. It gives Mum a break and gets him used to the place, know the staff, that sort of thing. It means, when the time comes…'

Tears welled up as Jen tried to finish the sentence. She busied herself with getting a beer from the fridge. As she handed it over, I pulled her to sit on my lap at the table.

'So, what do they do at these day sessions?'

Jen recovered quickly.

'All sorts. They can get massages, counselling sessions, learn new skills. They have a craft group that makes toys to sell in the shop. He seems to get a lot out of it.'

'Where do I come into it?'

'Dad suggested you might like to volunteer.'

'I can't massage old people, sorry,' I said, with more than a hint of panic in my voice.

'Don't worry. They won't let you anywhere near laying hands on people. They've got enough problems as it is.' Coming from anybody else, I would find this insulting. We both laughed and I could see the tension drain from Jen. 'He told me about his diary and what he'd asked you to do.'

'I thought that was meant to be a secret.'

'He was too excited and needed to tell me. I think it's a lovely idea. He wants to take it further. A lot of people at the hospice would benefit from being able to do that sort of thing, tell their story. Leave some kind of footprint while they can.'

'I still don't see where I come in. Surely, he doesn't want me to write books for everybody?'

'No. He knows we're going to be busy with the script. We think you should do one morning a week at the hospice and lead a group. Be on hand to get people started and support them while they write. A lot of them have never even used a laptop. You're great at that sort of thing and you got a lot out of my writer's group. You could do something similar for them.'

Normally, my first response would be to weasel out of something like this. I could find a host of reasons not to do it. Nobody was more surprised than me when I replied.

'OK. You're on. I can do that. One morning a week, you say?'

'Yes. Fridays. You start tomorrow.'

She kissed me and returned to making a snack for Charley. I had to get used to being outplayed like that. Best give some thought about how to get started.

9

'You'll be fine. I'll look after you,' said Ben. He was enjoying my discomfort and treating me like a five-year-old approaching school for the first time. My nerves weren't helped by having to squeeze into the final available parking space. We'd circled the car park twice before I committed myself. I decided it was probably therapeutic for Ben to laugh at me and grabbed the backpack from the rear seat before locking the car.

We entered through what had been the front door to a rather imposing Victorian house. A young woman greeted Ben at the reception desk like an old friend.

'You must be the star writer. I'll let Lucy know you're here.'

By the time we'd signed in, Lucy was shaking my hand. She was one of those women blessed with perfect skin and a smile that could light up Wembley Stadium.

'Ben's told us so much about you,' she said.

'I'll try to prove him wrong,' I said as we entered a large room to the left of reception.

'It's all good, don't worry. Ben, why don't you grab a coffee, and I'll give Frankie the tour? We'll be back in ten minutes and get started.'

By the time we crossed the room, Ben was in deep conversation with a small group clustered around a long table. At the far end, we reached an area of small tables, like an informal classroom.

'This is where we thought you could base yourself.' I took off my jacket and hung it over the back of a chair, dropping my backpack beside it. 'We've got a group of six for you today. Hope that's OK?'

'To be honest, I'm terrified. I've never done anything like this before.'

Lucy laughed and placed a hand on my shoulder.

'Don't worry, they don't bite. Except Barbara, she bites a bit. You'll be fine.' I felt something gently nudge the back of my legs. It was a dog. A beautiful black Labrador sat looking up at me. Lucy laughed. 'And this is Buster. He just wants to say hello.'

I bent and made a fuss of Buster. He seemed to be the most docile animal I'd ever encountered, just happy to be there. When he licked my hand, Lucy gently admonished him.

'Buster, why don't you go, and find Daisy?' Buster's ears pricked up, and he trotted off to a group of people clustered around a coffee table. Lucy gestured towards the door, and we started walking. 'Buster's a support dog. Everybody finds him very soothing. I think he understands what people are going through and does everything he can to help them. We all love him.'

'I can see why.'

'He's also our chief fundraiser. His image is on everything. Mugs, tea towels, badges. If we can sell it, Buster's on it.'

'You should do a Buster Dust-Buster Duster.'

'Great idea,' said Lucy. 'We always need creatives like you.'

'I'll visit the shop later and stock up.'

I meant it. Lucy was perfect for this job. There was something about her smile that just put me totally at ease.

She took me on a full tour of the building, greeting everybody by name, and introducing me.

We reached the main nurse's station. More introductions, this time Jane and Bella. I made a conscious effort to remember their names. Two men in dark suits approached the desk and Bella intercepted them. The three of them went through the door on the left. I was about to ask where they were going, but Lucy beat me to it.

'Through there is the main ward. I'll take you through later. It's closed at the moment.'

'Closed?'

Lucy gently guided me back down the corridor towards reception.

'The two men are funeral directors. I'm afraid we lost somebody this morning. We always close the ward to visitors while they do their stuff.'

This hit me hard. Of course, I knew the main reason the hospice existed, but it had all been so upbeat since I walked through the door. After a few steps, I paused, and looked at Lucy.

'Hope you don't mind me asking, how do you cope? Does it affect you?'

'Oh, it affects us all. I think if it doesn't, you're in the wrong job. We just have to come to terms with what we do. For me, I'm here to minimise the drama involved. We spend time with people. I think, in the end, most people have time to process things. They go through the stages of grief before they actually die. By the end, most people have found an inner peace. If I can contribute to that, it means so much. And from that point we try to help the families. It's those left behind that often have the most difficulty accepting what's happened. We try to help them too. Come on. Let's get you a coffee and you can get started.'

Raucous laughter greeted our return to the dayroom. It threw me for a second. I'd expected the place to be serious. People shuffling around in silence. It sounded more like the back room at The Crown. Lucy strode towards the group.

'Right. Hope you've all got an idea for your stories. This is Frankie. He's your guru and guide.'

Ben gave me the thumbs up as he slid away for his massage. Lucy ushered the small group towards the desks and nodded to a lady in a wheelchair.

'Frankie, could you do the honours for Daisy?'

I felt the panic rising. Here I was, a grown man, and I realised I'd never had to push a wheelchair. What if I crashed? Or worse, couldn't move it?

'Don't look so scared, love. I'm not that heavy.'

Daisy's laugh snapped me out of my panic. I spotted the brake without having to be instructed, and off we went. I even chatted with Daisy – just like a grownup.

To my amazement, when faced with half a dozen faces looking at me for leadership, I didn't freeze. In fact, I enjoyed myself. I remembered Jen on the evening we first met, nudging me to using pen, and paper to get started. The three laptops I'd brought stayed in my bag for now.

'I recommend you just write your story. Don't worry about if it's any good or what others may think. Nobody else has to read this if you don't want them to. Just let it flow.'

'What if we want people to read it?' said Daisy. One or two others murmured agreement.

'I'd still say the priority is to get to on paper. Then we can edit, make it better, correct the spelling mistakes.'

'Thank fuck for that,' said a voice from the back, triggering more laughter.

'Well put, Colin,' I said. 'For those who want to share their stories, I have an idea. Why don't we publish an anthology? I can help with self-publishing. We could even raise a few quid for the hospice. How does that sound?'

All of them agreed it would be great to see their names in print. We had another project. After half an hour, Daisy put down her pen. I squatted beside her.

'Everything all right, Daisy?'

'It's these bloody hands. Useless.' She was rubbing them together like she was cold. 'Neuropathy. From the chemo. Fingers are just about numb. I'm struggling to hold the pen.'

'Would you be better with a laptop?'

'Not really. Same problem. Maybe I should accept my limitations. Besides, I might not make it to publishing a book.'

She laughed, but she almost broke my heart.

'Hang on. We're not beaten yet. I've got an idea. May I?'

I pointed at the chair.

'Go for it.'

I released the brake and wheeled Daisy across to the corner of the room, away from the rest of the group.

'You making me sit in a corner? Like being back at school.'

'Just thought you'd find it easier away from the rest. Here, try this.' I dragged a desk across and one of the laptops. A few taps on the keyboard later, I was ready. 'Right. Watch the screen and say your name and why you want to write this.'

'Dozy bugger. Is it supposed to do it by magic? What the f…'

Daisy stopped mid-sentence, open-mouthed. She's obviously never seen the magic of dictation software as "dozy bugger" appeared on the screen.

'Don't worry about punctuation and stuff. We can tidy that up later. Just tell your story.'

I left her to it and went to check on the others. It didn't take long for the questions to start. They wanted to know what Daisy was up to. When I explained, suddenly everybody wanted a go. I had two more laptops and two of the group had iPhones. That was four more voices muttering their stories for dictation. Colin decided he was OK with his pen and paper.

As they all got busy, I phoned my partner in the software firm. Spud answered immediately. He asked about Jen and Ben. People seemed genuinely concerned. After establishing that all was well with the company, I launched into the real reason for my call.

'Do we still have a cupboard with loads of old laptops in?'

'We do. Not sure why we keep them, to be honest. Everybody manages to justify an upgrade, and the old ones just get stashed in case they come in handy.'

'That's what I was hoping you'd say.'

I explained my involvement at the hospice and why I needed the laptops.

'Sounds like a great idea. As I say, nothing wrong with the machines, and they'll be perfect for what you need. I'll need to wipe all our stuff, but not a problem.'

'Cheers, mate. I owe you one. I'll pick them up later in the week.'

It was a double win. Spud got rid of a pile of laptops that were taking up space. The hospice gained a valuable resource. I could provide everybody with one for next week. I was good at this.

All too soon, it was lunchtime. I started to pack up, ready to head off to the office for the afternoon to work with Jen.

'Where do you think you're going, young man?' It was Daisy. 'Stay for lunch. I'm sure it'll be OK. Besides, I need wheeling though.'

I was about to make an excuse, but Lucy appeared next to me.

'I was just about to insist that you stay. Come on. I bet you like meat and potato pie. You look like you do.'

It was impossible to take offence at anything that was said around here, and I wheeled my new friend through to the dining room. The pie was as good as advertised and quickly followed by rice pudding. Now, over coffee, we were chatting about families.

'And you're recently married?'

'Yes, to Ben's daughter. She's called Jen and, for some reason, decided I would do.'

'I'm sure she loves you very much. You've got a kind face.'

'Does that mean I can steal your chocolate Hobnob?'

'Dream on, sunshine. When you get to my age, you're never sure where your next biscuit is coming from.'

'Thirty-seven's no age.'

'Charmer. Add forty to it and you'll be closer,' said Daisy.

'Give over. I'd never have put you at eighty-seven.'

'Maths not your strong point then? Try seventy-seven. And before you say anything, yes, I do look my age. Didn't for years, but two strokes bugger up the beauty regime good and proper.'

'If you don't mind me asking, how long have you been in the chair?'

'Just over a year. Since the last stroke. I had it the same week as my husband died.'

'That's—'

'Shit. That's what it was.' Daisy took a deep breath. Why did I ask her that? Stick to the weather, idiot. 'Fifty-two years we had, me and Larry. Told him the sweets would kill him one day. He was a bugger for midget gems.'

'Heart attack?'

'Hit by a bus outside the newsagent. Still had the bag in his hand.' Daisy started laughing. It was a deep, all engulfing laughter that you just had to join in. 'At least he died happy. He still had two in his mouth when the paramedics got to him.'

She's obviously told the story many times. Maybe the laughter was her way of dealing with the nightmare.

'You got children, Daisy?'

It was like a cloud moved over her.

'No. Wasn't meant to be. We tried for long enough. In the end, we decided we were enough for each other. We were very happy, at least until the 486 did its thing. Just me now.'

'How do you manage, you know...' I nodded at the chair.

'Decided I didn't need the big house and now I live in my little flat. Sheltered accommodation. The warden's great. She comes round for a natter every morning. She fixed me up to come here. Then there's the carers that come in to make my meals and help me. Totally buggered without them, but I manage. It's a lovely place.'

'Sounds like just what I need for my parents. They need a bit of looking after now.'

'Get their names down where I am. There's a queue to get in but a regular flow of people leaving.'

'They leave?'

'We all leave in the end, son. Can't see me being that much longer.' Again, she erupted into laughter. Was this just bravado or had she really come to terms with mortality? 'I mean it. Remind me later, I'll get Lucy to give you the details. Now, tell me about what you've written,' she said.

'Have you seen a film called *The Hubberholme Syndrome*?'

'Loved it. Was that you?'

'Me and my girlfriend. Obviously, she's not my girlfriend anymore.'

'Sorry to hear that. Hope for me yet.'

Then I realised what I'd said.

'No. Don't get me wrong. We're married now. That's why she's not my girlfriend. Actually, I named my first ever character Daisy. *The Woman in The Yellow Raincoat*. She turned out to be a master criminal.'

'We all are, my dear. We all are.'

Whether that was all women or all Daisies I never established. My phone rang. It was Jen asking how things were going. We decided we could work for a couple of hours at the house rather than me dashing back to the office. I could give Ben a lift home to save Geraldine a trip. When I came off the call, people were drifting back to the dayroom. Daisy was pulling on her coat.

'Frankie, it's been lovely to meet you.'

'Not going, are you? I thought we'd be dancing this afternoon.'

'I'll hold you to that one day, but my taxi's here. Time I went home for a nap. Thanks for today. I really enjoyed it.'

'Me too. I'll see you next week. Can I assist?'

'Wagons roll.'

She waved regally to the rest of the group, and we made our way to the front door. I had to admit to feeling a bit deflated as the taxi trundled up the drive. Daisy was good fun.

'Have you forgotten me?'

'No. Of course not, Ben.'

I had. Another ten seconds and I'd have been on my way to the car.

'Good. I have to admit I'm knackered. So, that wasn't as bad as you thought?'

'I quite enjoyed it, if I'm honest.'

'Knew you would.'

Ben was fast asleep by the time we turned left onto the main road. I could cheerfully have joined him. It was only just after three o'clock, but the rush hour had already started. It took almost an hour to reach the end of our road. I was indicating to turn right when I caught a flash of bright yellow in the rear-view mirror. I tried to turn in my seat but was too late. The yellow raincoat, and its owner, had disappeared around the corner. Of course, I could be wrong. It was only in sight for the briefest of times. But Robbie was due for release this week. Could it have been her?

My heart was still pounding as I pulled the car onto Ben's drive. Some instinct in his brain kicked in and he woke up.

'We're back here quick. Thought it would be busy. Hope the kettle's on.'

PREDICTABLY, JEN WAS fussing with the teapot when we got inside. Gerry was sitting on the rug in the living room with her granddaughter. Some very involved game involving Barbie and a stuffed rabbit had them absorbed. I was more than a bit worried that the rabbit was twice the size of Barbie, who was probably being held against her will. Maybe I'd spent too much time writing about criminals. Ben was immediately called to action and took charge of Postman Pat. Barbie clearly didn't need the postman to ring twice. She had her hands full with the rabbit.

'My hero,' said Jen, as I hugged her. 'How did it go?'

'Don't tell anybody, but I enjoyed it. It felt weird at first, but everybody was so friendly. It felt nice to make a difference to their day.'

'How's Dad?'

'He seemed to have a great time. Tired now.'

We chatted for a few minutes.

'Maybe we need to rescue Ben from Charley's game,' I said.

'I'll do it. You pour the tea.'

'No need. Look at this,' said Geraldine.

We stood at the door of the other room. Ben and Charley were both fast asleep on the sofa. Jen took the light blanket from the back of the spare armchair and gently covered them both.

Back at the table, we sat and talked about nothing much. To be honest, my mind wandered. I was mulling over the clip I'd watched where Johnny Doc was talking about Roddy. Then the memory of what could've been a brief glimpse of Robbie reminded me of the database she'd given me a copy of. Her dad had kept records of all the criminals he'd ever had dealings with. It was a lot. I wondered if there would be anything about Docherty on it. It was a long shot. The guy was a celebrity. I had no reason to suppose he was a villain. I just took against him because of what he said about my friend.

The sound of Jen pushing her seat back from the table jolted me back.

'I just need to turn the oven down,' she said.

'Smells great. What are we having?'

'Roast pork.'

'With—'

'Yes. Crackling and roast spuds,' said Jen. 'Be nice to your mother-in-law. I'll be back in a minute.'

Jen disappeared upstairs. We chatted happily about our shared love of crackling. Geraldine looked around the room and smiled.

'You know, I've always loved this house. Jen's made it a proper home for Charley over the years. Now you've made it complete. It's cosy, warm, and happy. Trouble is, is it really big enough if…'

'You mean if we have more little ones?'

'Am I that transparent?'

'Shameless.'

'Jen always tells me to mind my own business. Is that what you're going to do?'

'I wouldn't dare speak to my mother-in-law like that. Let's just say I wouldn't be at all upset if Charley had a brother or sister to play with.'

'You'd definitely need a bigger house then. Shame, in a way. I'd really miss it. Then again, more babies would help me over it.'

'I'll see what I can do.'

10

Over the years, Saturday afternoons had meant many things. For most of my teens, it meant hanging around record shops, a regular meet-up for us music nerds. Then it was football, first playing (briefly), then watching. For a while, meeting friends for a drink before the game morphed into a drink instead of the game. Occasionally, that got very messy, merging as it did into Saturday night out with the lads. After that came the 'recovering from Friday night' years, when Saturday afternoon was spent asleep in front of *Soccer Saturday*.

Of all the versions, the current pattern took some beating. Weather permitting, I spent two hours in the park with Jen and Charley. Today, spring had definitely arrived. It wasn't exactly warm, but the sunshine on my face felt wonderful after the long winter. I'd shown off my football skills. Charley was impressed, particularly when I stood on the ball and ended up face down in the mud. That, apparently, was hilarious. A stroll around the lake was meant to tire her out before finally heading home. It wasn't working, but I was bushed.

Jen spotted the ice-cream van in the distance, and Charley upped the pace. I gave chase. Luckily, Charley stopped to laugh at my pathetic attempt to race. I really had to do something about my fitness. As soon as I'd had a 99. I struggled to get my breath back, then realised I knew the face inside the van. It was Justin.

'Good to see you still have the same turn of speed you had at school,' he said. 'Do you need a sit down?'

'I'll be fine once the wheezing stops.'

'Hi, Jen. What can I get you?'

'I'll have a choc-ice, an orange Calippo for madam, and a 99 for Mo Farrah here.'

This wasn't as funny as either Jen or Justin seemed to think. To make matters worse, they both expected me to pay. Jen thanked Justin before sitting on the bench to keep an eye on Charley, who'd made a beeline to talk to the ducks.

'We don't usually see you here,' I said.

'Just filling in. Next month, I start my tour. A few weeks at stately homes, then the festival sites.'

'Glad I bumped into you. I realised I didn't have your new number, and I wanted to ask you something.'

'Ask away,' he said, while fiddling with his phone. Mine vibrated as his contact details arrived. I loved it when technology worked.

'It was what you said about the *House Builders* programme being dodgy. Do you have any proof?'

'I'm not sure you could call it proof. More a pattern emerging so far. Why do you ask?'

'Oh, probably nothing. I'm always on the lookout for stories. To be honest, I saw an interview with Johnny Doc. What a twat.'

'He's that all right. If you're going to sniff around, I'd start with the producer of the show. I never actually met him, but he came across as a real arsehole in writing. If you like, when I get home tonight, I'll pull together what I've got so far. Mainly contact details for people in the same boat as me.'

'That would be great.'

'You and Jen out on the town tonight?'

'Not tonight. After chasing Charley round here all afternoon, I'm ready for the sofa and a good film. What about you?'

'Angel's doing a set for Joe early doors. Think we're just planning a few drinks afterwards.'

'Just you be careful. Joe is lethal when he gets going. And if he suggests a club, run for the hills.'

'I'll keep that in mind. Cheers, Frankie. See you soon.'

I walked towards the bench to sit with Jen. As I sat down, I looked across the lake just as a bright yellow raincoat disappeared behind the cricket pavilion.

'I think the Calippo was a mistake. If her face gets any more orange, she'll be running for president,' said Jen, pointing at Charley. 'How does spaghetti Bolognese and a bottle of Chianti sound?'

'Perfect, Mrs Dale. Just perfect.'

11

'What do you think?'

'It looks very nice. Well organised. You should have a trip to show them the website. See what they think,' said Jen.

We were talking about the sheltered accommodation complex where Daisy lived.

'Why don't we have a drive over there this afternoon? It's what Sundays are for. We could take Charley to the beach,' I said.

'Sounds like a great idea, except she's at a birthday party – remember? I'm helping with twenty of the little monsters, so I expect you to look after me tonight. But you should go. You said you'd see them more often.'

'True. I suppose I could set off late morning and still be home in time to cook something nice.'

'Or pick up pizza on the way back.'

'Twice in a week. Is that allowed?'

'Add peppers for a bit of variety if you like. Vitamin C and one of your five a day.'

'Even better.'

I figured I'd got the best of this deal. Much as I loved Charley, the idea of twenty screaming kids for the afternoon made my toes curl. This way, I got to play loud music on the drive to the coast, chat with Mum and Dad, fall asleep on the sofa before returning as the hero with pizza. I even had time to call in and see how far Angel and Justin had got with investigating Johnny Docherty.

It was Justin who answered the door.

'Our local celebrity.'

I gave Justin a look and followed him inside.

'What do you mean?'

'Angel's been telling me all about the writing and TV appearances. I had no idea.'

'Must admit to being a bit hurt that you never mentioned it. I assumed you were just playing it cool.'

'Totally oblivious, mate. Spent the last two years building a business and trying to learn Hungarian. More than enough for anyone. Never been one for checking Facebook every five minutes. Not much coverage of English celebs on Hungarian telly. No offence.'

'None taken.' For once in my life, I turned down the offer of coffee. 'Flying visit, I'm afraid. On my way to see my parents in Brid.'

'Say hello from me. Do you think they'll remember me?'

'Without a doubt. Even with the dementia, I suspect you'll still register.' Justin looked unsure if this was a compliment. 'No Angel this morning?'

'She's already out – busking in Leeds. Then she's meeting friends to watch the Bulls.'

'Didn't fancy the match?'

'Ice cream won't sell itself.'

'Fair enough. Just thought I'd see where you'd got with our friend Johnny Doc?'

Once again, I found myself at my old kitchen table, hunched over a laptop, scribbling in a notebook.

'I'll email a copy of this spreadsheet. It's not very impressive, to be fair. I started gathering contact details of people who lost their houses after being involved with the programme. Plenty of similarities between my case those who've got in touch so far.'

'What actually happened to you? Obviously, I know the firebomb-y bits but still a bit vague about what led up to that.'

'Long story short, we bought a house that needed a lot of work. I say we. It was me, but with our money. Meant to be a nice surprise. That's what pissed-off Angel initially.'

'Initially?'

Justin nodded. 'It gets worse. I was between jobs, so I decided I would do a lot of the work myself. I moved in while it was still a building site so I could save on rent.'

'Didn't know you were a builder.'

'I'm not. I'd done a bit in Italy. We built a kitchen extension on the farmhouse. Very basic stuff. A whole house was much more complex and I figured that out very quickly. That's when I called in a professional. A bloke called Vic Jackson. He reckoned he could do the work but would need proper plans, that sort of thing. He put me in touch with an architect, Samantha Crow. Looks exactly like her name suggests.'

'She sounds lovely.'

'Anyway, she passed my details to Trowel Productions. Sven Trowel is the producer of *House Builders*, at least on paper. I never met him, but he signed all kinds of stuff. They said they would pay a fee if I agreed to be on the show. Seemed like a no-brainer. The fee would cover the extra costs of the plans and builders. I quite fancied being on telly too, if I'm honest. As you know, things went wrong with the build. Jackson blamed Crow. Crow blamed Jackson. They both blamed me. It was a mess. We had delay after delay, and I ran out of money. The bank was about to take the house. Angel took exception to the idea, blamed me, and you know the rest.'

'So, what makes you think there's a pattern with the others?'

'Similar story of delays. No firebombs but, in all three cases, Trowel acted as an intermediary to a mystery buyer. They stepped in and offered us less than we'd have got from the banks. The benefit was no bankruptcy on our credit records. Same result – no house. We all went for it. Now the houses are all finished and worth several hundred thousand more than what they paid.'

'How long's the show been going?'

'Fourteen series now, twenty episodes in each. They're all still available online.'

'Why don't we do a bit of digging? Watch as many episodes as we can, make notes of the ones that go wrong. See if we can trace them.'

'You're on. Will take a while, there's a lot of them.'

'You take the odd numbered series, and I'll do the evens. See where we get to.'

'OK. Now, I need to go. Otherwise, the kids will be rioting in the park if I'm not there.'

'And I'm off to the seaside.'

THE DRIVE TO the coast was uneventful. At this time of year, the roads were quiet. Once Easter was upon us, the crowds would flock, and the roadworks would start. The one thing that never occurred to me was to call ahead. Mum was always there, especially on Sunday afternoon.

They weren't there. I'd picked the one day in living memory they were out. How could they? Getting into the house wasn't a problem. I had a key. Sure enough, the place was deserted. I called both mobiles and, as expected, got no answer. For a moment, I had visions of interrupting a Sunday afternoon of passion. The trauma could stay with me for years. To my relief, Mum's coat wasn't hung up. They were definitely out, and I had no way of knowing when they'd return.

At least I could have a cup of tea before I went home. As their only child, I felt sure they would want me to raid the biscuit barrel as well. What I saw next shocked me. Duchy Organic Orange and Dark Chocolate – two packets. Just when you thought you knew somebody, they blow your inheritance on luxury biscuits. I helped myself to two.

Before I sat down, I pulled open the kitchen drawer. A sixth sense told me there would be a notebook in it. There was. And a pen clipped to the cover. I could leave them a note if they didn't get home in the next half hour. As I took out the pad, the pen snagged against a large envelope. Being a writer meant I'd developed a heightened sense of curiosity. OK, I was a nosey bugger. It was a letter, confirming their appointment for a valuation of the paintings as part of *Johnny Doc's Treasure Trove*. I was just about to push the two sheets back into the envelope when I noticed the letterhead. Trowel Productions. That was the second time today they'd cropped up. Once I thought about it, it seemed reasonable that both of Johnny Doherty's shows were produced by the same company. Given what Justin suspected, I was suddenly uneasy that my parents were getting involved with them. At least it was only a couple of worthless paintings they were risking.

I wrote a note and included the website name for them to look at the sheltered housing. It would be better to walk them through it, but it could be hours before they returned. I finished my tea and rinsed the cup. As I reached the door, I couldn't resist going back for another biscuit. It was their fault for having such expensive treats in the cupboard. I locked up and headed back to the car.

By the time I reached the main road, the phone rang. I glanced at the name, saw the D, and hit answer.

'Dad, where are you?'

'I hate to break it to you, but I'm not your dad.'

What? No breaking it to me gently? Then I heard the laugh. It wasn't my dad. It was Demus.

'Sorry, mate. I was expecting—'

'Your dad, by any chance?'

'How did you guess? Shall we start again? How are you?'

'I'm fabulous. Actually, scrub that. Joanne's away for a few days and I'm a bit bored. Just thought I'd call to see how you're getting on with *The Sting*.'

'Still at the ideas stage, to be fair. We'll start fleshing them out in the office tomorrow. Why the rush?'

'I just get twitchy if I've got nothing to do. I'm not used to it.'

'You could do some detective work again.'

'Seriously? I'm in. I loved all that last time.'

'It's not particularly exciting at the moment.'

I told him all about Justin and his theory that Johnny Doc was dodgy.

'Never liked the odious little shit,' he said.

'You know him?'

'Sort of. Been on the same chat shows, met at awards ceremonies, that sort of thing. A friend of mine worked for him years ago. Touchy feely, if you get my drift. She left after a couple of months.'

'Do you know everybody?'

'It's a very small world in TV. The same faces popping up at different companies. Now, what do you need me to do?'

I explained about gathering evidence by watching the shows, in particular the ones where the build went wrong. To my surprise, he was enthusiastic.

'If I can do anything to expose the git, I'll do it.'

I explained Justin was watching the odd numbered series. We divided the even ones between us. While I was on a roll, I tried my luck.

'I don't suppose you know anything about getting paintings valued?'

'I played an art expert in an episode of *Silent Witness* when I was younger.'

'How did that go?'

'Horribly murdered, as you'd expect.'

'Does that make you an expert?'

'No, but I know one. My sister owns a gallery in Manchester. She sources stuff for us. A bit of a hobby with Joanne that's turning into an obsession. What do you need?'

'My parents have a couple of paintings that they're taking to Docherty for his *Treasure Trove* show. Just want to make sure they don't get ripped off.'

'Sounds easy enough. I'll have a word with Gabby – that's my sister. I'll get back to you. Right, I've got research to do.'

'Glad to help. I'll call you through the week.'

Demus was a very useful person to have around. Did I mention he was a big star and my mate? All this and pizza coming up. I added to the note I'd just scribbled to let them know I'd taken the paintings with me to get them valued. Once in the car, I put my foot down and headed for home.

12

I woke with a start, my heart pounding. Things had never quite been the same since the break-in last year. I was just keeping an eye on the house while Jen and Ben were off on their coast-to-coast walk. These days, the slightest noise woke me. There it was again. The bloody fox was back. Now, I love nature as much as the next man. Unless the next man was David Attenborough. Nobody loves nature more than him. But why did the fox have to make so much noise at – I peered at the radio – 4.27 in the morning? Because he's a cocky little shit. That's why. At least it wasn't a burglar coming through the kitchen window. Shit. Why did I think of burglars? Now there would be no more sleep.

Between four and five hours was the tipping point in my sleep pattern. Long enough that my brain wanted to get going for the day, but short enough that I would feel crap all morning, and have to go for a nap in the afternoon. Just like a baby. I'd come a long way in forty years.

Jen must've sensed I was awake. She was almost asleep as she spoke.

'What's up?'

'Nothing,' I whispered. 'Go back to sleep. I might get up.'

'No. Sleep. Come cuddle…'

Her last act before returning to a deep sleep was to clamp her right arm across my face. She had me in a headlock. An affectionate headlock, but a headlock, nonetheless. I breathed in the subtle moisturiser. Oxygen, however, was in short supply. I had to move if I was not to expire in the next couple of minutes. My mind flashed back to watching the wrestling on telly with my dad. Somehow, I slid down the bed, towards freedom, taking the duvet with me.

'Come on, referee…' said Jen.

Jen's right hand was now flapping, chasing the errant duvet. Luckily, she was still fast asleep. I reunited her with the warm duvet, pulled on my jeans and T-shirt, and slipped out of the door. I made it as far as the bottom of the stairs, where I froze. Two eyes were staring through the window beside the front door. The urge to go to the toilet was almost overpowering. I kept my eye on the figure as I searched for a weapon. Then I realised the figure moved at the same time. It was my reflection. I was wearing a Stevie Wonder T-shirt featuring a picture of the great man himself. He may be a musical hero, but he'd scared the living shite out of me.

The kitchen was where the burglar had come through the window, so I swerved the coffee I craved, and slipped into the living room. Back in my old house, the music would've been playing by now. With Jen and Charley upstairs, I had to be quiet. I thought of headphones but was still a bit too freaked to be cut off like that. If I had the volume on really low, I could start the marathon watching *Johnny Doc's House Builders*.

Within seconds, the first download was ready to go. I shivered and grabbed the blanket from the back of the other chair and settled in to watch.

Docherty oozed across the introduction. They were somewhere in Essex. The subject was a small, square set fifty-year-old with a lazy eye. He was going to be a disaster. When the main contractor pulled out, I reached for my notebook. Failure number one coming up. I fast forwarded through the ads as the man got stuck in. Turned out he was a grafter and knew what he was doing. A surprisingly impressive home appeared from the muddy building site. I was rooting for him as the crane winched in the enormous window, just as the snow started to fall. By the time the lambs were gambolling in the field next door, his family had moved in, and they were sharing a glass of red with Docherty.

I was disappointed. I'd actually enjoyed the programme, which was not the aim. The second show was similarly heart-warming. A fresh-faced, round couple from Aberdeen building a perfectly acceptable modern box. They were immensely pleased with their bi-folding doors. I'd harrumphed when I saw them on the plan but had to admit – I wanted some.

Show three was more promising. It was from Leeds. This made me realise I should ask Justin which episode he was in, as I should watch that, too. Anyway, the bloke in Leeds was a teacher. His wife was a nurse. They inherited money from his parents and were pouring their life savings into a barn conversion. I knew a bit about this, having been through one in a previous life with Robbie. They were such a nice couple but soon appeared well out of their depth. The money seemed to run through their fingers. The final shot showed them both sitting on a wall, looking at the barn. It was uncanny, like the night I'd done the same. Except mine didn't have a Johnny Doc voiceover lamenting the death of their dream and the sale of the half-built home.

I was just finishing my notes when the sounds of movement came from upstairs. I would have to google the episode later and track down the exact location. We were underway, and I desperately wanted to return to bed.

'Am I that boring?'

I finished my magnificent yawn before answering.

'Course not. Sorry. Just tired.'

'You don't seem very fired up for this project. Are you sure there's nothing wrong?' said Jen.

She pushed her seat back and put her feet on the desk.

'Nothing. Honest. Let's try a different tack. I think we're trying to make the idea too perfect. Have everything mapped out before we start. We never work like that. Could we make a start on the bits we know?'

'Even if we don't really know what the story's about?'

'But we do,' she said. 'A bit. We know that the bad guy has done a bad thing. The hero wants to avenge the bad thing that was done to his friend. We know there has to be a clever plan to do a thing. Then do the thing and engineer a big finish.'

'When you put it like that, it virtually writes itself.'

'Would a chocolate biscuit help?'

'Couldn't harm,' I said. Jen put her head on one side. It barely took me ten seconds to pick up on the hint. 'Shall I make the coffee then?'

'That would be nice,' she said.

I yawned again as I made my way to the kitchen. By the time I returned, Jen was on the phone. She took the mug I was offering and chose the Twix over the KitKat.

'He's back. Hold on, Demus. I'll put you on speaker.'

'Hi, Frankie. I hear you're feeling a bit uninspired.'

'I'm sure we'll be fine once we come up with a clever idea,' I said.

'How about a distraction for a minute? I spoke to Gabby, my sister. She's happy to take a look at the paintings for you. I'll send you her contact details. Could you get over to Manchester in the next couple of days?'

'I'm sure I can manage that.'

'Great. I think she gets a bit bored in the gallery by herself all day. She'll be glad of the distraction. Sorry. I need to go. Another call coming in. Just a thought for *The Sting*. How about art fraud? Copy of a masterpiece, that sort of thing. Switch the paintings at the last minute. I'm sure you two could work your magic on that.'

'But I don't know anything—'

'Great idea, Demus,' said Jen, cutting off my protest. 'We'll get cracking straight away.'

Demus went to his other call.

'Do you really think we could base the story on that idea?'

'We can at least make a start. What we don't know, we learn. If the whole thing is terrible, we think again. Sometimes, the best way to get out of this kind of slump is just to start writing. Something will come to us.'

When it came to writing, I couldn't argue with Jen. She was always right with her suggestions. I picked up the Post-its and wrote the words 'art fraud'.

We were up and running.

13

Jen had encouraged me to take this trip. What she actually said was that I would be as good as useless until I got it done. Same thing really. I clutched the securely wrapped paintings to my side and stepped off the train. Little did the throng of people in Piccadilly Gardens realise that the brown paper parcel could be worth millions. Then again, it was probably just some old junk that had been in the loft for forty years.

Demus had explained where the gallery was, and I soon found the turning off Market Street. He'd said that Gabby worked in a gallery. What he failed to mention was that it was her name picked out in foot-high letters across the facia of the double shop front. The Gabby Wolf Gallery looked impressive, stylish, and completely devoid of customers. The real-life *Vogue* model who greeted me could only be Gabby. I would've picked her out of any lineup as Demus's sister. It must be the bone structure. She greeted me like an old friend.

'Frankie. Demus told me so much about you.'

'I hope not. At least you should just believe the good bits.'

'Don't worry. It's all good. We both agree that you and Jen have the magic touch when it comes to scriptwriting. Drink? I have a rather nice Sancerre in the back. I wouldn't usually, but this seems like a special occasion.'

'In that case, it would be rude not to. Thanks.'

'Come into the sanctum.'

She led the way through the white painted door at the back of the large space. Come to think of it, all the walls were white too. I'd be worried about not being able to find the office if it was mine. In contrast to the pristine gallery, the office was chaotic. Piles of books and invoices seemed to cover every surface.

I picked up a sheaf of papers from a chair by the desk. An outsize bulldog clip held it all together. I glanced at the top page.

'Here, let me take that out of your way,' said Gabby.

'Interesting title. Is there really much lost art from Manchester?'

'You'd be surprised. There's more than I thought when I had the idea for the book. I'm discovering all kinds of dark shenanigans.'

'I love a dark shenanigan. Do you have a publisher lined up?'

'Yes. Dead keen.'

'When's it due?'

'Two years ago. Treat 'em mean, keep 'em keen's always been my motto. This place takes up so much of my time.'

Gabby pushed the manuscript into a desk drawer. I looked around. Framed pictures were stacked five deep against two of the walls. A huge print hanging above the desk dominated everything. It was the classic Andy Warhol design with four different coloured images. Instead of Marilyn Monroe, it was Gabby who smouldered over the office. She saw me gazing.

'My pride and joy. I couldn't bear to part with it, so it stays in here.'

'Did you produce it yourself?'

'God no. I don't advertise the fact, but the photograph is a Warhol original.'

I couldn't help laughing as I took the wineglass from my host.

'Come on. You can't have been born when Warhol died.'

'I was three. But the picture isn't me. It's Granny Wolf. Of course, she wasn't Granny back then. She was a young artist, learning from the master in New York. I made the print as a sort of tribute when she died.'

'It's fabulous. I can see why you'd keep it. You're very talented,' I said.

'If only. No. I'm competent, that's all. And self-aware enough to know from an early age that I couldn't compete with true genius. I figured the gallery was a better match for my skill set.'

'It seems to be going well.'

'It keeps the wolf from the door, so to speak. Cheers.'

'Cheers.'

'To business. Mr Dale. Show me what you've got.'

I handed over the neat parcel. Jen was very good at wrapping. Gabby moved a large frame from the workbench and carefully extracted the paintings.

'Very nice,' she said, laying the two frames side by side on the table. 'You say they've been in your parents' loft for the last forty years?'

'Near enough. I suspect you're going to tell me to put them back.'

'Not at all. At the very least, I would have them on the wall.'

'But not priceless?'

'Maybe not. I may as well tell you now that they're not by Lowry. I take it that's what you were hoping for?'

'It would've been nice. Better than a kick in the slats, as my dad would say.'

'I'd need to get a friend of mine to confirm it, but I think they're by Cedric Sherry.'

I started to nod, as if I'd heard of him, but decided to look blank instead.

'Never heard of him.'

'Not many people have to be fair. He was an accomplished painter in his own right but specialised in Lowry lookalikes. This really prevented him from developing his own style and becoming famous. His wife – on the other hand – you will know. Deidre Campbell. She went for big, colourful abstracts. She gives Hockney and Dali a run for their money when it comes to value. If you find a couple of them in the loft, you might want to give me a call.'

Now, Hockney and Dali, I knew of. I had to admit I'd heard the name Deidre Campbell but wouldn't have been able to tell you what type of painting she did.

'Can I hold on to these for a week or so? I have a friend in Cardiff who'd be able to confirm everything for you. As luck would have it, I'm staying with him this weekend. In fact, Joanne and Demus will be there too. I can send them back with Demus, if that's OK with you?'

'Sure, if it's no trouble? My mum and dad will need them next month.'

'Demus said they were taking part in *Treasure Trove*. Keep an eye on them. He's a shark if ever there was one. They should be OK. My guess is that the paintings are worth about £500 to £2000 each, assuming I'm right. Not enough for Docherty to rip them off.'

'Do you think he's dodgy?'

'There are rumours. Nothing proven. I shouldn't slag him off. He's a regular here. He has a decent eye. Bought a few decent pieces over the years.' There was a discreet but audible beep. Gabby glanced at the monitor on the other wall. 'Excuse me. Potential client. Back in a minute.'

I watched on the monitor as she swept into the main gallery. She was soon in deep conversation about one of the beautifully lit pieces on the wall. I sipped my wine. OK, so not by Lowry, but she thinks they're nice paintings. At least Mum and Dad would enjoy their fifteen minutes of fame. I bet they'd have tea and scones on the day out as well. What more did they want?

IT WAS PROBABLY a very nice rucksack, as far as these things go. My nose had pressed against it for the last hour and the novelty wore off around fifty-nine minutes ago. To say the train was full was an understatement. It was hot, smelly, and unpleasant. I dreaded to think what it would be like at rush hour. How could people do this day after day? Being able to work from our little office, a ten-minute walk from home, was such a blessing. As we pulled into Halifax, the platform looked like Wembley Way on cup final day. Around half of the carriage pushed for the exit, and for a moment, seats were visible. I dropped into the nearest one with a sigh. My pleasure was short-lived as another backpack clattered into my arm. If anything, the train was even more packed than it was before. At least I had a seat.

In theory, I could watch another episode of *House Builders* on my phone. In reality, the signal was so bad I gave up after a few seconds. Staring out of the window seemed like the best option. Eventually, we crept towards Leeds. After a ten-minute wait just outside the station, the platform edged into view. A flash of yellow raincoat caught my eye. I was fairly sure it was Robbie, picking her way through the crowds towards the exit. Strange that she was out of prison but hadn't been in touch. Then again, why should she? I'd made it pretty clear that my future was with Jen. I'd kind of underlined that point by getting married. She appeared to have taken my advice and was getting on with her life.

The train finally lurched to a halt, and the scramble for the doors started. I was prepared to sit patiently and wait, but the tutting from beside me forced my hand. I dipped my shoulder and pushed my way out, clutching my ticket as if my life depended on it. My hatred of automatic barriers went back years. It was the way it sucked your ticket out of your hand and spit it back at you. On a good day, the barrier opened like a bad-tempered bouncer waving you through. Then there was the risk of being flattened by those behind if it barred your entry. I could feel the tension mounting as I approached. My palms were sweaty. What if my sweaty hands had damaged the ticket? Swept along by the crowd, I proffered the key to freedom. With a frankly aggressive attitude, the ticket disappeared, the barrier opened, and I was free.

'Fancy a pint?'

Not the reaction I expected. I paused and was promptly shoved out of the way. Robbie was beside me, grinning.

'Robbie. I heard you were…How did you know I was here?'

'I saw you as your train pulled in. How about that pint?' Part of me wanted to run away, but even I realised that would be stupid. 'It's just a pint for old times' sake. I promise I'll be able to keep my hands off you. Half an hour, then Jen can have you all to herself.'

I weakened.

'Why not?'

We strolled through the station, heading towards Friends of Ham. I felt strange chatting with my ex-fiancée. The bar had been a favourite when we were together. It felt like I was being disloyal to Jen. I told myself not to be so stupid. It was just a drink.

'So, what have you been up to?'

'Largely, being in prison, to be honest.'

'Sorry. Stupid question,' I said.

'Not your fault. It's just nice to get out and about again. I was on my way home from Wakefield when I saw you. Interview for a job.'

'Any good?'

'What do you think? Call centre. Minimum wage.'

'Sounds lovely. Will you get it?'

'Already told them to shove it. It was my mother's idea. Wants me to stay out of trouble.'

'And will you? Stay out of trouble?'

'I've got no intention of going back inside, believe me. Straight and narrow from now on. Although, I do have a couple of scores to settle.' I paused and looked at her. 'Don't worry. I've still got lots of contacts in the logistics game. Thought I may start up under my own steam. Small scale to start with. I've got a potential option already.'

'And what about settling scores?'

'Longer term. Will take me a while to work out how to do it. But I will.'

Then something hit me. I stopped in the middle of the crowded pavement.

'I'm not on the list, am I?'

'You? Why would you be? I loved you. Still do if I'm honest. I'm deeply sorry about everything that happened. I wish I could turn the clock back.'

We resumed walking.

'So, who's on your list?'

Robbie seemed to consider her answer carefully as we paused at the crossing.

'There's a very senior police officer who took money from my father for years. He thought he was buying loyalty, a bit of protection. When he needed a friend in high places…'

'You can't seriously be talking about bringing down somebody from the police?'

'Keep your voice down. He's not just any old police officer. Very senior. I thought you'd have come across some of the evidence already. Make a good book at some point.'

'Me? Why me?'

'The database.'

'Crookipedia?'

Robbie let out a snort of laughter.

'Is that what you call it?'

'Thought it was quite a good name. I'd almost forgotten about it, to be fair. It helped us to track down the Fifth Man, but I haven't needed it since.'

'I thought you would've been all over it. Would be a great source of story ideas, I'm sure.'

We reached the door of Friends of Ham. A large group of middle-aged women were just leaving. Judging by the shopping bags and raised voices, it had been a good day. In that moment, it hit me.

'Sorry, Robbie. This is wrong. I need to be home. Jen's expecting me.'

'It's just a pint. You sure I can't tempt you to stay out? I'm meeting Angel and Justin at Headrow House later. There's a new band she wants to see.'

'Who is it?'

'No idea. New music has kind of passed me by for the last couple of years.'

I nodded sympathetically. Would Jen mind if I had a night out? What the hell was I thinking?

'No. Honestly, I'd best be off. It's been nice to catch-up. Good luck with the new business and enjoy the band.'

Robbie just stood there, holding the door open. Was I expected to kiss her? A peck on the cheek was just friendly, surely? I was about to lean in when Robbie stuck out a hand. I shook it, rather formally.

'Thanks, Frankie. Good to see you.'

I scurried up the hill. My heart was still pounding as the taxi edged out into the traffic.

'YOU SHOULD'VE BEEN here half an hour ago.'

'Why? What happened?'

I was trying for levity, but I could see Jen was pissed off.

'I should be at the community centre by now. You're meant to be looking after Charley – remember?'

'Shit. Sorry.'

The writers' group. Jen still ran the group where we'd first met. I felt bad that I'd made her late. She picked up her bag.

'I called one of the girls. They're opening up for me. Where've you been, anyway?'

'The train was late. Then I bumped into a mate in the station.' Time to cleverly change the subject. 'I could murder a beer.'

'All right for some. Right, Charley's fed and watered. She's in her room chatting with Issy on her iPad. Ten minutes, then she needs a break before you read to her. Don't suppose you got to IKEA for the units?'

I sensed this was a rhetorical question, as Jen had put her coat on and was heading for the door. I followed her.

'I am really sorry. I'll get my finger out tomorrow.'

'Got to go. Lamb tagine in the oven.'

Jen kissed me on the cheek and hurried off to her car. I'd never seen her like that. I could see her point. She was very committed to the group, and I had said I'd be home in time. I closed the door and trudged back to the kitchen. The lamb smelt wonderful, but I was no longer hungry. My first reaction was to open the fridge for a beer but stopped myself. I could at least wait until Charley was asleep. Instead, I poured milk into a saucepan and busied myself making hot chocolate.

Why had I said I'd bumped into a mate? Jen would've understood if I'd said it was Robbie. There was still some animosity after what happened years ago, but she'd been the one who'd insisted I visit Robbie in prison. We'd have a chance to speak properly when she got home.

I took the two cups of hot chocolate upstairs. The sound of giggling through the bedroom door was infectious, and I started to feel calmer. Leaving the cups on the windowsill, I slipped into the bathroom. After changing into jogging bottoms and a fleece, I tapped on Charley's door.

'Time to say goodnight to Issy, sweetheart.'

'Ten more minutes.'

'If you have ten more minutes, you won't have time to drink your hot chocolate.'

'Got to go, Issy. See you tomorrow.'

She was very decisive. I think she got it from her mum. I perched on the tiny stool beside Charley's bed and we both savoured the chocolate drink. At least she noticed the blob of chocolate on the end of my nose. Her laughter was the best cure for feeling like a bit of an arsehole. By the time we'd finished, Charley was already looking sleepy. The story was a short one. My audience was spark out.

I rescued the tagine from the oven. The last thing I wanted to do was appear ungrateful that Jen had cooked such a tasty meal. After I finished eating, I stacked the dishwasher and settled down to watch another *House Builders*. The first one I watched was straightforward. Nice couple, bit of drama, end up with a nice enough house. It was the second of the evening that made me think.

First, he was local. I recognised the area as being just a few miles from me, close to the Leeds Ring Road. It backed onto the last remaining green space for miles around. Wayne, the subject, was a single thirty-something with big plans. He was converting an attractive 1930s bungalow into an ultra-modern shag-pad. Quite how he got planning permission for the huge extension on the back was a mystery. Once a big digger finished excavating where the lovingly tended garden had stood, his problems started. Estimates seemed to count for nothing, and his projected costs rocketed. One by one, ambitious features got pared back or abandoned altogether. What he ended up with was a charmless bungalow with an astroturf back garden. It did not bring him joy (nor, I suspect, the sexual delights he'd envisaged).

I was just finishing a few notes when I heard the door. Jen was back, and I sprang into action.

'Hello, love. Can I get you a drink? Wine? Tea?'

'Tea would be nice. Splitting headache.'

'You sit down. I'll bring it through with a side order of paracetamol thrown in.'

I realised I was being over the top jovial. The rebuke from Jen earlier had stung. I threw in a few biscuits for good measure.

'Listen. I'm sorry about earlier. It was thoughtless of me to be late back,' I said.

'You have to remember you have responsibilities now. If you say you'll be here to take care of Charley, then…'

'And I'm sorry. It won't happen again.' Jen was still a bit frosty. This was a new side to her. 'I'll sort the units out this week, I promise.'

The cheeky grin didn't seem to have its normal impact. Jen reached for my hand but stared straight ahead.

'I'm sorry. I didn't mean to take it out on you.'

'What is it, Jen? You're worrying me.'

She took a deep breath.

'It's Dad. He's not as well as he's making out. I'm sure they aren't telling me everything. They were both evasive when I asked about his latest scan, and he just tried to change the subject. I'm worried that the treatment isn't working.'

'But you don't know for sure?'

'No. Just a feeling.'

'Anyway. Even if it's not working – it's happened before. They change to another drug and he improves.'

'True. But there's a limit to how many different drugs they can try.' She started to sob. 'I'm scared we're going to lose him.'

'Come here.' I held out an arm, and she snuggled in close. I was powerless to do anything else.

14

There it was again. The bloody fox. Was it picking on me, or did it visit every garden in the area and make as much noise as possible? It was 4.41. He was late. The thought reminded me of Jen being annoyed with me. Was I overreacting? Was she? It was hard because, in all the time we'd been together, we'd hardly had a crossed word. Maybe I needed to make that grand gesture after all. I ought to look at a few more properties. I should also look at the properties from *House Builders* if I was serious about investigating Johnny Doc.

It seemed I was wide awake. I slipped out of bed, desperate not to wake Jen, grabbed my clothes, and let myself onto the landing. Once downstairs, rather than switching on the TV, I took my jacket from the hook, scribbled a note for Jen, and stepped out into the darkness. I checked the garden for the fox. I hadn't thought far enough ahead to work out what I would've done had he confronted me. Were foxes aggressive? This one was so horny I wouldn't put anything past it. Anyway, the garden was now a fox-free zone.

It was starting to rain, so I took the car. Five minutes later, I was letting myself into our office. As usual, I found the place a bit creepy when it was dark and switched on all the lights. Music and coffee soon followed, and by ten past five, I was at my desk. Then I realised I'd left my notes at home. Cursing under my breath, I used Google Maps to search the area where the shag-pad bungalow was. Thanks to Street View, it wasn't difficult to work out the address. While I was there, I did the same for the barn conversion. I was about to watch the next *House Builders* episode when an email popped into my inbox. It was from Angel. She'd attached three more properties that she and Justin had identified. What was she doing sending emails at this time? I hit reply to ask the question and the phone rang immediately.

'I'm waiting for my taxi to the airport,' she said. 'What's your excuse for being up at this time?'

'Couldn't sleep. Thought I'd make a start on the day. Why are you going to the airport?'

'Easiest place to catch a flight.'

'Let me put it a different way. Where are you going?'

'I'm going to Spain for a couple of days with Flic. We're scouting for locations for the Peterson film.'

'The what?'

'You haven't been reading your emails, have you? Flic, and by extension you, are producing a film written by Trent Peterson, the crime writer. What's so urgent that you've not heard of it?'

'In my defence, I'm working on *The Sting* with Demus.'

'How's that going?'

'Slow, to be fair. This Johnny Doc stuff has sidetracked me.'

'Same with Justin. He really needs to concentrate on the new ice-cream flavours. The season starts in a couple of weeks, so no distracting him.'

'But I need to ask him something. It hit me last night. Do we know if there are more cases of people losing houses who weren't featured on the show? I wondered if they worked on some projects that never made it far enough? The numbers could be a lot bigger than we thought.'

'Interesting thought. I'll start doing a bit of digging.'

'How will you go about it?'

'Oh. You know me. I find stuff out. Sorry, my taxi's here. I'll let you know what I come up with.'

Angel appeared to be making herself indispensable. She seemed to know more about what was going on in the production world than I did. She would definitely track down any properties we didn't know about. She was very resourceful. Not always legal, but very resourceful.

After watching another *House Builders* episode, I was getting twitchy. It would be at least three hours before Jen got to the office. Time for a road trip. Now that I had addresses for two of the nearby properties, I wanted to see them in real life. It didn't really make sense, but it was better than just sitting around.

The morning crawl around the Leeds Ring Road was in full swing as I joined the queue towards Horsforth. Maybe this wasn't my cleverest idea. The satnav reckoned I would be there in ten minutes. Twenty minutes later, it still insisted I'd be there in ten minutes. It then changed its mind and decided we'd reached our destination.

I parked the car and looked around for the bungalow. It wasn't where I expected it to be. I don't mean it was being playful and hiding. It wasn't there. I checked the houses on either side of where I thought it should be. Number 70, then number 74. There was no number 72. Instead, there was a newly created access road to a vast building site that was readying itself for another day's activity. A sea of mud and mountains of breeze blocks and pipes had replaced the pretty green space. The shag-pad had been well and truly shagged and replaced by a small estate. My phone rang.

'Where are you?'

'Morning, love. I couldn't sleep so I went to the office early.'

'Guilty conscience?'

'About what?'

'Steady. I'm only joking. I'll see you in the office once I've dropped madam at school. Bacon butty?'

'Perfect. I'll see you soon. Love y—'

The line had gone dead.

WAS IT MY imagination, or was Jen still borderline cool with me? She'd arrived with a takeaway breakfast, but…It just felt strange.

'You seem subdued this morning. Everything OK?'

'Fine.'

'Only, you seem a bit – quiet?'

'Mmm.'

We were still throwing ideas about for the big plotline, but nothing was working.

'Fancy some music?'

'Later.'

She sighed. Now, I'm no expert – something I've proven time and again over the years – but something was wrong. I sensed that probing may get my head bitten off. Another two Post-its were thrown in the bin, the ideas rejected. I excused myself and went to hide in the toilet for a minute. When I came back, I stood behind Jen and put my arms around her.

'It doesn't seem to be working today. Why don't we take the day off and go do something nice?'

'Like what?'

'I don't know,' I said. 'We could go to a spa, have a swim, bit of lunch. Or a walk in the Dales. We haven't done that for ages. What's the point of being our own bosses if we can't skive for a day?'

'We need to get this done. Demus is relying on us and, so far, we've got bugger all. Besides, it's a short day today. I'm taking Dad to his appointment with the oncologist. They changed the day on him and Mum's at the dentist. I'm afraid that means you're on Charley duty.'

'No problem. Are you sure there's nothing wrong?'

'Apart from my dad getting more ill every day and a work project that's going nowhere?'

'So, I haven't done anything wrong?'

Jen gave me a look that made my stomach turn over. She seemed about to say something but stopped herself. After a moment, she spoke.

'It's not you, don't worry. Come on. Let's get stuck in. If we can crack the idea for the main plot, you can make your special chicken casserole for tea.'

Maybe that was what I needed to hear. By two o'clock there was a breakthrough – we had a story outline we agreed on. Jen still didn't seem particularly happy, but with the visit to the hospital coming up, that was understandable. When she left to pick up Ben, I had half an hour to kill before I was due at school. I hit the property websites. The dream home had to be out there.

OF ALL THE conversations I'd had with Ambrose, this was our first at the school gates. We'd both officially joined the group of parents (mainly mums) picking kids up.

'How's it going with the cinema?'

'You know Joe as well as I do. He's obsessed. It looks like he's going to be on telly.'

'*House Builders*?'

'Yeah. I told him I'd run a mile before I appeared on it so he's "the face of the project" as he likes to say. We met with the architect. She has some great ideas. Not cheap.'

'Would that be Samantha Crow?'

'Yes. Scares the bejesus out of me. There's something about her. I just need to keep reining Joe in. He'd have everything in gold leaf if I'd let him. The building is beautiful enough without going over the top. It's going to be a cinema and a music venue. It'll be dark for most of its working life. You must come and see the place, though. It's stunning. Look out, here they come.'

Issy and Charley ran towards us. How they could find so much to giggle at was sometimes beyond me, but their joy in each other's company was lovely to see. The constant chatter continued.

'Daddy. Can Charley come to tea? Can she? Please,' said Issy.

'I think we need to ask Uncle Frankie, don't you?'

'Uncle Frankie. Can Charley come for tea? Please.'

'What are you having?'

Issy looked up at Ambrose.

'We are having boiled turnips and deep-fried wardrobe monsters with liver ice cream for pudding,' said Ambrose with a straight face.

The two girls looked at each other and let out the same cry of revulsion.

'Do you still want to come, Charley?'

'Yes, please.'

Ambrose knew when to accept defeat and looked at me.

'How do fish fingers and beans sound?'

'Perfect. Are you sure you don't mind?'

'Not at all. They'll keep each other occupied while I get to watch *Pointless*,' said Ambrose. 'Why don't you pick her up about six-thirty?'

'Cheers, mate. I owe you one.'

We walked back to Ambrose's car, and I waved them off before sending a text to Jen. The reply came immediately.

Clinic running late. Not sure what time home x

I replied with the promise of a glass of wine waiting for her when she arrived.

Back at the house, I got a text from Daisy. I replied in overly formal language and received a stream of laughing emojis. This had become a regular part of my days since we met. For somebody in her situation, she was a lot of fun to be with. It was great to make friends so easily and quickly. Hearing from Daisy got me thinking about Ben. I hadn't made much progress with the diary, but I had a bonus couple of hours thanks to Ambrose. I settled into the armchair with my laptop and opened the document.

Half an hour later, I was close to tears. Ben wrote simply, but the depth of feeling was so clear. He wrote about how he felt holding Jen for the first time. His love for his wife and daughter was everything. Somehow, I felt I was getting to know the whole family far better than I had over the last couple of years. Maybe it was time to call my mother-in-law Gerry like Ben did, rather than the more formal Geraldine. Above everything, the diary emphasised how close Ben was to Jen. When the time came, Jen was going to be devastated. Somehow, I had to help her through the grief.

I made notes as I went along, suggestions for restructuring, but on the whole, the writing was excellent. The next entry punched the air from my lungs. What? Surely not. I went back and read the paragraph again, assuming I'd misunderstood the first time. No. There it was, in black, and white. What the hell did I do now?

AMBROSE WAVED FROM the doorway and Charley fell asleep in the back of the car. A whole day of chattering had worn her out. I carried her upstairs and put her straight to bed. Technically, it was a bit early, but she'd slept through me almost clattering her head against the door frame, and the subsequent outburst of swearing. I figured she'd sleep through to morning. There was still no word from the hospital, and I was worried about Ben. Then there was the diary. I really needed to speak to somebody about what I'd seen, but that person was Jen, and she was the one person I couldn't consult about it. What a mess.

From what I could tell, the chicken casserole was surviving its extended stay in the oven. I turned it down and opened a bottle of Sauvignon Blanc. At last, there was the familiar sound of the car door closing.

Jen looked pale when she came in.

'What is it? You look terrible.'

'Thanks. Just what a girl needs to hear.'

'Sorry. It's just…Drink?'

Jen nodded and sat at the table. I poured another glass and covered Jen's spare hand with mine. She downed the wine and poured another.

'The good news is that they're starting a new chemo drug tomorrow. Trouble is, we've got to the end of the list. If this doesn't work…'

The sobbing that she'd held at bay engulfed her. I held out my arms, and she moved across to sit on my lap, burying her face into my shoulder. We sat for a while before Jen's stomach made the kind of noise that got volcanologists twitching.

'When was the last time you ate something?'

'Does a Twix count?'

'Not really.'

'Breakfast then. Something smells nice. Actually, I'm starving.'

Jen got up and moved towards the oven. As she retrieved the casserole, I got plates and broke the large baguette in two, arranging the pieces delicately on the bread board before moving the lot to the table.

We ate in silence for a couple of minutes.

'This is nice,' said Jen.

'One of my specialities.'

'I didn't mean the chicken, although it is. I meant just sitting here. With you. In our house. By the way. What have you done with Charley?'

She smiled, and the room lit up.

'Worn out. She fell asleep on the way home. I put her straight to bed. Needs to clean her teeth twice in the morning to make up for tonight. Good news is, she's already dressed for school.'

'She'll survive. Not the first time she's ended up in bed still wearing everything. On one occasion, it was a full crocodile outfit. Would've terrified burglars.'

Jen was right. It was nice just sitting here and chatting. I knew I needed to ask more about Ben, but didn't want to trigger more tears. It was Jen who broke the silence.

'I'm sorry about this morning. I was a mardy bum.'

'No. I needed a kick up the arse, and you provided it. You helped me focus on the task. Now we've got the outline of a good story.'

'Maybe. But I could be motivational without giving you a hard time so – sorry.'

'Thanks. But don't worry about me. Tell me more about Ben's appointment.'

Jen broke off a piece of bread. She was about to chew on it, but changed her mind, and pulled a tissue from the box beside her.

'It's not great, to be honest. Like I said, they've decided the current drug isn't working. They want to try something new, starting tomorrow.'

'But that's good news, the fact there's another drug.'

'It's the last one.' The sobs came again. 'The oncologist basically said this may buy some time, but…'

I pushed back from the table and moved across to put my arms around Jen. Whatever else we were worrying about could wait. Ben was Jen's priority. Jen was mine.

'Does he need us to do anything?'

'Mum's taking him to oncology tomorrow for the treatment. He still wants to go to the day care at the hospice on Friday. Are you OK with taking him?'

'Yes, of course. Whatever he needs.'

I wanted so much to tell Jen it would be OK, that the drug would work, but she'd see straight through that. We had to prepare for the worst.

15

On Thursday morning we worked hard. The ideas were flowing and a structure for the story was in place. I think Jen was glad of the distraction, rather than thinking of Ben and his latest chemotherapy session. But by the time we broke for lunch, she was getting twitchy. She checked her watch for the third time since I'd started my tuna wrap.

'Are you sure you're OK?'

'Sorry. Just wondering how the patient is getting on,' said Jen.

'Why don't you give him a call?'

'He turns his phone off while he's in the room. The only thing he's moaned about when he's there is people being loud on the phone while he's trying to have a nap.'

'What time's he due home?'

'About two-ish.'

'Why don't you go to their house, see for yourself how he is?'

'What about the script?'

'We've done well this morning. I'll stay and start sketching some dialogue. I'll pick up Charley and see you back home.'

'Thanks. Just for that, you get this.'

She slid her unopened Crunchie across the desk.

'Do you really love me that much?'

'Of course. It's not as if it's a Twix, is it?'

'Fair enough.'

She pulled on her jacket and moved around the desk for a kiss.

'I'll see you about six. Take something out of the freezer when you get in. And don't forget to take the lunch boxes home.'

I saluted, and Jen left me to it. The Crunchie would be my reward for doing another hour's work. In truth, I loved this bit of the process. Writing dialogue for the opening scenes of a new project didn't feel like work. It felt like breathing life into new creations, hearing the names on the page start to talk. Before long, I had the opening scene where Johnny (our hero) is fleeing the scene of his latest con. It was only at the end, when we cut to the police arriving, that I got distracted. It was thirty-three minutes after starting the afternoon session. That was close enough to an hour. Time for coffee and Crunchie.

The second chocolate bar of the day was probably a bad idea, but I couldn't refuse Jen's token of love. As I ate, I pondered how the appearance of the police in the scene had triggered my thoughts and disrupted the writing process. It was no good. The thought of what I was about to do gave me the shudders. The need to get to the truth overrode the awkwardness, at least for now. I had to speak to Robbie about Ben's diary. Would she still have the same phone number? Only one way to find out. She answered on the second ring and suggested we meet in the park.

Don't ask me why, but I was relieved when it was a different ice-cream van that was parked up. I could do without explaining to Justin why I was meeting my ex-fiancée on a Thursday afternoon while my wife was visiting her seriously ill father. I needn't have worried. There was nobody in the van. On the bench nearest to it was a familiar, yellow rain coated figure. She smiled as I sat beside her.

'You got here quickly,' I said.

'I was already here when you called.'

'Must be nice, spending your day sitting on a bench in the park.'

'I'll have you know, I'm working,' said Robbie. She even managed to look offended before breaking into a big grin. She nodded towards the empty van.

'What? You're selling ice cream for a living too?'

'Not just selling. I'm now a major shareholder of a food manufacturing, retail, and distribution company. Angel said that Justin was looking for an investor. I was looking for an opportunity. It's a perfect fit. And I'm my own boss. Means I can shut up shop for a while when a friend needs to talk. Not too long, mind. There could be riots if I'm denying ice cream to the masses. It sounded urgent on the phone. What's up?'

How the hell did I tackle this? Why hadn't I rehearsed this bit? I looked across the lake to the ducks, but they were no help.

'It's difficult.' I paused, gathering my thoughts. 'Jen's dad is seriously ill. It looks like the chemo could have run its course.'

'Rupert mentioned it. I'm sorry. He was always good to me when we were at school. What can I do?'

'I don't think any of us can do much, except support Jen and Gerry.' The ducks were still no help. 'Ben's been keeping a journal. In fact, it's more like a memoir. He's asked me to turn it into a book, a keepsake for Jen as much as anything. I read something last night…'

Robbie looked uncomfortable, as if she knew what was coming.

'About me?'

I nodded.

'Is it true?'

'Depends what he's written, but it's probably true.'

'So, the real reason you cut Jen out of your life was down to Taylor Willis?' Robbie put both hands to her face. I waited as Robbie stared across the lake. 'Talk to me, Robbie. Tell me what happened.'

'Superintendent Willis is the senior police officer I'm determined go after. One day. Not only is he corrupt, but he also preys on young girls. I was fourteen when I met him. Dad was sponsoring a match at Rochdale. He'd invited a lot of his mates to the hospitality lounge. Football was everything to me in those days. It didn't seem odd he talked to me about the game for ages. I was just glad to be part of the group. A fan, not a kid. After that, he came to the house quite a lot. I found out later that Dad was paying him to look the other way when some of the less legal stuff was going on at the warehouse. Willis got more brazen, finding reasons to hang around the house when Dad wasn't there. He always seemed to have some excuse to talk to me, put an arm around me, that sort of thing.'

'Did you tell your dad?'

'No. I told Mum. They had a big row that night. I heard him say something about Willis being important and not to upset him. He could cause big trouble. They did nothing.'

'So, your dad was allowing him to harass you?'

'You know him. Nothing got in the way of making money. I was just part of the deal. It came to a head when Willis cornered me in my room. He made it very obvious what he expected to happen next.'

'What did happen next?'

'I kicked him an absolute beauty. Right in the Rees-Moggs. He went down like a sack of spuds. Threatening blue murder. I legged it and left him there. The only place I felt I'd be safe was Jen's house. But she wasn't in. She'd gone to see her grandparents with her mum.

Ben could see I was upset. I told him everything. Eventually, he took me home and read the riot act to Dad. There was a huge row. Ben threatened to go to the police. You can imagine how that went. Anyway, that's when the hassle from the police started for Ben. I found out later that they stopped him nearly every night when he was driving home. Willis made sure I knew what was going on. Eventually, he threatened Ben with charges of child abuse. Said he could make it happen if he ever said anything. I decided that the only way I could protect Ben was to break off all contact with them. When Dad made-up the story about being mugged, I backed him up. You know the rest.'

'So, for the last twelve years, you let your best friend think you'd betrayed her when you were really protecting her family?'

Robbie nodded and dabbed at her eyes with a tissue.

'How did Willis react?'

'You mean after screaming that he was going to kill me? He backed off. Suppose I showed he didn't scare me. He was still best buddies with Dad, right up until we were all arrested. Couldn't see him for dust then. I know what we did was bad, and I apologise again for buggering everything up. But seeing how he betrayed Dad on top of the stuff with me…I want to take him down. And I will. Just may take a while.' She smiled up at me, then blew her nose. 'I wish I could make it up to you somehow. Don't get me wrong, I'm not suggesting we get back together. I don't deserve that, and neither does Jen. Being in prison made me realise friendships count for a lot. I couldn't have got through it without Angel. She's quite a special character.'

'You can say that again.'

'But so are you,' said Robbie. 'If there is any way for me and you to get back to being friends…'

I looked again at the ducks. One of them gave a loud quack. I took that to be encouragement.

'And what about Jen? She lost her best friend all those years ago. She needs as many friends as she can to get through the next few months.'

It was Robbie's turn to stare at the ducks.

'But it's been years. She hates me.'

'Jen's not capable of hating anyone. She's the most loving person I've ever met.'

'Can I think about it?'

'On one condition.'

'Let me guess. You want an ice cream?'

'Spot on. And don't take too long with Jen. Ben's probably not got that long left, to be honest.'

I ZIPPED MY fleece right up to hide the stain caused by dripping ice cream and waved to Robbie. After so much sweet stuff today, I needed a walk, and set off around the park lake. I was kicking myself for leaving my earbuds in the car. Instead of my usual music, I would have to settle for thinking. I realised how many memories featured this place. Impromptu picnics with Robbie and then Jen. The bench where I chatted with Flic and agreed to join her start-up production company. From where I was, I could see the swings that Charley loved so much.

I turned the corner and walked along the path that ran parallel to the road. I'd always envied the people who lived in the houses overlooking the park. Unusually for me, I even got as far as viewing a cottage before I bought my first house. The shared back lawn had put me off. There was a line down the middle where the neighbour had stopped mowing, only doing his side. That set off all kinds of alarms for me. Better to be opposite the pub. Stick to what you know.

Then again, we had more money now. I'd always admired the house that was set back a little further on the road, elevated slightly. It looked imperious. That was a word the younger me would never have come up with. I realised I was looking at the house now. What caught my eye was a blue van that parked up outside. My dad would've described the man who got out as a 'brick outhouse', when he was being polite. He was at least six foot four and almost as wide, and was soon emerging from the back of the van with a sign attached to a wooden stake. One blow of his hammer was enough. He got back in the van and drove off. The house was for sale.

I'm not what you'd call a spiritual person. But surely, this was a sign. Well, of course it was literally a sign, but you know what I mean. To spot the house going up for sale, as I just happened to be walking past. A house I'd admired for ages, opposite the park where we spent so many Saturday afternoons. What were the chances?

The path would lead me back round the lake to the car. Instead, I doubled back and took the fork up to the road. I was about to climb over the wall, then spotted a gate up ahead. That would be much more sensible. From the road, I would see the estate agent's number, and called them. They promised to call me back once they'd spoken to the owner to arrange a viewing. It was irrational, but I felt disappointed. What was I expecting? Would you like to pay cash or card, sir? I'll have it wrapped and sent round immediately.

Should I call Jen and tell her or surprise her later? Calm down, idiot. The whole place could be riddled with dry rot, whatever that is.

Imagine the surprise when I heard a voice call my name.

'Mr Dale.' I looked around, then saw a man of about seventy walking towards me from the house. 'Mr Dale?'

'Yes,' I said, and walked towards him, without considering the car that was being driven sedately up the road. The driver confirmed his brakes were working before calling me something less formal than Mr Dale. I scurried the rest of the way across and shook the hand that was extended towards me.

'I'm Tom.'

'Frankie.'

'The estate agent said you wanted to view the house. Would you like to come in now?'

'If you're sure it's no trouble, that would be great.'

My new best friend led the way into a bright, welcoming room. Within seconds, I wanted to ask when I could move in. The place would've been perfect even without the wall of shelves that housed an impressive record collection. No visit to IKEA for me.

'You like your music?'

'A bit of an obsession to be fair,' Tom said, moving across to the shelves. It struck me that he'd be about the same age as my dad. He had a similar taste. We chatted for a while about the merits of Ziggy and Aladdin Sane before he led the way to the back of the house. The garden stretched off into the distance. To cap it all, bi-folding doors. I wanted this house.

'Can I ask why you're selling, Tom?'

'Downsizing, I think they call it. Now it's just me.' He glanced at a wedding photo in a silver frame on top of a bookcase. 'My daughter lives in Southport. Wants me closer. At least it's by the sea.'

'It's certainly a beautiful house.'

'Do you have children, Frankie?'

'Just one at the moment. My stepdaughter is six, Charley.'

'Does that mean there's going to be more?'

'Hope so. That's the plan.'

'It would be nice to think there'd be children here again. My girls were very happy here.'

After a cursory look at upstairs – it had bi-folding doors and record shelves – I shook Tom's hand again and promised to be in touch soon. I was due at the school in five minutes, but the plan was coming together.

CHARLEY WAS SITTING on the rug in my old living room. Somehow, she was engrossed in her colouring book while wearing Angel's crash helmet. We'd finished the game of bumping into things wearing the helmet with only minor damage to a vase of daffodils. Angel had somehow produced the colouring book and pens, but Charley insisted the helmet stayed.

Angel joined me and Justin at the table.

'So, what are you suggesting?' she said.

'I'm suggesting that there is something very dodgy about Trowel Productions. It can't be just a coincidence that so many people lost their houses because of being involved with *Johnny's House Builders*.'

'I've got a couple more contacts to add to the list,' said Justin, taking another biscuit.

'I've been doing some digging online,' I said. 'The company is jointly owned by Johnny Docherty and a Sven Trowel. Now, if that sounds like a made-up name, it's because it probably is. I've found no trace of him before 2004. He seems to appear out of nowhere and teams up with Docherty. They formed Trowel Productions and land a commission to develop *House Builders* – despite having no track record of any other shows.'

'But Docherty would've had connections in the business,' said Angel.

'True. Whichever way they got the go-ahead, the show was a success. A slow burner at first, but the ratings grew. The first suspicious property was towards the end of that first season. I checked the land registry and the figures are interesting. A supermarket manager called Mike Newsome bought the house for £97,000. The build was a disaster, he ran out of funding, a familiar story. Trowel offered to introduce him to a company that would buy the house from him. With the bank about to repossess, he took the deal. A shell company bought it for £47,000. They finished the build, and the house sold three months later for £289,000. Even allowing for the cost to finish the job, the profit was around two-hundred grand. I know that because the accounts for the company show a dividend payment of £100,000 each to its two shareholders. Would you like to guess who those shareholders were?'

'Trowel and Docherty, by any chance?'

'Give the man a coconut. Now, I haven't had time to check the other examples, but my guess is they would show a similar pattern.'

'Sounds like the sort of research I enjoy,' said Angel. I'd hoped she was going to say that.

'While you're at it, do you think you could dig around in Doherty's finances? His lifestyle seems fairly lavish for a B-list celebrity, if you ask me.'

'Consider it done,' said Angel, leaping into action to rescue Charley from a sneezing fit. I didn't want to think what the inside of her crash helmet was like, but Charley thought it was hilarious.

'The next one we should look at is this.' I slid my phone across the table. It had the photograph from where the house on the ring road had disappeared, and the building site beyond. 'The road goes through what used to be a little bungalow. Trowel acquired it after a project went wrong. Suddenly, planning permission for the land behind it was forthcoming. Previous applications had been turned down flat. It would be interesting to see how that all changed.'

Angel looked closer at the picture.

'Doesn't Robbie know the bloke that was the head of the planning committee?'

'Unpleasant piece of work called Sir Alan Durham. He went down at the same time as Dexter. Still inside. Maybe this was another of his dodgy deals? This whole thing got me thinking. If *House Builders* is dodgy, what about the other shows produced by Trowel?'

'What else do they—' The doorbell interrupted Justin. 'I'll get it.' He was back within seconds. 'We have another visitor.'

It was Robbie. Angel jumped to her feet and hugged her friend.

'We were just talking about you.'

'Nothing good, I hope,' said Robbie, taking the fourth seat at the table. She didn't seem to register how uncomfortable I was.

'Your mate, Sir Alan Durham. We think we've found another of his dirty little deals,' said Angel.

'That wouldn't surprise me.'

'Did you ever come across Sven Trowel?' said Angel.

'Not that I remember. Who's he?'

Angel explained the story so far. Robbie looked at me.

'Have you checked Crookipedia?' I glanced at Angel and Justin. I'd been sworn to secrecy about the existence of the database. Financial ruin and kneecapping were on the cards if I even so much as acknowledged its existence. She'd even referred to it by the name I'd given it. 'Don't look so worried. I shared a cell with this woman. There is nothing, and I mean nothing, she doesn't know about me and my life.'

I blew out both cheeks, trying to get control of my heart rate again.

'I checked for Johnny Docherty, but there's nothing. Trowel's name emerged later. I'll check again as soon as I get home.'

'So, I take it we are the team to take down Trowel Productions? Excellent,' said Robbie.

It appeared we were now a team of four.

'Frankie,' said Justin. 'You were about to tell us which other shows we need to look at.'

'Yes, of course. There are two. *Johnny Doc's Treasure Trove*—'

'We used to watch that on Sunday nights,' said Robbie, laughing with Angel.

'You and several million others. It's huge during the summer. As is *Johnny Doc's Millionaire's Row*. It's a bit of a *Who Wants to Be a Millionaire?* rip-off. Again, hugely popular.'

'And you think they're dodgy?'

'That's just it, Robbie. I've no idea, but if they're willing to rip-off Joe Public on one show, why not?'

'OK,' said Robbie. 'You're the boss. What do you want us to do?'

I was suddenly back in project manager mode.

'OK. Angel's already agreed to look into the finances of Trowel and Docherty. Justin, you carry on gathering info on all the people who lost houses to this lot. Robbie, Crookipedia – see what you've got on Trowel. I've got some telly to watch. I want to see if there's an angle on the other shows that could be bent. It's also time to get Charley back for her tea, so I'd best be off. How about we meet back here on Saturday morning?'

Everybody agreed. Time to go.

16

Maybe I was being a little oversensitive, but Jen had seemed cool again this morning. She's always cool as in laid-back, classy. This was more of a distance. Not quite frosty, but not my Jen. I tried everything I knew, but she insisted there was nothing wrong. She would go to the cottage and work on the story outline while I went to the hospice with Ben. I offered to skip it for this week, but she wouldn't hear of it. A commitment was a commitment.

Ben helped to cheer me up. He was so positive about life, even when faced with the prospect of losing it. Today's challenge was his first watercolours class. I was quite envious, if I'm honest. Not of the whole chemotherapy bit. Painting was something I used to love and don't really do much of these days.

I dropped Ben by the door and unloaded my box of goodies from the back of the car. Six reconditioned laptops donated by my mate Spud. Ben offered to carry the box inside, but we both knew he was bluffing. Instead, he sat on a wall while I went off in search of a parking space. When I got back, both Ben and the box had gone. I solved the mystery when Lucy met me in reception.

'I put the laptops in your corner. Are you sure we're OK to use them?'

'Better than that. They're yours. Consider them a donation.'

'Really? That's very generous, thank you. Ben's already settled in the painting group. Do you have everything you need for your session?'

'Apart from coffee, I have everything,' I said.

'Make yourself at home. *Mi café es tu café*,' said Lucy, grinning, and answering her phone.

'*Gracias*,' I said, and made my way into the dayroom.

The group was smaller this week. Had I really been that bad? More to the point, where was Daisy? I was soon busy getting everybody started. Before long, I was working my way through, and giving feedback on the stories produced so far. Assessing the writing of others was something I'd never been comfortable with. What made me such an expert? Then I reflected on how much Jen had taught me. How many manuscripts had been successful and relaxed a little.

With half an hour to go before lunch, I needed the bathroom. On the way back, I glanced through a window to where the painting group was gathered. There was Daisy, happily hunched over her artwork. Lucy was at the next table, leaning across to watch what Daisy was doing. I was relieved that Daisy was OK, but felt a bit let down that my new friend had deserted me after just a week. Maybe I should finish the session and head back to the office to work with Jen.

I trudged back to the dayroom. A sheet of paper taped to the door announced fish pie for lunch. A faint aroma confirmed this, and my stomach gurgled. Maybe I'd stay for lunch, then go. That was the polite thing to do. I opened the door and tried to concentrate on helping the group. The rest of the session went quickly. I distributed my email address so everybody could send me anything for review during the week and we all trooped off to the dining room. I joined the short queue before I felt something nudge the back of my legs.

'Who does a girl in a wheelchair have to sleep with to get some help around here?'

I couldn't hide my smile as I turned.

'Hello, trouble,' I said. 'Where've you been hiding?'

'Helping a damsel in distress. Not all superheroes wear capes, you know. If you get me a fish pie, I'll tell all.'

I wheeled Daisy across to an empty table and returned to the counter. As expected, asking for two plates brought good natured ribbing. This place was so friendly. Food secured, I slid in beside Daisy.

'So, what have you been up to? My session not good enough for you?'

'Don't be daft,' said Daisy. 'I'll be back next week, assuming you'll have me.'

'I'll think about it,' I said, trying to play hard to get. 'How come the painting took priority this week?'

'Special favour to Lucy. She knew Lowry was my favourite and wanted me to share my technique. They're doing abstracts next week, can't be doing with that. Besides, holding a brush is quite difficult these days. Dare say I'll pay for it over the next few days, but it was worth it.'

'I'd love to see some of your work.'

'Is that a way to get me to invite you to see my etchings? Dirty bugger. I'm old enough to be your grandmother.'

I could feel the blush rising from my feet to my scalp. The loud cackling drew attention from all over the room. Daisy thought she was hilarious. Actually, it was quite funny. She put down her knife and fork and tapped at her phone.

'Here. That's one of mine.'

I looked at the image on the phone. It was extraordinary.

'You did that?'

'Sure did. I was good before the hands started to go. Not watercolours, obviously. That's acrylic on canvas. Once I got into Lowry's head, I found the rest quite simple. Made a few quid with them in my time.'

She tapped the side of her nose and winked like a music-hall comedian.

'You mean you forged them?'

'All right, keep your voice down. I prefer to style myself like a tribute band. Like the Björn Again of art.'

A glint of an idea started to form.

'I may have a favour to ask you at some point.'

'Sounds exciting. Whatever you want, just ask. That way, you'll owe me a favour.'

'Name it.'

Daisy scooped the last prawn into her mouth and pushed her plate away.

'I need you to come with me.'

'I'm not looking at your etchings, no way.'

'Dozy bugger,' said Daisy. She laughed and pretended to slap my hand. 'It's silly, I know. I've been coming here for ages, but I've never done the full tour. I've never been onto the ward. Felt weird when I first came. Now I think I need to see it, so I know what to expect, you know, when…'

'Of course I'll come with you, but why me? You've only known me a couple of weeks and all we do is take the piss out of each other.'

'Never undervalue the effect of having a laugh. I know you won't let me get all maudling. The warden at home offered. She's lovely, but she'd do the head on one side bit and end up blubbing. Don't need that. What d'you say?'

'When do you want to do it?'

'Today. Pudding first, obviously. Not doing this without sticky toffee pudding inside me. Especially if you were getting off your backside to get it.'

'Charmer. Custard?'

'Does a bear sh—'

'Behave.'

As I waited for the puddings to be dished up, I looked at Daisy. She was pushing a plastic box into her handbag. An impressive cluster of pills had appeared on the table, and she worked through them. Apart from her struggling with the keyboard last week, this was the first sign of just how ill she was. She swallowed the last tablet as I reached the table.

'Caught me taking my stash.'

'Very impressive it is, too,' I said, trying to keep things light.

'Surprised I don't bloody rattle. That last one's a bugger. Tastes foul. That's why I need the pudding. What's your excuse?'

'I'm a growing lad.'

'Not surprised, all that pudding.'

'You need to be careful with that chair. It'd be terrible if the brakes failed.'

The spoon stopped before it got to her mouth, and she stared at me. Had I gone too far? Then came the familiar cackle.

'You're OK, Mr Dale. Where've you been all my life?'

'I wasn't born for most of it.'

'Cheeky bugger. Now, finish your pudding. We've got stuff to do.'

Arrangements must've been discussed, because Lucy appeared at the table.

'You all set? I take it your chaperone agreed to escort you?' said Lucy.

'He has. We're ready, assuming he's not going to try to lick the pattern off that plate.'

I looked at Lucy for support, but she just laughed. She whipped the plates away while I took charge of Daisy's wheelchair.

'You sure about this?'

'I am. So long as her upstairs knows I'm only looking today and doesn't get any ideas.'

'So, you think God is a woman?'

'Who said anything about God? I meant Jane, the manager up in her office.'

Lucy held the door open, and we were off. The walk through the building took a while. Daisy seemed to know everybody by name and had something to say to all of them. She knew the names of their children, partners, even pets. She was a remarkable woman. Even Buster, the black Labrador, joined us. Could he sense Daisy's nervous state? We reached the doors at the end of the corridor.

'Right, madame. This is the bit you haven't seen yet. Nothing scary. Think of it like a hotel corridor,' said Lucy. She pointed to the first door on the right. 'That's our quiet room. A small lounge for visitors to chat to the doctors or just have five minutes.' The next two doors were closed. 'Siesta time for some.'

'Great idea if you've had a couple of margaritas with lunch,' said Daisy. 'Take note, young man. We should do that one day.'

'Neither of us is allowed to drive this thing when we're drunk.'

'I'm sure Lucy would help.'

'I'd be right there with you, thank you very much,' said Lucy. 'And this one is unoccupied just now.'

She pushed open the fifth door. We stepped into a large, airy room that was a cross between a hospital and a hotel. Functional, but with some pleasant touches. The first thing Daisy spotted was the large Lowry print on the wall between the two windows.

'Bloody hell. I've got the same picture above the fireplace at home. I'll take that as a good sign.'

Daisy seemed to relax. I parked the chair next to the bed. Sunlight streamed in through the large windows. As it reflected off a table, it bathed Daisy in a warm glow. It was as if she had her own halo. She smiled.

'I think this'll do. Nice big telly. I take it we are en suite?'

'But of course,' said Lucy. 'Would madame like to tour the facilities?'

'That's all right. I believe you.'

Lucy's phone vibrated. She checked the screen.

'Sorry, got to go. Take as long as you like. I'll see you before you go home.'

I moved around the room and sat in the visitor's chair.

'She's such a bundle of energy,' I said once Lucy was out of earshot. 'Always so warm and friendly, but totally in control of this place.'

'She's lovely. A damned good painter, too. Took me five minutes to explain my technique today. Then she was off and running. Next thing, she's teaching the others as if she'd been banging out perfect copies for years. She could make a lot of money if she wasn't so wholesome.'

'Don't you be corrupting her. Anyway, this place. What do you think?'

'It's fine. I was just scared to come here. Daft, I know.'

'Understandable, given the circumstances.'

'Thanks for bringing me. Means a lot.'

'Happy to help. But if we sit here much longer, I'll need to stretch out and have a nap.'

'Same here. Come on, my taxi'll be here in ten minutes. Let's go and wave to everybody.'

Ben had been his usual busy self at the hospice. He seemed to have made genuine friendships in the short time he was there. I admired his painting from the morning but couldn't help noticing that the 1930s crowd heading towards a football ground seemed to be watched by a spaceship.

'I got a bit bored towards the end,' he said. 'Annoyed that I got the scale wrong, spoils the perspective.'

'It could just be further away that we think.'

Ben shrugged and made himself comfortable in the passenger seat. I was glad we had half an hour together in the car. I needed to speak to him about Robbie. As usual, the Friday afternoon traffic was busy. I edged out of the car park and took a deep breath.

'Ben.'

There was no response. For a horrible moment I thought the worst, then realised he was fast asleep, still clutching the painting. He looked just like Charley – if Charley had aged sixty years and lost a couple of stones over the last few months. It hit me once more how ill Ben was, yet this morning was proof that he was determined to wring every last drop from life. Learning a new skill and taking pleasure from adding a spaceship to his painting. A wave of affection and admiration for this man swept over me. The conversation would have to wait. He needed to sleep.

Gerry was waiting for us as I pulled up outside the house. As if by magic, Ben woke up. He thanked me for the lift. I turned down the offer of tea. I had work to do.

JEN WAS STILL at the office. She was leaning back in her seat, feet crossed on the desk. She stretched to return my kiss.

'You look very relaxed,' I said.

'I'm in ponder mode. Often mistaken for sitting with your feet up and staring into space,' she said.

'My mistake. What's up?'

'Probably nothing. Just wondering if we've got the right type of con in the story.'

'OK. Why don't I make us a cup of tea and we can work on it?'

'Done. How's Dad?'

'He's had a great time. Tired him out. I suspect your mum is fussing over him as we speak.'

Any of the frostiness from this morning seemed to have gone. Maybe Jen really was just worried about Ben. Before I could take my first sip of tea, my phone rang.

'Demus…Hi.'

'Hi, Frankie. I'm in your neck of the woods and I have your pictures. Can I drop them off?'

'Of course. We're at the cottage.'

'I know. I can see you through the window.' Sure enough, as I opened the door, Demus was taking a parcel from the boot of his car. 'Sorry I didn't call earlier. I was up the road with Flic, and I lost track of time.'

I ushered him inside. It was still strange that this big star was our friend and business partner. Jen hugged him and I was sent off to make more tea. Five minutes earlier, I'd resisted the biscuit barrel. This was different. We had a guest.

When I got back from the kitchen, Demus was just finishing the funniest story Jen had ever heard.

'What have I missed?'

'Nothing, mate. Just me being silly,' said Demus. Jen was dabbing at her eyes with a tissue. 'Never mind that. Gabby's mate confirmed what she thought about the pictures. Excellent imitations in the Lowry style, worth about five hundred quid to two grand on a good day.'

'Thanks for trying. I still think Mum and Dad will be more than pleased. Just being on telly with Docherty will keep them going for years.'

'Talking of our friend Johnny Doc. I may have a theory. Sounds a bit daft, to be fair,' said Demus.

'Frankie always says there's no such thing as a daft idea. Usually, when he has a daft idea,' said Jen. She got the giggles again. Had she been at the sherry? I ignored the comment and looked again at Demus.

'I think he might use *Treasure Trove* to supplement his own art collection.'

'Gabby mentioned he was a keen collector.'

'He is, but I think he's definitely dishonest. I watched a few more episodes of *House Builders*. I'll email you a list of the episodes I think are dodgy. Then I switched to *Treasure Trove*. He makes a big thing in the press about how any artwork they buy as part of the show is sold on and the proceeds donated to charity. I think he's telling porkies. Can I Airdrop a couple of files for you?'

'Of course.' I tapped at my laptop and two files appeared.

'Have a look at the first one.'

Jen used the remote control to switch on the big screen on the wall. I opened the video clip. Johnny Doc appeared on the screen, introducing a painting that was valued by the show's experts at £70,000. The crowd went wild at this point. The old lady in a tweed suit had bought the painting for £50 at a car-boot sale. She couldn't believe her painting was worth so much. Of course, under the rules of the show, she had to pick a door. In theory, she could receive millions, or a cabbage. The various experts went off stage to secrete themselves behind the prop doors for the climax of the show and Docherty introduced the latest partially clad teenage karaoke singer. The camera cut to the stage performance. Thankfully, Demus had edited out the next three minutes, and we were back to Docherty. He smiled, hyping up the end of the show for all he was worth. A full two minutes later, the old lady got to see what was behind her chosen door.

She looked devastated as Docherty theatrically counted out the £2,000 hidden behind door three. So much for it being her lucky number. The clip finished with a close-up of the picture. It was by an artist I'd only heard of just recently. I concentrated hard, then realised I'd heard the name at the gallery with Gabby. Deidre Campbell, the wife of the man who'd painted our two Lowry-style pictures.

'Right. So, at this point we have a disappointed old lady who's just made almost two grand profit on a painting she's owned for six months. We should also have a donation of around £70,000 to her chosen charity. Would you care to guess how much the charity actually received?'

'Is it less than that, by any chance?'

'Seven hundred.'

'What? Did they sell it and keep the money?'

'I can't find any record of a sale. Open the second image.' I clicked on the file. 'This is a screenshot of an interview that Docherty did for the *Sunday Times*. A four-page spread in the 'Home' supplement. The image shows his library. He's very proud of it. Just zoom in on the picture on the far wall. I almost missed it.'

I magnified the image and adjusted the view. There was no mistaking it. Pride of place went to the picture we'd just seen on the TV show.

'What a twat,' I said.

'Precisely,' said Demus.

'But I think he's just given me an idea for our script.'

'SHE'S OUT LIKE a light. Barely two pages into the story and she was sparko.'

'You've got the magic touch,' I said.

'To be honest, I was disappointed. I know that makes me a terrible mother, but I was looking forward to spending time with her. I feel like I've neglected her a bit recently.'

'You've got a lot on. Charley understands that Grandad's poorly and you need to be with him a lot.'

'Maybe. But it's not fair to her. Not fair to you either. I don't know how I'd be coping if you weren't around. Look, I'm sorry, you know, if I've been a bit…'

'Arsey?'

'Difficult.' Jen slapped my arm playfully. 'OK, arsey as well. Sorry. I just get a bit…'

'No need to apologise. In sickness and in health. That's what we said, and it applies here too. Why don't you put your feet up? I'll do the dishwasher and bring a bottle through.'

'Sod the dishwasher. I'll do it later. Just bring the bottle.'

Who was I to argue? We settled on the sofa. Jen had picked the new Yola album again, and I handed her a glass as I sat down. She wriggled closer and pulled my arm around her as she rested her back against me. I loved sitting like this.

'We did good work today,' she said.

'Demus has a real eye for what makes a story work.'

'He does, but you came up with it. I don't doubt it will make good TV. Are you sure you can pull it off in real life? Writing a script is one thing. Exposing a fraudster is another level.'

'You heard what Demus said. It'll be fun. We've already started putting our team together, just like in *The Sting*. Angel's good at this sort of thing, as she proved last year. Justin sees it as payback, so he's engaged. Demus just likes mischief, and he'll rope his sister in.' I was about to mention Robbie's involvement but decided now was not the time.

'And the woman from the hospice you mentioned? Do you really think she'll be up for it?'

'I think it'll be right up her street. I'll charm her, don't worry.'

'That's exactly what worries me. Just be careful. Hope you understand why I can't commit to much. Dad has to come first.'

'Totally understandable. Don't worry. What could possibly go wrong?'

17

Jen had taken Charley to the local pool. Normally, I would go too. This time, I suggested Jen might like some concentrated time with Charley. My sacrifice earnt me many brownie points for being so thoughtful and a Saturday morning to myself. Who says nice guys come second?

My first port of call was The Roxy to see what progress Joe was making. The sight of multiple skips in the car park worried me. The last thing I wanted was to be distracted from my mission by having to do some actual physical work. I'd been grateful in the past for the efforts of Rupert and Ambrose when we were clearing out our first office. But this was different. Quite how, I wasn't too sure. I needn't have worried. The first thing I saw when I walked inside was Joe, sitting in a deckchair with a clipboard.

'Frankie. I saved you a seat.'

Sure enough, there was another deckchair by his side.

'How did you know I'd be coming?'

'Intuition,' he said. 'That, and I bumped into Jen and Charley. I was just leaving the pool as they arrived. Jen mentioned you were thinking of coming for a nosey.'

'I didn't know you were an early morning swimmer.'

'Rupert's idea. He gave me three options. Running with him, swimming, or die of a heart attack.'

'I see why you went for swimming.'

'Don't tell him, but I'm quite enjoying it now. Hell at first, but now I'm thinking the Olympic trials can't be far off.' The familiar laugh boomed across the old building. 'Treasure pile, over there.'

Joe was addressing one of four muscular men in hard hats who were hard at work, stripping the old building of years of accumulated rubbish. A framed poster for the film *Jaws* made its way to the corner.

'I thought you'd have your sleeves rolled up to do this yourself,' I said.

'Alas, the demands of high office are such that I must give leadership from the sidelines these days. Besides, I get to sit here and admire these hunks.'

'Sounds like a wise move. Surprised you're making progress so soon.'

'This lot? Just clearing out junk today. Still working on the plans.'

'How's it going with your architect?'

'Ms Crow? She's good, so far. Her ideas seem to stack up. No sign of skulduggery. The TV company were due on-site next week to film the opening shots, but I've cancelled. There was a cooling-off period in the contract. After your research, I don't trust them as far as I could chuck 'em. I'm glad you warned me.'

'I know you can keep a secret.'

'Is that sarcasm, Mr Dale?' said Joe, pretending to take offence, before shuffling his seat closer to mine.

I told him all about the plan for exposing the production company, and Johnny Docherty in particular. Joe was excited and offered all the help he could.

Activity from the labourers appeared to have stopped. Tea break. Joe got to his feet.

'Entertainment's over for the next fifteen minutes. Come on, I'll show you the first-draft plans.' He led the way to an office just inside the front door. 'This was the ticket office originally. Previous owners seemed to use it to stash soft-porn magazines, judging by what we found.'

There was none in evidence as Joe spread the rolled-up plans on a trestle table.

'Impressive,' I said.

'I love it. I know it would've made a spectacular home, but now I'm so excited to restore it to an entertainment venue.'

I nodded wisely as Joe talked me through each cross-section drawing. To be honest, I'd always struggled to visualise how buildings would look in reality just from looking at the plans. The architect certainly seemed thorough.

'Any idea of cost?'

'Let's just say a lot. But it'll be worth it.'

We both looked up as the familiar sound of diesel engines clattered into the yard. Two ice-cream vans pulled up, side-by-side.

'You expecting lots of sightseers?'

Joe laughed.

'Eventually. Justin mentioned he needed somewhere to park the vans, so a deal was done.' The sound of crashing plasterwork from the main auditorium distracted Joe. 'What the f—?'

'I'll let you investigate. I need a word with Justin.'

'OK. Don't leave without popping back in.'

With that, Joe was gone, barking instructions like Tony Soprano. Outside, Justin was getting busy with a power wash. Robbie was just finishing wiping down the counter on one of the vans. I smiled as she looked up.

'I could watch people work all day,' I said.

'Stand still around here and somebody'll put a cloth in your hand. A clean van is a happy van.'

'I'm glad I bumped into you. I looked at Crookipedia last night, but didn't understand what I found.'

'Strangely enough, so did I.'

We moved out of the way so that Justin could turn the hose on the second van. He waved before returning to his task.

'Trowel?'

'Yes,' said Robbie. 'What you couldn't see were the other entries that are for my eyes only.'

'I forgot there was an entire section you keep secret from me.'

'Not a secret. Private. No point giving away all the best bits, is there?'

I had to concede she had a point.

'So, the entry I saw just said *Trowel 100k July?* What did you find?'

'I think that my beloved father was setting up a deal to launder money through the TV company.'

'And you didn't know about it?'

'No. Nothing unusual about that. Dad did the deals. I did the accounting. The entry was dated January. The deal looked like it was going to start in July with £100k.'

'Start?'

'A trial run. From the notes Dad made, it could've been up to a million a year they could do.'

'How the hell were they going to do it?'

'He didn't explain. I think we need to do a little more digging. If this was true, and we can expose it, the fraud from *Treasure Trove* and *House Builders* would be trivial. We could be talking a long prison sentence for Docherty.'

'I like the sound of that. What do you think we should do next?'

'Easy. Work out what they were up to and a way to expose them.'

'I suppose that was a stupid question.'

I had some thinking to do.

AFTER PROMISING JOE that we'd have a night in his bar soon, I got back to the car and checked for emails. The one I wanted had just arrived. It included an open invite to call anytime and an address. I programmed the satnav, sent a reply saying I'd be there in ten, and drove out of the car park.

The building wasn't what I'd expected. The pictures on the website had shown a functional modern tower block. That appeared to be a separate building around the back. This was on an impressive scale. I guessed it dated from the early part of the last century and had started life as a rather grand house. The gardens were still impressive, but the number of parked cars suggested at least six apartments. The ramp to the front door looked like a relatively recent addition. I pressed a button and heard a phone ring from inside the building.

'Give it a push. First on the right,' said the tinny voice.

Inside, the hallway was as grand as the outside suggested. A high ceiling and wide staircase to the upper floors. I followed the polished-wood floor to the door that had just opened.

'Come to see my etchings after all?'

'Morning, Daisy. Just you behave. I'm at a very impressionable age.'

'Kettle's on.'

I followed Daisy into a spacious modern kitchen. The work surfaces were all adapted for her wheelchair, and she skilfully manoeuvred around, collecting cups, milk, and sugar.

'Can I help?'

'Just grab the coffeepot, thanks.'

'This is all very nice. You have a lovely home.'

'Thanks. I've always been very happy here.'

'Must make it a lot easier, having things adapted for the chariot.'

'It does. Cost a fortune, mind. I decided I was worth it. No point snuffing it with loads of money in the bank.'

'No wider family to leave it to?'

'No. Just me now. Don't tell anyone, but I think I'll leave most of it to the hospice, assuming I haven't spent it all on gin and dubious young men by then.'

'How's that plan going?'

'I'm still hard at work on the gin, but the stock market seems to make the pile bigger as each year goes by. If I thought about it too much, I could be pissed off that I'm not seeing the world from the deck of a first-class cabin on a cruise ship. But what would be the point? This is the hand life dealt me. May as well enjoy the time I have left, which includes an endless supply of Fox's Luxury Biscuits. Top drawer over there, if you don't mind.'

I found the biscuits.

'Plate?'

'Plate? Just bring the packet, posh boy. By the way, I don't want you feeling sorry for me. I've had a good and entertaining life.'

'I bet you've a few tales to tell.'

'One or two. I may even tell you a few one day.'

'Hang on a minute. When we spoke about my parents needing sheltered accommodation, you told me that's where you lived.'

'And I was telling the truth. A warden calls twice a day to make sure I'm OK.'

'But isn't this place a bit...'

'Grand? I suppose it is. There're five other apartments in the house and a modern block at the back. All one complex.'

'Who did you sleep with to get this one?'

'Let's just say I know the owner of the whole complex. In fact, I helped to set up the charity that runs it. Did you mention it to your parents?'

'My dad would love somewhere like this. Not sure his pension and selling a cottage by the seaside will stretch as far as this.'

'That's detail. Like I say, I know the owner. There's always deals to be done. I can pull a few strings if you like.'

'That's incredible, Daisy. Thank you.'

'Leave it with me. I'll have a word in the right ears and get back to you. Back to today. Your email intrigued me. Tell me more.'

I put my mug on a coaster and explained about Johnny Docherty. How he'd ripped off Justin and other self-builders. How he was potentially about to rip-off my parents on *Treasure Trove*. Finally, how he'd talked about Roddy Lightning in the interview.

'Ripping off innocent people is one thing, but I loved Roddy Lightning. For that alone, I'm in. What do you need me to do?'

I outlined the plan, explaining that I wanted to use the template for our TV script as a real-life scam to set up Docherty and get the evidence we needed to get the police involved.

'So, you want me to produce these three paintings?'

'If you agree, yes.'

'But what about provenance? This series of pictures is purely fictional. How will we fool Docherty?'

'We have access to a master of deception. Demus Wolf is a personal friend. He's capable of fooling anybody. He'll become our expert valuer and sell the entire story.'

'But Docherty will just do his research, surely?'

'We'll invent the whole back story. Let's just say I have contacts to create any number of websites and articles to prove they've been the holy grail of modern art for years. We can even produce books by eminent art dealers. Well, one eminent art dealer.'

'Won't that take years to set up?'

'We've got nearly three weeks. We can make this happen, honest.' Daisy looked concerned. 'You don't think we can do it?'

'I'm sure you can make all these things happen. It's me. I'm not sure my hands are up to producing three pictures of sufficient quality in that time. If I lose much more feeling…'

I slumped back in my seat. It was like somebody had let the air out of me.

'Sorry. I suppose I get carried away sometimes. It's one thing making up stories for books and scripts. I get a bit mixed up when real life is involved.'

Daisy looked at me and grinned.

'Fuck it. We won't know until we try. I'll give it a go. What else am I going to do? Sit and tick off the days until the grim reaper comes knocking? This could be fun, just like the old days.' I raised an eyebrow. 'Don't ask. Not yet, anyway. Needless to say, that pile of money in the bank had to come from somewhere. I'll need to see the two pictures you have already to make sure the materials match.'

'They're in the car.'

'Don't just sit there. I want to get started as soon as.'

CHARLEY WAS GRUMPY. Thick black clouds had given way to torrential rain. We had officially cancelled the Saturday afternoon park visit.

'But I want to go,' sniffed the sulking six-year-old.

'Really? Look at the weather. We'll get wet through,' said Jen. In this situation, she had the patience and skill of a UN negotiator. 'Why don't we play hide and seek? You hide, and I'll come and find you.'

The change in Charley's demeanour was instant and absolute.

'No peeping,' she said, and ran off to hide under her bed. It's what she always did, and it always took Jen ages to find her. For all her qualities, my wife was rubbish at the seeking bit.

As Charley disappeared, I whispered, 'You know, there's a theory that there's no such thing as bad weather, just inappropriate clothing.'

I earnt a look that suggested I should join Charley under the bed.

'The last thing I need is dressing up in a wet suit to feed the ducks. Don't worry, I'll let her burn off some energy, then we can all settle down to fall asleep in front of Pixar's finest. Deal?'

'Perfect.'

'Coming. Ready or not,' she said, before heading off to the stairs.

For the next five minutes, I could hear Jen's running commentary on all the places she reckoned Charley was hiding. The loud giggling still suggested she was under the bed.

I got busy chopping vegetables. This was my new superpower. Not just chopping, but turning them into a superb vegetable curry that had become Charley's favourite. Spaghetti hoops rarely got a request these days. Jen's superpower appeared to be teaching me how to cook. It was all part of my new life as a family man, and I loved it. Saturday nights had certainly changed. That reminded me to check the fridge for white wine supplies.

I opened the door at the same time as a Tasmanian devil erupted through the kitchen, laughing and screaming. Charley showed her superpower by ducking under the fridge door and veering around the kitchen table before Jen doubled back and scooped her up in her arms.

As I kept busy in the kitchen, several more rounds of running up and downstairs appeared to do the job. Mother and daughter were officially tired. It was film time. As the microwave did its thing with the popcorn, I turned the heat down and left the curry to simmer. The three of us huddled on the sofa. It didn't matter that we all knew every word of the film. The rain was hammering against the windows. We were cosy, and all was good with the world.

Thirty minutes later, I realised two-thirds of the audience were fast asleep. It would be easy to join them, but something had been playing on my mind all day. How had Doc been planning to launder money for Dexter?

Tentatively, I reached for the remote, and paused the film. No reaction from Charley or Jen. Seconds later, thanks to the on-demand service, I was watching the first episode of *Johnny Doc's Millionaire's Row*. It was the last of the three shows produced by Trowel. If the other two were dodgy, why would this be any different?

It soon became obvious. The show was a straightforward rip-off of *Who Wants to Be a Millionaire?* OK, they'd changed the structure of the prizes, added cheesy graphics, and an American-style, super-excited audience – but it was very similar. Above all was the syrupy bonhomie of Docherty. The audience loved his antics. I thought he was a dick.

With generous use of the fast-forward button to cut out the worst of Docherty, I reached episode three. The first two prizes given away hardly justified the hype. Twenty grand in the first episode and two in the second. Hardly entry to *Millionaire's Row*. The third show introduced us to Maya from Northumberland. She was obviously nervous, eyes shooting all over the place as the camera focussed on her. Docherty always kicked off with a very simple question – just to settle the nerves. In Maya's case, it didn't work. She got it wrong.

'Don't worry, Maya. That was just for fun.'

Docherty gave a withering look to the camera, and the audience fell about laughing. Question two would net her £500 – if she got it right. She didn't. I was squirming as Maya got more flustered. The ever-oily Docherty told us she'd lost her standby life. From now on, it was sudden death. Even that hardly raised the tension, as humiliation seemed only a question away. Aside from the low-cut top, Maya seemed to have little going on upstairs.

Question three was about the film we'd just been watching, so I knew Charley could answer it. The camera focussed on Maya as Docherty read out the four options.

Come on, Maya – it's B. It's obviously B.

The top button of the under-pressure top appeared to have surrendered to the inevitable. Not only was Maya's general knowledge falling apart, but her wardrobe was too. Droplets of sweat appeared on her forehead. Music that mimicked a heartbeat grew louder. Maya's face revealed the mental contortions she was going through. The camera cut to the audience members, each concentrating on giving the answer telepathically. Back to Maya.

B, Maya. It's B.

'B,' she said.

Docherty rushed forward to embrace her. The crowd roared their approval, and somehow Maya had £500. As Docherty released Maya from his embrace, the errant button had somehow fixed itself. I paused the recording to check. Sure enough, not just one button was refastened, but two. The sweat had disappeared from Maya's forehead, too. I rewound to look again. I was right. OK, understandable that they'd edit that bit.

They'd actually gone to a lot of trouble to make it look like it was all one shot. So what? It was telly. I dismissed the professionalism that Docherty had shown. The embrace was presumably a tactic to allow the edit to look seamless.

From that point, Maya seemed to grow in confidence. Her answers were almost instant and required little thought. In no time at all, she faced the £250,000 question. Docherty dropped his voice as the studio lights dimmed, just Maya's head brightly lit.

'Maya, for £250,000, answer this question. The song 'Suffragette City' first appeared on which David Bowie album. Was it: A – *Low*. B – *The Rise and Fall of Ziggy Stardust and the Spiders from Mars*. C – *Black Tie White Noise*. Or D – *Hunky Dory*?'

That was another Charley would get. She'd been brought up on Ziggy, and my silly stories about the spiders. We played the album in the car on every road trip. Maya, on the other hand, didn't have a clue.

'D.'

'Do you want me to lock that answer in, Maya? It would *be* wrong to rush you. *Be* careful before you give me your answer.'

Hang on. How many times could Docherty suggest it was B? Was that my imagination? I rewound. No. Definitely coaching her. I let the recording run.

'Is it B – *Ziggy Stardust*?'

'I'm locking in B – *Ziggy Stardust*.'

Docherty wasn't hanging about for Maya to change her mind again. He locked the answer in, and they cut to a commercial break. I fast forwarded through the ads. The oily host was building the tension again. When the answer was finally revealed, the audience went wild. Maya just looked like she wanted to be sick.

'Maya, you've just won £250,000.' Again, the hug from Docherty. 'Now, would you like to gamble that win and turn it into £500,000 by answering one more question?'

Again, I was worried we were going to see Maya's breakfast. She did not look well. Eventually, she shook her head.

'No.'

'You want to stick at two hundred and fifty grand?' Docherty didn't wait for an answer. He went for another hug. The music started, and the crowd celebrated. Maya's turn in the spotlight was over, but somehow, she was richer to the tune of a quarter of a million quid. You'd think she could let her face slip. Some people are never happy.

'What on Earth are you watching?'

I hadn't noticed that Jen was awake.

'Sorry, did I wake you?'

'No. I only needed five minutes.'

I didn't mention she'd been spark-out for an hour.

'It's a game show hosted by that creep Docherty we're digging for dirt on.'

'From what I saw, it was pretty basic stuff. You'd do well on it.'

'Was that a compliment or not?'

'Yes. She got two-hundred-and-fifty-grand for knowing one fact about Bowie. With your intimate knowledge of every last thing he ever did, you'd be quids-in. A quarter of a million, tax free would go down nicely at the moment.'

'Tax free?'

'Yeah. Any winnings on game shows are tax free. Easy money.'

'Jen, you're a genius.'

'Thanks very much. Don't suppose that entitles me to a cup of tea?'

'Anything for you, my love.'

I went to put the kettle on. Was that really how Docherty was laundering the money? A large payment received by Trowel. A stooge, such as the hapless Maya, is fed answers and wins two-hundred-and-fifty-grand. Somebody walks away with perfectly laundered cash. Trowel makes a large commission on the transaction. The TV company handover the prize fund in exchange for a hugely popular prime-time show. Even Maya managed, despite looking terrified through most of it. Then again, for this to work, Maya would have to be the one laundering the money.

It was a nice theory, but a gigantic leap. How the hell could I prove I was right?

18

A recent change to our lives had been the addition of supermarket home deliveries to the heady mix of domestic excitement. It had been my idea, mainly because I always got mardy in shops. The trade-off this week was that I got to wait at home for the delivery while Jen and Charley went on a tour of the many shoe shops in Leeds. Officially, it was for new school shoes, but I knew what Jen was like. More than anything, she knew she was going to miss Charley this week. Jen had a two-night trip to London. Charley was off to stay with her grandparents for more spoiling. The unspoken point was that it could be Ben's last chance to spend concentrated time with his granddaughter.

The delivery had gone smoothly. It was only when I was putting things away that I noticed the suspiciously large number of identical paper bags. They each contained two aubergines. There had to be a mistake. I remembered ordering four aubergines to create a mega curry for the freezer. Just before I called the supermarket to complain, I looked at the receipt for the phone number. A little voice told me to check the printout. Sure enough, I'd ordered four kilograms. That was a lot of aubergines. We were going to need a bigger freezer.

I was just wondering where to hide the evidence that I was an idiot when my phone rang. It was Daisy.

154

'Hope you don't mind me calling on a Sunday?'

'No. Of course not. I was just hiding my aubergines.'

There was a brief silence at the other end of the phone.

'I'll never understand men. Whatever rocks your boat, I suppose. I just called to say I've almost finished the first painting.'

'That's great. You work quickly.'

'Glad of the excuse to stay up all night. It felt good to be useful again. Trouble is…my hands are complaining. I'm starting to struggle to hold a brush.'

'Your health has to come first, Daisy. I understand. We'll think of something else. Don't worry.'

I was trying hard to fight the disappointment when Daisy jolted me from any self-pity.

'Thing is, I've come up with a Plan B. I just need your approval.'

'Go on.'

'I think I should recruit Lucy.'

'Lucy, Lucy? From the hospice? Isn't she too…'

'Wholesome?'

'That's a good word.'

'Don't let appearances fool you. Yes, she's probably the nicest person in the world. But she's got an awful lot to her. She's tough. You have to be to do the job she does. And she's pragmatic. She's not against breaking rules if that's the best thing to do. We've had a couple of long talks over the last few months. She knows what I did for a living. I think she'd be up for it, and we can trust her.'

'Is she a good enough painter?'

'She will be, by the time I finish with her. Do I have your approval to ask her?'

'Yes, if you think she can do it.'

'Good. She's on her way over. I'll call you later.'

Thinking of Johnny Doc had set my mind racing. Aubergines would have to wait. I powered up my laptop and opened Crookipedia. This was a long shot. I typed the word *Maya* into the search box. Nothing. Where had she been from? I remembered and typed the word *Northumberland*. Nothing. How would I find out if Maya from Northumberland needed access to a money laundering service? Not the sort of thing Google would answer, but I knew someone who could. Angel had a knack for finding stuff out.

I called her but it went to voicemail. What was she doing that was more important than answering my impossible questions? I left her a near incomprehensible message and hung up. My next call was to Demus, but he too invited me to leave a message. When Justin's phone did the same, I decided a rethink was in order. This thing was getting to be a bigger project. We needed a meeting. Flic had recently introduced me to some new software. I'd never heard of the company behind it, but decided a Zoom account would be just what we needed. Half an hour later, I'd sent out invitations and had my first meeting scheduled for Monday at five o'clock. Angel, Justin, Demus, Gabby, Spud, Joe, Rupert, Ambrose, Daisy, and probably Lucy. All these people had roles to play if we were going to execute this plan. Oh, and we had a six-part TV series to write. No pressure then.

Feeling pleased with myself for getting so organised, I returned to the aubergine mountain. May as well get the first batch of curry started. Baba ghanoush seemed like a decent option for a starter tonight. While I was at it, what would they taste like with custard?

19

I'd had a few practice goes at the software, so I knew what to expect. At five o'clock, I started my very first Zoom meeting. Jen had left earlier to pick up Charley and left me to play. It was weird, being able to see every member of our little team on one screen. Why hadn't I thought of creating software like this? There must be a vast market for it.

'All right, shall we get started? Can you all hear me?'

There was a resounding chorus of affirmations, followed by a loud howl of feedback from somewhere. I could see Rupert whip off his headphones and mouth something uncomplimentary.

'Can I suggest we all go on mute when we're not speaking?' At least five voices asked how to do it. After a bit of frantic screen searching, I found the icon, and everybody followed my instructions. 'OK, first meeting of the *Down Johnny Doc* working group. Some of you on this call knew Roddy Lightning. It seems that Docherty cheated Roddy many years ago. He also appears to have cheated the public through several of his TV shows. Trowel Productions make all three shows: *Johnny Doc's House Builders*, *Johnny Doc's Treasure Trove*, and *Johnny Doc's Millionaire Row*. The company has just two shareholders, Docherty and Sven Trowel.

I'm fairly convinced Sven doesn't actually exist, and it's a front for Docherty.

'The plan I've sort of got in my head is to gather evidence that he's cheated people and, if possible, drop him right in the shit with the police. Justin, why don't you introduce yourself and tell us how you became a victim?'

I made a tick on my notes for the meeting, before realising the meeting had gone quiet. I looked at the screen in a panic. Sure enough, Justin was telling his tale, but none of us could hear him. Then I realised why.

'Justin, you're on mute.'

Even though we couldn't hear, I knew the exact word Justin had used. Eventually, he found the button.

'Is that better?'

We all nodded. A happier Justin ran through his story about the appearance on *House Builders* and subsequent disaster. He confirmed that he now had contact details for nine other victims and was compiling as much evidence as possible. Ambrose sat forward and unmuted himself.

'Justin, when I was a solicitor, property was my speciality. I'd like to help with the evidence gathering. Sounds like my area. I'll get Stella involved too.'

Brilliant. This is what I was hoping for when I floated the idea of a meeting. When Justin finished, I set out my theory that *Millionaire's Row* was potentially being used to launder money.

'I have to stress. At the moment, this is just a theory. Angel, I need you to work with me to see if we can come up with the evidence. Tracing Maya from Northumberland would be a start, but watching every episode of the show is time consuming.'

'I can help with that,' said Rupert. 'Watching telly is one of my specialities.'

'Cheers, mate. I'll give you as much help as I can with that. OK, I've saved the *Treasure Trove* scam until last because my plan revolves around it.'

I was determined to sound cool as I introduced my big-star mate, Demus. Most people on the call already knew him, but it still sounded cool. As you would expect, his run-through of what he'd found about *Treasure Trove* had his audience rapt. He really was good at this. When he'd finished, I gave a brief outline of my plan.

'My parents have two paintings in the style of LS Lowry. They've been invited to take part in Docherty's programme. According to their letter, it will go out live on Saturday night TV. If we pull this off, we expose him as a crook and there's no way back for him. I think between us, we can make this happen.

'We're going to turn those two paintings into a series of five and build a backstory to make the set so valuable, Docherty won't be able to resist. His greed will do the rest.'

I was hoping for wild enthusiasm. What I got was objections. Gabby went first. She introduced herself to the group, then poked at my plan.

'I can see that Docherty's weakness is art. He's a keen collector, and he knows his stuff. You want us to pass off some Lowry copies as priceless works of art? Don't you think he's going to check the provenance?'

'Yes. And I'm hoping we have the skills within this group to build a convincing story. It all revolves around you, if you're willing to help.'

'Whatever I can do. I'm no fan of Docherty, even if he is a good customer.'

'You told me at the gallery that you're working on a book about great lost artworks. Could you write a chapter about a theoretical, long-lost Lowry series? I believe a series of five is called a pentaptych?'

Gabby smiled.

'Somebody's been doing some research.'

'Very basic, obviously. But I'm banking on Docherty not doing much more. Again, we've got the skills here to create a story from scratch. Between the two of us, we should be able to construct a believable back story. Angel and Spud can handle fake websites that will convince Docherty that you're onto something.'

'Frankie, can I offer something?' It was Daisy. 'First of all, Lucy is on board. She sends her apologies but couldn't make the meeting. Now, aside from actually painting copies, one of my skills is ageing paper. Given enough time, I'm sure we could splice new pages into an old reference book and make it look convincing. We'd need a book that's out of print, so Docherty couldn't get hold of his own copy. Sounds like just the kind of thing Gabby would have for her research.'

'Perfect,' said Gabby. 'Let's swap numbers.'

'This is good,' I said. 'I'll make sure everyone has everyone else's contact details.'

'I still see one problem,' said Gabby. 'I can buy we might be able to convince Docherty, but what about his valuers on *Treasure Trove*? They will see through this…'

'That's where your very talented brother comes in handy. Somehow, we need to get him hired as an expert on the show.'

'You make it all sound so easy. Is it?'

'No. But I was hoping no one would notice. We have to be ready for that live broadcast. It's the only way we get access to the show.'

'OK,' said Rupert, 'Say we manage to produce fakes that fool him. How does that expose his as a crook?'

Demus spoke up.

'The beauty of the plan is in starting small. The two pictures alone are worth relatively little. If we get the story right, the value only comes from having all five paintings. Each time we dangle one in front of Docherty, we up the stakes and draw him in further. By making the fifth one the jackpot, we can demonstrate to the police that he was working towards this all along and was happy to cheat Frankie's parents. Put that alongside the evidence of fraud from the *House Builders* show and we've got him. As for the timescales, anything's possible in showbiz. Leave it with me.'

The first meeting had gone well. I was pleased. Assuming we could get Demus hired as an expert on a popular TV show, we had a plan. I confirmed the list of actions, set the date for another meeting, and wished everyone a goodnight.

20

Jen was dropping Charley at school and meeting me at the cottage to work on the TV series for a couple of hours. After that, I was driving her to the station for her train to London. I'd set off early to visit an old haunt, just five minutes from the cottage. I had another favour to ask. The community centre was where everything started. I'd met both Jen and Robbie there on one memorable night. I'd ended up renting an office on the top floor. When the writing took off, I moved operations to the cottage. The IT side of my business empire stayed on at the centre. Spud had been my partner for a couple of years now. You'd think he'd be used to my great ideas.

'Are you crackers?'

Not the response I'd hoped for. I tried again.

'It doesn't have to have bells and whistles. It just has to look superficially superb.'

'That'll be OK then. Seriously, we've already started building a couple of fake websites to back-up the art story. Now you want a fake auction site?'

'Should be easy enough, man of your talents.'

'Normally, flattery would get you everywhere, but this is a lot of work. Why don't you roll your sleeves up and pitch in?'

162

'I'd be a drain on resources. I'm too rusty. Besides, I've got money launderers to track down. What other work do you have on?'

'Just your run-of-the-mill stuff that pays the bills.'

'Couldn't you get a contractor in to cover that, free up Rupert to do the auction site?'

Spud made a show of tapping at his keyboard, then rubbed his chin.

'OK. You win. One condition.'

'Name it,' I said.

'Get me a part in the TV series with Demus.'

'I can't do that.'

'Course you can. You're a partner in the production company.'

'Fair point. I keep forgetting that. OK. You could play the IT geek who builds the fake auction site for the big sting.'

'Typecasting, but you're on. How long have I got?'

'Two weeks?'

'Impossible.'

'Great. Knew you wouldn't let me down. Got to go, meeting Jen in five.'

'AND YOU'RE ONLY going for two days?'

'The suitcase isn't that big. Anyway, you want me to look fabulous when I'm painting London red, don't you?'

'I want you sitting in your hotel room, shedding a tear, and telling me you'll never go away without me again.'

'Dream on,' said Jen. 'A premiere is a premiere. I shall be fabulous, darling.'

'And he just happened to need a meeting in London that coincides with his premiere?'

'Come on, it makes a great final chapter for the book, you have to admit.'

'It does, and I'm just winding you up. I hope you have a wonderful time.'

'Admit it. You'll enjoy having a couple of days to yourself.'

'I shall miss you every second you're away. Are you sure your parents don't mind having Charley?'

'You try to stop 'em. Full on grandparent spoiling coming up. I know you're new to this parenting business, but if we're serious about adding to the family, you need to learn to grab every chance of a bit of peace and quiet. Let my parents take the responsibility. Besides, Dad might not have…' Jen struggled to finish her point. I was just about to change the subject when she did it for me. 'What was that bong?'

I looked at the car's dashboard.

'It's that red light that just came on. Did it yesterday as well.'

'What does it mean?'

'No idea. It went off yesterday, so I assumed it was OK. There you go, it's gone off again.'

'Red warning lights on cars are usually not good. You need to get it looked at.'

'I will, I promise.' We'd reached the train station. 'Shall I park up and come to wait on the platform with you?'

'No, don't be daft. Just drop me here. I'll be fine. You fly free and enjoy yourself. No nights out with Joe and Rupert, though. You know what you were like after the last one.'

'Good point.'

'Don't forget, call me if anything happens to Dad. I can be home in a few hours if I need to be.'

'Nothing's going to happen. You enjoy yourself.'

'You too. Oh, one more thing you have to do while I'm away.'

'IKEA, I know. I'm on it.'

'All right, two things. The other is to eat more bloody aubergines. I want them gone by the time I get back. Besides, they're good for your fertility. If we're trying for a baby, you need to be in tip-top condition.'

'Are aubergines really good for my bits?'

'It's more that having them lying around the kitchen might be bad for them. I may cut them off.'

It's never easy to decide when Jen's joking. I got her suitcase out of the boot. We said our goodbyes, and I watched as the love of my life expertly bounced the case down the stairs to the platform. I should've added a few aubergines while she wasn't looking.

As the train pulled in, Jen waved from the platform, and I got back in the car. It was only then I realised I'd no idea what I was going to do next. Jen presumably assumed I would head to Joe's bar and settle in for a few drinks. No. I had research to do. I would head for home and watch more episodes of *Millionaire's Row*. I turned on the ignition.

Bong.

The red light was back.

'What do you mean, bong? I want vroom, not bong.'

I tried again but, despite a good talking to, the car refused to cooperate. What the hell was I supposed to do now? I knew how to open the bonnet, as Jen had shown me. Something about water in the windscreen wipers. Once I'd opened it, I'd reached the limit of my potential. I'd achieve no more without help. Thanks to some loud, not to mention rude advice, from the drivers stuck behind me, I closed the bonnet and set about pushing the car away from the blocked drop-off point. It was a shock to realise how difficult this was until I remembered to take the handbrake off. When it was finally moving, the queued drivers behind me gave friendly encouragement. Once the car was safely out of the way, I got back inside, and sulked.

What would Jen do? She'd call the AA, that's what. She'd even offered to enrol me, but I knew better. Or thought I did. Instead, I did what I always did in times of crisis and turned to Google. Twenty minutes later, Big Mick from the local garage had finished sucking in his cheeks. I stood forlornly and watched my car being towed away with a promise it would be ready by Friday.

With no car and no Jen, what else could I do? I went to the pub.

21

Some nights out are born great. Others have greatness thrust upon them. Then there are the ones where you wonder what the hell happened. What have I done to deserve this? I needed to go back to bed. Correction. I needed to go to bed, having just woken up in the armchair.

Last night started well enough. I heeded Jen's instruction not to have a night out with Joe and Rupert, as they always lead me astray. One drink in The Crown to get over the imminent repair bill for the car. What I failed to consider was that Angel now lived in my old house, directly opposite the pub. She spotted my arrival and wanted to know why I was planning to drink alone. Then Justin arrived. There was a quiz involved, lots of bags of crisps, something undrinkable called a Woo Woo, and a takeaway curry back at Angel's. I'm fairly sure there was a phone call from Jen, a group singalong to 'Big Country' on the jukebox, and some kind of plan for today.

I could do with coffee. More urgently, I needed a bathroom. Twenty minutes later, I was showered and feeling more human. My new plan involved toast, more coffee, and going back to bed for a couple of hours. I was just plugging my phone in to charge it when I got a reminder on it.

Road trip with Angel – have a shower and bring the box.

Hang on a minute. How did Angel know about the box? Oh no. How much did she know? This story was not meant for public consumption. Alcohol is not my friend. The murkiness in my brain was clearing. Angel had tracked down Maya from Northumberland and wanted to visit her. She'd put the reminder on my phone and thought it hilarious to add the shower instruction. Then came the awful realisation that the alert meant I had fifteen minutes before she'd be here. I should phone and cancel. Going back to bed was my priority. Who was I kidding? You didn't cancel on Angel at the last minute. Add to that, I desperately wanted dirt on Johnny Doc.

I was still eating the first slice of toast when I heard a car pull up. I grabbed my jacket and the box before I headed outside to be met by an ancient, battered-looking Citroen 2CV. Had Angel bought a car? If she had, why this one?

'Don't just stand there looking gormless, get in.'

I did as I was told. Angel opened her window a couple of inches.

'I see you decided against the shower.'

'I—'

'Only kidding. This is Justin's pride and joy, apart from me, obviously, so no being sick.'

'Well—'

'Fasten your seat belt. There are mints in the glove box.'

'But—'

'I was almost late, temporary lights just up here.'

'We—'

'OK, we can stop for coffee on the way.'

'But—'

'I hope you're not going to be like this all day. This'll be fun.'

Fun? Would this thing get to the end of the road in one piece?

'Tell me again what I signed up for.'

'I know you were bad last night, but you must have some memory? I've been tracking down Maya. She's Maya Christodoulou. Or at least she was. She appears to be back to Maya Brown these days. Her husband is, or was, Chris Christodoulou. According to Robbie's lowlife father's database, the guy was responsible for half the armed robberies in the north of England and a lot of its drug trade. Nasty piece of work, but exceptional at evading prosecution.'

'Hang on. Why are we heading towards him if he's such a bastard?'

'We're not. We're going to see his ex-wife.'

'Same thing in my book. Stop the car. I want to go home.'

'Stop being a wuss. Maya would love to see her ex behind bars, but he's not our target, don't forget. We want dirt on Docherty, and I think she's got it.' I tried to relax but the soft suspension felt weird. Angel noticed. 'Nice car, isn't it?'

'It is. Not the most aerodynamic choice. About the same as Justin's van.'

'Can't go on dangerous missions in an ice-cream van. Besides, this is chic.'

'Something like that.'

'It has more character than modern cars.'

I was about to point out there was nothing wrong with the car I had before I remembered where it was. They would phone me today with an estimate for the repairs.

'Shit. We need to go back. I've left my phone at home. It's charging.'

'Relax. You can survive a few hours without it. I've got mine for emergencies.'

'What if it runs out of battery?'

'These things never die. Don't think I've charged it in a month.'

I'd forgotten Angel was one of the few people yet to succumb to the charms of a smartphone and still had an ancient Nokia. For someone who'd mastered a huge range of technology, it still felt odd. When I'd challenged her about it, she'd muttered something about Big Brother and tracking before changing the subject.

'We're almost on the A1. I'll have you back to your little lifeline in no time,' she said.

She was right, of course. It was a lifeline. Ambrose reckons the average person picks up their phone over two hundred times a day. If that's true, somebody's slacking. I must be heading for a thousand every twenty-four hours. Now I was without it for the best part of a day. My stomach objected as Angel lurched onto the motorway. Nothing I could do now. May as well enjoy the ride.

'Tell me more about Christodoulou.'

'Not much to tell, really. Robbie says her dad avoided doing business with him. They lost a couple of consignments when trucks were targeted. Dex seemed to know who'd done it, but there was no way he was going to the police with the information.'

'You think he was scared of him?'

'She reckons everybody is scared of him.'

I chewed over this latest exchange.

'Can I say again, why the hell are we doing this?'

'Relax. We're off to have a nice cup of tea with his ex. That's all.'

'So, she's expecting us?'

'Now, where would be the fun in that?'

Angel did seem to be having fun. I'd almost forgotten how infectious her enthusiasm was.

'How do you know where she lives?'

'Have you met me? I'm very resourceful.'

That was true. Some of her methods were even legal. All of them were very effective.

'Do you really think she'll just dish the dirt on Docherty to two strangers on her doorstep?'

'I think if the alternative is the police turning up, yes.'

'But the police aren't involved.'

'And she doesn't know that.'

We lapsed into silence.

'Where are we going?'

Angel had turned off the A1.

'It turns out, Maya of Northumberland is now Maya of Middlesbrough. Which is handy. A lot closer for us.'

Before long, Angel's scribbled directions were taking us past row upon row of red-bricked, terrace houses. Some painted, others pebble-dashed. All very neat and tidy. Even allowing for the fact that we weren't in Northumberland, this was not where I expected Maya of Northumberland to be living, given her husband was some big-time gangster.

There was nobody about as Angel pulled up outside a bright-red door. It was number thirty-seven, but the seven was loose and hanging at an angle.

'Come on. With a bit of luck, she'll have the kettle on.'

Angel strode to the door with a certain confidence. I shuffled along behind her. After the second knock, a head appeared around a neighbouring door.

'Try the pub. King's Head.'

An arm pointed to our right, then disappeared behind the closing door. Strange. But helpful. Angel buttoned her coat, and we set off.

IT WAS BARELY noon, but it was clear Maya of Northumberland liked to start her day early. She looked crumpled. That's the only way to describe her. She seemed thirty years older than the glamorous contestant on *Millionaire's Row*. The remains of a black eye didn't help. Angel almost whispered.

'Maya?'

'Fuck off.' Maya of Northumberland raised a shaky glass to her lips and drank the dark liquid. I guessed it wasn't just Coke in the glass. 'There's no money and even if there was, I'd give you nothing. Fuck off.'

She seemed adamant. I took a step back, ready to retreat to the car. Angel tried again.

'Maya, we're not after money. Maybe we can help. Another drink?'

'Bacardi and Coke. Then you can fuck off.'

Angel turned and nodded at me. I got the message that I was going to the bar. In that case, it was time for a hair of the dog. I ordered myself a pint and an orange juice for Angel. She was driving. As I waited for my change, a loud cackling rang out from behind me. I turned to see Maya of Northumberland and Angel helpless with laughter. I took a sip of my pint before picking up the three glasses and heading to the corner.

'And this is Frankie. He's not that bad, really.'

This provoked another bout of hysterics that Peter Kay would've envied. I passed over the drinks and waited to be admitted to the joke. I wasn't. Maya downed half the rum.

'Cheers, Frankie. You're OK, Angel, you'll do for me. So how can I help?'

'We're interested in Johnny Docherty.'

'He can fuck right off.' Interesting. More emphatic than when she told us something similar. 'He's just as big a criminal as my miserable runt of a husband.'

Maya slammed the now empty glass on the table. I looked over my shoulder at the barman. He nodded and grabbed another glass. He didn't bother asking if he should make it a double and brought the drink over. I gave him a tenner.

'Keep the change, mate,' I said, and sat back, happy to leave the questions to Angel.

'How long were you married, Maya?'

'We still are. He calls himself a churchgoer. Greek Orthodox. No chance of a divorce. Been fifteen years altogether.' There was a hint of a smile. 'Had a great life. At first.'

'What went wrong?'

'Made the mistake of hitting him back one night. Went down like a sack of spuds. Trouble is, he got up again. Knocked seven shades of shite out of me. Flung me out. Had the dressing gown I was wearing. All I had to show for all that time, helping him rack up the cash. Moved his young tart in the day after, apparently.'

'What did you do?'

'Set off walking to my sister's. A taxi driver picked me up. Gave me a lift. Said I could pay him when I was back on my feet. Still waiting. Two years later and here I am. And I'm sick of it. So, yeah, if you want dirt on him, ask away,' said Maya.

'Tell us about *Millionaire's Row*. How did that come about?'

'Thirsty work, this.' The barman was already on his way over and I slipped him another tenner. 'He was all cosy with Docherty. They were always drinking together. One night, he tells me I'm going on this quiz show. I told him he was mad. I know fuck all about fuck all. Sorry. My language…'

'Not a problem,' said Angel. 'Did they feed you the answers, make sure you won?'

'Could you tell?'

'Only because we were looking for it.'

'From what I could tell, it was a trial run. Docherty had this idea that he could turn dodgy money into legitimate cash. I was never sure what the con was. I know it had something to do with Chris paying Doc a big bag of cash. Then I won £250,000, so he got his money back. Meanwhile, I got to look an idiot on telly. Never understood it.'

'We think Docherty would accept a large sum, say £300,000 of illegal money that somebody like your husband could never explain to the authorities. You won £250,000 back. That's tax free and from a legitimate source. Your husband is happy. The show's sponsors will probably pick up the 'official' bill, so Docherty walks away with a fortune, too. We think he's done that at least once in each series. It's a lucrative business.'

'And I got bugger all.'

'Maybe it's not too late,' said Angel. Where the hell was she going with this now? 'Our beef is with Docherty, not your husband. A friend of mine knows good lawyers. The kind of lawyers who could get you a nice pension, assuming your husband wants to stay out of prison. We just want to expose Docherty as the sleazy lowlife he is. Would you be willing to help us?'

'What would you need me to do?'

'Well…'

BACK AT THE car, Angel looked across at me.

'Right. I've waited long enough. Tell me the tale about this box. You were both very evasive last night.'

'It's just an old money box. Useless without the key.'

'Hand it over.'

Reluctantly, I reached to the back seat.

'Like I said, it's useless without the key.'

Angel took a bunch of what looked like Allen keys from her pocket. She looked closely at the lock, flicked through a few of the keys, and settled on a particularly slim one. Within seconds, the lock was open. Is there anything this woman couldn't do?

Before she could look inside, I took the box from her and placed my jacket over it.

'Thanks for that. Time we were getting back.'

'Dream on. I have to know what's in the box that was so important to you and Justin all those years ago.'

'It's nothing.'

'Rubbish. It meant you lost touch with a good mate for over twenty years.'

'It doesn't show either of us in a good light.'

'Now I have to see. Come on. Spill the beans.'

'This goes no further. It's a bit, embarrassing.'

I opened the box and retrieved the small packet from inside.

'Condoms? You fell out over a packet of three?'

'It wasn't like today when you can just wander into a supermarket and help yourself. Trying to buy them was a traumatic experience for a school kid.'

'But you were eighteen. Couldn't you just get them from the pub toilets like any normal human being?'

I felt my face flush.

'I'd had them a while.'

'How long?'

'About three years. Stop laughing. I knew I shouldn't say anything.'

'But I still don't understand why you fell out.'

It was pointless trying to keep it secret now.

'We'd just finished our exams. There was a big party to celebrate. Let's just say, I'd had my eye on a girl for a while. She hinted, you know…'

'She was up for it?'

'I was trying to be delicate. Yes. She was well up for it. Trouble is that your fuckwit of a boyfriend also fancied her. He wanted to kibosh any chance I had. Little did I know that he'd stolen the key from my pencil case earlier that day. I managed to entice the object of my passion back to my place on the understanding that I had the necessary in my room. At the vital moment, I discovered his treachery and the key's absence.'

'Useless without a key,' said Angel through what was now, quite frankly, hysterical laughter. 'So, what did you do?'

'What could I do? She stormed off.'

'Not even a—'

'No. Just a slamming door that woke my parents up. It was a disaster all round, and it was all Justin's fault.'

Angel tried hard to compose herself. As she started the engine, she couldn't resist one last dig.

'At least you've got them back. A bit of something for the weekend.'

This set her off again, and we were another five minutes before we could wave goodbye to Middlesbrough.

As soon as I arrived home, I checked my phone. A missed call from Jen, and a voicemail. *'Just a quick call. Presume you're busy doing something clever. Just spoken to Dad. Sounds like he's having a better day. I wanted to rub it in that I'm in a limo on the way to the premiere. Don't worry about calling me back. I'll ring later.'* She signed off with a big kiss. I seemed to have got away with being offline all day.

Faced with an evening alone, my usual instinct was to head for the pub, or a takeaway menu. The sight of the bags of aubergines triggered something deep in my subconscious. I had to at least try to get through them. My kitchen skills were improving, thanks largely to Jen. She was a superb cook, and I was learning from the best. The cupboards provided onions and a jar of curry paste. The aubergine population reduced by two. As it was simmering, I reasoned that if it was awful, there was always the back-up option – cheese and crackers.

Dad called. It was funny how the calls now came from him rather than Mum. She seemed to drift off when she spoke on the phone and either hung up or left the handset on the chair arm. Dad was being chased by Trowel to submit the pictures for an initial valuation. I agreed to use a courier to get them delivered.

Jen called at around ten o'clock.

'I can report that two more of the purple beasts have found their way into a rather tasty curry,' I said, sounding pleased with myself. I looked guiltily at the last of the cheese on my plate. Jen didn't need to know how foul the curry had been. I just needed to destroy the evidence before she arrived home. 'How was the premiere?'

'Not as good as ours for *The Hubberholme Syndrome*, but OK. At least it was an early start. I've left them all getting steadily drunk in the bar. I much prefer a natter with my husband and an early night.'

We chatted about the various celebrities she'd met at the premiere. None of them were as impressive as Demus.

'Enough about me. What's your day been like?'

'I'm hot on the tail of the suspicious deals on *Millionaire's Row*. Just about to watch my fifth episode of the night. We even tracked do—'

'Hang on a minute, love. Room service just arrived. Back in a second.'

I could hear the muffled conversation from the other end and tried to work out which nightcap Jen'd ordered. Part of our ritual in hotels was to order large brandies, just to feel we were being extravagant.

'Sorry about that. They do an amazing hot chocolate that's more like a meal in itself. What were you saying?'

'Just that we're making progress tracking down some of the contestants on *Millionaire's Row*. I think we may have proof that they're laundering money through the show. With a bit of luck, we can expose Docherty.'

'Look, I know he did the dirty on Roddy but just be careful. I came close to losing you on the A1 last year. Shit.'

'What?'

'I just dropped chocolate covered marshmallow on the sheet. That's going to take some explaining.'

'Do you need to go? Concentrate on your chocolate.'

'As long as you don't mind and you're OK?'

'I'm fine. We can speak longer tomorrow night and you'll be home the day after. I'll let you know if I've got the car back by then and I can pick you up from the station.'

We went through the familiar back and forth, who should hang up first. I always did, in the middle of asking a question. It had made Jen call me straight back when I first did it. Now she just likes the routine. Two minutes later, I had a text from her made-up of sleeping emojis and, more worrying, two aubergines. I texted back.

What the f—?

I meant the curry xx followed by a blushing face.

I removed the evidence of the curry while I remembered, scooping it into its own bin liner before burying it deep in the main kitchen rubbish. As an extra precaution, I took the lot outside and sneaked it into next door's bin. That should do it. I locked the back door and went back to *Millionaire's Row*.

22

'**J**ustin.' We were on our second Zoom call, and everybody had finally settled down. 'How're you doing with the list of dubious deals on *House Builders*?' He picked up a sheet of paper. 'Justin, you're on mute.'

'Bugger. That better?'

'Loud and clear.'

'So far, we've got nine, including me. Profit for Trowel would appear to be over three million.'

Ambrose raised his hand as if he was back at school. Justin told him to go ahead.

'We're pulling together a decent dossier to hand to the police whenever you give us the nod. I'm confident we're building a decent case, assuming we can get the police interested in the first place. Without the smoking gun, they could give us the brush off.' He glanced down at his notes. 'So far, they all follow a similar pattern. Private residents using the same, unknown to them, architects, are put in contact with the show's producers to appear. After the point of no return, costs rise way beyond initial budgets. They have problems with suppliers. Orders go missing, items not available, credit withdrawn for no reason. Most have had builders walk away from the job. I'm wondering if there's been intimidation, or the building firms are also in on it. Still looking for proof of either, or that they're innocent pawns.'

'That's great work. Well done, both of you.' I took a deep breath. 'OK. *Millionaire's Row*. We may have had a breakthrough yesterday. Angel tracked down an address for the first suspicious-looking winning contestant. We paid her a visit, and it seems she was coerced into appearing by her husband, a distinctly unpleasant local villain. Luckily for us, he's now an estranged husband, and she's not averse to a bit of revenge. I've also got a few names we need to check out. They all won £250,000 and seemed dodgy.'

'Send them over,' said Angel. 'I'm enjoying this. How many million-pound winners have there been?'

'None, so far. Still got lots of shows to watch but I have a theory about that. Do you think winning the jackpot would attract a lot more scrutiny from the press? They'd be bound to go digging. This way, it's still sizeable sums but relatively low key.'

Everyone on the call seemed to nod at this. I continued.

'This brings us to their third con and our sting operation. I'm convinced that Docherty uses *Treasure Hunt* to top-up his personal art collection and pocket a tidy sum from ripping off pensioners. When you put that together with cheating Roddy, I'm more determined than ever that we take him down. It'll be difficult. We're up against some tight deadlines, but you're all doing great work. Gabby, why don't you run us through your progress so far?'

Even in the small Zoom window, Gabby exuded class and poise.

'Thanks, Frankie. Just to recap. Our plan revolves around convincing Docherty of the existence of a series of five paintings by the great LS Lowry. Now, Docherty has a reasonable eye, but he's no expert. He relies on specialists in the business to authenticate and value his targets. For some years, I've been his contact for northern artists. He owns a Hockney and several McKenzie Thorpe originals. He craves a Lowry. The thought of five in a long-lost series may make his head explode. Thanks to Daisy and Lucy, we're well on the way to having three more paintings to add to the two owned by Frankie's parents. The trick will be to convince Docherty that they are long-lost masterpieces rather than expertly done, but still damp, imitations.'

'Is that really possible?'

It was the first time Joe had spoken, but he had a point.

'It depends how authentic we can make things look,' said Gabby. 'Spud, Rupert, and Angel have been doing great work building a series of websites and social media profiles to plant the backstory of how they came to be lost. Bear in mind, Docherty would rely on me to do his in-depth research, so a superficial bunch of historical, online stories should be enough. The clincher could rest on having another expert valuer. He always wants a second opinion.'

'Surely, a second opinion would spot the con?'

'You'd think so, Joe. However, I have every confidence that Alexander Defoe will fit the bill as he doesn't exist – yet.'

'That's where I come in,' said Demus. 'I've already begun prepping for the role. That's what the beard's all about. Once it's a bit longer, we'll take photos for the various websites. I can always call on our make-up artist if we need it quicker.'

'I believe I can convince Docherty to use Mr Defoe as an expert on the show. That way, we get an inside view of what goes on and know that the backstory will stand up,' said Gabby, as if it was the easiest thing in the world.

'How long before we're ready?'

'A week? Maybe ten days.'

This was suddenly moving quickly. My phone burst into life. I thanked everyone for their time and ended the meeting. I needed to take the call. It was Gerry.

'SORRY TO BOTHER you, Frankie, but with Jen in London, I...'

'Not a problem, Gerry. What is it?'

'I'm just waiting for an ambulance.'

'For Ben? What's happened?'

'No. It's for me. Ben's fast asleep upstairs and knows nothing about it. On the other hand, ended up sitting at the bottom of the stairs with what I suspect is a broken ankle. I'd just been to check on him and was rushing to get to a pan that was boiling over. Anyway, lost my footing, and heard a crack. I've got myself up and turned it off, now, so don't rush, but—'

'Do you need me to come with you?'

'No. Could you come here? I don't want to leave Ben by himself. If you could be here, I don't even need to wake him.'

'I'll be there in five minutes.'

It was then I remembered I didn't have a car. It was still at the garage. I looked at my watch – as if I knew what time a bus was due. Or which one I needed. It was only when I opened the front door and saw Jen's car. She saved the day again. The key was in a box in the hall, as usual.

I still had Ben and Gerry's house key from plant-watering duties when they'd toured Spain last year. My heart was still pounding as I let myself in. My mother-in-law was sitting on a dining chair.

'Thanks, Frankie. I feel such an idiot. This is the last thing we need.'

'At least you managed to turn the pan off.'

'Not very ladylike. Dragged myself through on my backside.'

'Once the ambulance has been, I'll call Jen, let her know.'

'No need. She'll only insist on coming home early. Let her finish what she's there for and she can come tomorrow.'

I was about to argue, but there was a loud knock on the door. Two paramedics soon had Gerry in the back of an ambulance. An oxygen mask had restored colour to her face.

'Are you sure you'll be OK?'

I got a weak thumbs up. The doors closed, and the ambulance pulled away. What was I supposed to do now? May as well put the kettle on. While I was waiting for it to boil, I washed the two mugs that sat on the counter. The offending pan still held the soup Gerry had been making. The rest of the kitchen was immaculate. Anything I did would only make it worse. Within ten seconds of the kettle boiling, I could hear shuffling from upstairs.

It had only been a few days, but I could see a difference in Ben. He looked older. A dressing gown hung loosely over his gaunt frame.

'Hello, son. Didn't know you were coming.'

'Hi, Ben. Tea?'

'Please. One of my superpowers, hearing that kettle from upstairs.' Ben didn't need telling to sit down. I noticed him grimace as he did so. 'I'm sensing Gerry got you over to cover for her on Ben-watch. Where is she?'

For a brief second, I wondered whether to lie. Then I realised a big pot on her foot may be a giveaway.

'Don't worry, but she's at the hospital.'

The instant that you tell someone not to worry, they worry.

'What's wrong?'

'She fell. We think she may have broken her ankle. She didn't want to wake you, so got me round to make tea, and get the biscuits.'

Ben took the hint and pointed at the cupboard.

'I'll just have this,' said Ben. 'Then I'll get down there, make sure she's OK.'

'You'll do no such thing. I'm under strict instructions to use force if necessary to keep you here. I have a black belt.'

'Holding your jeans up, I know. Think a little finger would stop me at the moment.'

'How do you feel?'

'Crap. In fact, I could do with a shot of my magic juice.' I must've looked puzzled. 'Tupperware box, top shelf, by the sink, if you would?'

I retrieved the box and removed the lid. Ben's hands shook as he filled a small plastic syringe with liquid from a bottle. When he was happy with the exact level, he put the end of the syringe in his mouth. The look of relief on his face was almost instant.

'Should you have something to eat with that?'

'Good point,' he said. 'I suspect Gerry saved my sandwich from earlier.'

I crossed to the fridge. Sure enough, there was a cling-film wrapped sandwich. We sat in silence as Ben ate slowly.

'How long have you been taking morphine?'

'Just this week.'

'Aren't you worried about getting addicted?'

Ben let out a chuckle.

'Hardly think that's going to be a problem, do you?'

'Shit. Sorry. I…'

'Don't worry. You get used to it. Look, both me and Gerry know this is it for me. The latest chemo may buy me some time, but not much. I've had time to get used to the idea. Don't get me wrong. I'd rather we were planning where to go for our holidays, but it ain't going to happen. Would be nice to hang around to see another grandchild, if you don't mind getting your finger out.'

He grinned at me.

'I'll see what I can do,' I said.

'Actually, there's one other thing I'd like to see. I take it you've read my diary by now?' I nodded. 'Could you get Robbie and Jen to patch things up? They were such good friends. I hate thinking my weakness caused them so much pain.'

'Weakness?'

'I gave in too easily.'

'Nonsense. From what Robbie says, you were up against a powerful enemy.'

'So, you've talked to her about it?'

'She told me the full story the other day.'

'Does that mean she's out of prison?'

'Yes. I thought you knew. Let me work on it.'

'Don't take too long. I'm kind of on a meter here.'

Ben finished his tea and hauled himself upright.

'Need a lie down, sorry.'

'Can I help?'

The man who'd always seemed so full of energy just nodded. I put his arm around my shoulders and gently guided him to the sofa. By the time I'd covered him with a blanket, he was asleep. I eased the door closed and moved back to the kitchen. I'd just had another sip of tea when Demus called.

'Are you OK to talk?'

'Yes,' I said. 'I need to keep the volume down. I'm with Ben and he's just fallen asleep.'

'How is he?'

'Not great, to be honest.'

'Give him our love. He's a great bloke. Kept us all in stitches at the wedding.'

'I will. How are you getting on?'

'Which do you want first? Good news or slightly less good news?'

'Better start with the good.'

'Alexander Defoe just got his first email. It's from Trowel. Thanks to Gabby singing his praises, they want to offer him a place as an expert on *Treasure Trove*. It's conditional on passing a screen test.'

'That shouldn't be a problem for you, surely?'

'Not for me, certainly. But that brings us to the slightly less good news. The email came from Docherty's assistant, Yasmin Franklin.'

'And is she particularly difficult to please?'

'Far from it. The trouble is, I pleased her a bit too much. We had a thing some years ago when she was a runner on a film I was in. Even with a good disguise, she's bound to recognise me.'

'Bugger. How is that just less good news? It's a disaster.'

'In my business, we call them opportunities. This is yours.'

'To do what?'

'Become Alexander Defoe.'

'No way. I'm not an art expert.'

'Neither am I, but we know someone who is.'

'I'm not an actor.'

'Maybe not, but you know someone who is. And you're lucky.'

'How so?'

'He already speaks like you and looks a bit like you as well.'

'How do you know?'

Demus sighed.

'Because he's made-up. He can be anything we want.'

'There has to be a better way.'

'Not from where I'm sitting. You want to do this for Roddy? Would he have given up at the first hurdle?'

'He'd probably've gone on a bender or run away.'

'No, he wouldn't. He was a singer who became a great actor. If you can be a writer who becomes an OK actor, we've cracked it. So, who's Alexander Defoe?'

'Looks very much like I am.'

Bollocks.

23

Could I really pass myself off as an expert art historian? I'd seen Demus transform and fool an old man into believing he was his long-lost son, but he's a professional. At best, I'd describe my acting experience as limited. Admittedly, I nailed it as a shepherd in the nativity at school. At least, I did until Barney nudged me and I fell backwards off the box I was perched on. Now I think about it – that was probably my only acting experience. Then again, what choice did I have? I was doing this for Roddy and all those who'd lost fortunes to Docherty.

'Shit. Look at the time.'

With Gerry at the hospital, nobody was picking Charley up from school. Ambrose was at the dentist with Issy, so he wasn't an option. What did I do about Ben? A quick look in the living room confirmed he was fast asleep. I scribbled a note on a pad by the phone and left it next to Ben. I would only be half an hour. The phone calls started before I made it to the front door.

'Mrs Frobisher, hello. I'm really sorry, Charley's grandmother had a fall. She's at the hospital. I'm on my way to you now…OK…five minutes. Thank you. Bye.'

It had been a while since I'd felt a naughty schoolboy. On the surface she'd been very nice, but I could tell she wasn't best pleased. I started Jen's car just as she called.

188

'Where are you? The school just phoned. Where's Mum? What's happening?'

Eventually, I got to speak.

'Nothing to worry about, love. I'm on my way to the school now. Charley's fine.'

'What about Mum?'

Did I break the promise I'd made not to tell Jen? I wouldn't last two minutes under torture.

'Don't worry.' Shit. Now she was going to worry. 'She's fine, but she had an accident. We think she's broken her ankle. She's at the hospital. I've been sitting with Ben. He's asleep, so I'm on my way to get Charley.'

'When were you going to tell me all this? Seems you're very good at keeping things secret at the moment.'

'What does that mean?' I sounded snappier than I intended as I was trying to manoeuvre the car one-handed with the phone clenched to my ear. 'Sorry, Jen. I'm in your car so no hands-free. I'll call you as soon as I get Charley home. Don't worry.'

I cursed myself for the worry comment. Jen hung up. She was angry with me. I'd forgotten to pick up Charley, but it wasn't really my fault. And what did she mean about secrets? Why was that blue light flashing behind me?

'Is this your vehicle, sir? Oh, hello, Frankie.'

It was Tinkle, otherwise known as PC Kate Smith.

'Hello, Kate. Sorry about that. Bit of an emergency.'

I explained about the fall, Charley, and the bollocking from Jen.

'Follow me. We'll catch-up later.'

With that, Tinkle got back in her car, and, to an accompaniment of blue flashing lights and sirens, our mini convoy cleaved through the busy traffic. It was hard not to pretend I was in an episode of *Line of Duty*. In no time at all, we made a rather undramatic approach through various locked gates to the school entrance. I spotted Charley through the door to the hall behind the reception desk. She was happily engrossed in a book while the rest of the after-school club shrieked their way through some high-speed chasing game. I apologised profusely to the young woman in charge when she delivered Charley to me.

Back outside, she seemed none the worse for the delay and was delighted to see Tinkle. Before long, she was wearing the police cap and threatening to arrest me if she didn't get fish fingers for tea.

'How come you're flying solo?' I asked Tinkle.

'Cuts. Somebody high up noticed they could reduce costs by sending me out to face the violent criminals alone.'

Charley was busy arresting a cocker spaniel. I could see Tinkle's point.

'What about your partner in anti-crime?'

'PC Newhouse is currently on a course and will shortly emerge, butterfly-like as DC Newhouse. No more pounding the beat for him.'

'That's great. Surely, you're pleased for him?'

'I am. Just miss him. We had a laugh when we weren't combatting crime at its grisliest.'

The cocker spaniel was now licking the giggling six-year-old special constable into submission. Its owner was doing her best to drag the dog away. The least I could do was the same for the giggler. I scooped her up.

'Come on, you. Your mother would have a fit if she knew you were being slobbered on.'

Tinkle tickled Charley before helping to load her onto the back seat of the car.

'How is Jen?'

I dropped my voice.

'She's a bit pissed off with me, to be fair. Maybe I deserve it. Forgetting to pick this one up didn't help.'

'It can't be easy for Jen, what with her dad and everything.'

I was about to tell her about the house I'd seen when a blast of static came from the radio on Tinkle's jacket.

'Sorry. Got to go. Love to Jen.' She was almost back in her car when she remembered to retrieve her hat. 'Bye, Charley.'

I got back behind the wheel.

'Right. Grandad needs one of your special hugs. With a bit of luck, he'll have some fish fingers in the freezer.'

I pulled out into the traffic. At least one crisis was sorted.

CHARLEY COPED WELL with the transition from police officer to doctor. Somehow, Ben had produced a tiny white coat for Charley to wear as she inspected Gerry's foot. The protective boot proved fascinating to her, and she couldn't see why it wasn't a suitable option for a Christmas present.

I suspect we all enjoyed the emergency meal of fish fingers, chips, and beans. Between Doctor Charley and me, we made sure Ben and Gerry had everything they needed for the night, including a flask of tea beside their bed. They tried to hide their relief as they received goodbye hugs and we left them in peace, with a promise to return in the morning.

Once again, I felt out of my depth as a newly established parent when we were in the car.

'Will that boot fix Grandma's foot?'

'Yes. In a few weeks, it'll be as good as new.'

Charley considered this for a minute.

'When she's finished with the boot, I'm going to give it to Grandad, so he gets fixed. He'll be good as new.'

Luckily, the smile I gave her seemed to be enough, and I went back to rapid blinking. We navigated the bath and bedtime routine without further upset. Charley was looking forward to her mother being home the next day. So was I. This looking after people was exhausting.

With Charley asleep, I settled down with a cup of tea to check my emails. There was one from the estate agent asking if I was ready to bid on the house. They reckoned they already had a couple of offers. I clicked again on the pictures. It really was ideal. I heard a key in the door.

'Jen? What are you doing here?'

'Couldn't settle, so I got on the train.' Jen hugged me but pulled back from a kiss. 'Garlic?'

'Sorry. I blame the aubergines.'

'Hope they're all gone. Any chance of a cuppa?'

'Of course. Sit down. Back in a minute,' I called through from the kitchen. 'Can I get you something to eat?'

'No, thanks. I had a sandwich on the train.'

I was chattering away happily as I brought the tea through. Jen had a face like thunder.

'What's this?'

She pointed at the laptop.

'That, my love, could be our new home.'

'And when did you decide this?'

'Decide? Nothing's decided. I just looked at it. It's in a perfect place, look.'

'I wasn't aware there was anything wrong with where my house is.'

'There's nothing wrong...Hang on. *My* house? I thought it was *our* house.'

'Certainly can't miss your stuff making it untidy.'

She pointed at the records, still sitting in the corner.

'Sorry. Look, I had to look after Ben, and Gerry had her fall. It's been chaos. I'll go to IKEA tomorrow. I promise.'

'I seem to remember you promised before.' I couldn't believe we were having our first proper row. Where had this come from? 'Then I find you secretly planning to move house. But then, you are really good at keeping secrets.'

'Secrets? What does that mean?'

'Why didn't you tell me Robbie was out?'

'It honestly didn't seem that important. We've both been busy,'

'Not too busy to have a nice little catch-up in the park. You were seen.'

I started to ask who'd seen us but realised quickly that wasn't the point.

'Look, I'm out of my mind with worry about Dad. What with everything else, I can't do this now. I'm going to bed.'

With that, she was gone. I was shaking. This can't be happening. I slammed the laptop shut.

'Fucking bi-folding doors.'

I stared at the wall and choked back the tears. What could I do now? Something stopped me storming out and going to the pub. It must've been an hour that I just sat. I was numb. Apart from my bladder. That was full. There was silence from upstairs. I crept up and used the bathroom. Our bedroom door was closed. Should I go in? I put my hand on the handle, then decided against it. Charley was asleep. She didn't deserve to hear us arguing.

At the bottom of the stairs, I spotted the framed envelope on the wall. Joe said to open it when we had a row. I think tonight counted. Back on the sofa, I pried open the clips on the back of the frame and retrieved the envelope. How could this help? Only one way to find out. I opened the envelope and extracted a sheet of paper. The message was simple.

You are an arsehole. Call me – NOW. Then apologise unreservedly once you've used the enclosed to buy flowers. Love Joe & Rupert x

I smiled, despite everything. He'd taped a fifty-pound note to the bottom of the letter and a second envelope was addressed to Jen. It was eleven o'clock. Early for Joe. He'd still be at the club. He answered on the first ring.

'I'm an arsehole. Where the hell do I get flowers at this time of night?'

'You opened the first envelope? Oh dear. Where are you?'

'Home.'

'Don't move. I'll be there in twenty minutes.'

The line went dead. Sure enough, twenty minutes later, there was a tap on the door. Joe stood there with the biggest bunch of flowers I'd ever seen.

'Where did you get those at this time of night?'

'Contacts. I won't come in. Keep the fifty quid and put it back in the envelope for next time. Now, go and apologise.'

Without another word, he turned, and walked back to the cab that was waiting. No time for thinking. I did as I was told and tapped on the bedroom door. There was no answer. I crept inside. Jen was sitting in bed, clutching her knees to her chest. She looked like she'd been crying for hours.

'Where did you get those from?'

'Contacts.'

'They're lovely. But you're still an arsehole.'

'I know. Joe just told me that. It's true. I'm an arsehole for keeping secrets from you, but I swear, nothing is going on with Robbie. There's no way I'd risk what we have. You mean everything to me. There's no affair. I'm just an arsehole.'

'Arsehole.' I was relieved when Jen took the flowers and didn't hit me with them. 'If I find out you're lying to me, I'll cu—'

'Honestly. I am just an arsehole.'

'Arsehole.' I think we'd now firmly established I was an arsehole. Jen dropped a disintegrating tissue on the bedside table. I offered her the box. 'Ta.'

'Surely, you can't believe I'd ever do the dirty on you. I meant those vows we made. As we've already established, I can be an arsehole at times, but I'm a loyal arsehole.'

'And don't think you can get round me with flowers, even if they are very nice.'

'What about IKEA units?'

'More likely.'

'How about I order them online and get somebody to build them when they get here?'

'Good idea. What's that?'

I remembered the second envelope and handed it to Jen. She ripped it open. Half a dozen Polaroid pictures fell onto the bed. They were all from our wedding. Jen's face crumpled. She was crying and smiling at the same time as she scanned each in turn. I produced another tissue.

'Sorry,' she said. 'I'm so worried about Dad. It's all a bit...'

'Shite?'

She nodded and blew her nose.

'OK. I might still be mad at you. I haven't decided yet. You can get in, but no funny business.'

'Of course. Whatever you say.'

Ten minutes later, there was funny business.

24

Ben called early the following morning. He insisted he wanted to go to the daycare session at the hospice. I could hear from Gerry's comments in the background that she thought he should rest at home. He was adamant, and I agreed to pick him up at the usual time. The car was due to be delivered in perfect health this morning, so all looked possible. In fact, after more funny business earlier, anything seemed possible.

Jen had apologised. She said the pressure was getting to her. I told her it was all my fault and promised no more secrets. Delighted that her mum was home earlier than expected, Charley announced she was planning to be a doctor when she grew up.

'Why don't we ditch work for the day? You could come to the hospice and help with the session,' I said.

'You mean I could have a look around and see where Dad's going to end up?'

I kissed the top of her head.

'That as well. I think you'll like the place. Everybody's so nice. And you can meet my other woman…Shit…I meant Daisy. She's seventy—'

'Relax. I knew what you meant. You've done a lot to convince me. Just don't give me any more reasons to get mad at you. Deal?'

'Deal. Does that mean you'll come?'

196

'May as well. Are you sure they won't mind?'

'It'll be fine. They'll welcome you with open arms.'

We dropped Charley at school with no drama. Things were looking up, and we headed off to get Ben. Gerry again argued that he shouldn't be going, but she seemed happier that Jen would be there too. It helped that Jen turned up with the first three books of *Chocolat*. Gerry loved Joanne Harris, and the fourth book was due out this week. We left her with strict instructions to put her foot up and read all day.

Ben smiled every time he looked at Jen. He was chatty in the car and determined to enjoy the day's activities, whatever was lined up for him. When we arrived, Lucy intercepted Jen and took her for the tour. I got Ben settled with his watercolours. Daisy was already passing on tips to two of the group.

'Morning, Daisy. Does this mean I've lost you from the writing group?'

'Hello, love. Certainly not. I'm only filling in until Lucy gets back, then I'm all yours. Just showing Jimmy how to make his plums pop.'

'That's a hell of a boast,' I said. Jimmy was blushing furiously.

'Still life. We're doing fruit, as you well know, young man. I'll deal with you later. Are you OK, Ben? You look pale. Well, paler than usual.'

I looked at Ben. He was somewhere around Wimborne White, bordering on Salt. The Farrow & Ball colour chart was one of my party tricks. I'm a hoot at all social gatherings.

'Glass of water, please.'

Ben's voice was barely above a whisper. I was two strides from a water cooler. Ben took a sip as Daisy dabbed at his brow with a handkerchief. I set off for help just as Lucy and Jen came through the door. Lucy's calm professionalism was impressive. Within seconds, she'd produced an oxygen mask, loosened Ben's collar, and restored his face to something approaching Middleton Pink.

'How does that feel, Ben?'

'Much better, thanks. Not sure what happened. One minute, I felt fine then…'

'Let's play it safe. I'll ask the doctor to have a look at you. Give me a minute.' Jen fussed over her dad, and in seconds, Lucy was back with a wheelchair. 'We've got a bed free. I'll take you for a lie down. The doctor'll be about five minutes, OK, Ben?'

Ben nodded. I was now an expert, so I pushed while Lucy got the door. Jen walked beside the chair. By the time we got into the corridor, conversation levels in the room behind us were back to normal.

Lucy led the way down the familiar corridor to the empty bed. It was behind the fifth door. Ben was just grateful for somewhere to rest. He accepted Lucy's expert help in getting from chair to bed.

'Dad, do you need your Oromorph?'

Ben nodded. Jen extracted a familiar bottle from Ben's shoulder bag. Lucy made quick work of using the syringe to measure the dose and held Ben upright while he swallowed. I squeezed Jen's hand. She looked terrified.

A new face appeared at the door. Lucy introduced him as Dr Hall.

'Morning, Ben. Do you mind if I give you a quick MOT?'

Ben managed a smile and a nod. Lucy gently ushered Jen and me outside. She led the way back to a door marked '*Family Room*'.

'I thought it was worth us getting out of the doctor's way. He'll only be a few minutes.' Lucy spoke quietly but had a wonderful way of making everyone else feel better. 'Has Ben been like this before, Jen?'

'Not really. He seems to be more reliant on the morphine, the pain is definitely more frequent.'

'And how's your mother coping? Gerry, isn't it? We met at his induction day. He talks about her a lot.'

'Until the last couple of days, she's coped very well.'

Jen explained about the broken foot and how she was planning to spend more time looking after both of them.

'Can I make a suggestion? And don't read more into it than I'm intending. How would you feel if Ben moved in here for a few days? We have the bed. He would get looked after and Gerry gets a rest. You all must be exhausted. It's amazing the difference a few days recuperating can do for all of you.'

'What about his chemo?'

'Don't worry about that. We're used to transporting people.'

'It just seems a big imposition on you,' said Jen.

'It's what we're here for. It's not just about Ben, either. You all need rest.'

'Shouldn't it be Ben's decision?' I said.

'Yes. And I'll have a word with him if you agree. Jen, why don't you speak to Gerry, and I'll pop in to see the doctor?'

Jen patted her pockets. I took the hint and offered her my hankie. Once Lucy had gone, I put my arm around Jen.

'What do you think?'

'I don't know…I always thought once you came in here…'

'But you heard what Lucy said. It's common for people to come for a break. He'll end up treating it like a spa knowing Ben.'

Jen managed a laugh, then blew her nose.

'I think I'd rather speak to Mum face to face.'

'Of course. We'll pop back to see Ben, then I'll take you home.'

'No. You stay. People are waiting for your session. I'll take the car, then I can bring Mum this afternoon to see him.'

'OK. Why don't you bring a few pictures and stuff? Make the room look a bit more like home.'

There was a knock at the door. It was Dr Hall.

'How is he, doctor?'

'He's better now the pain relief has kicked in. He's agreed to stay for a few days. We can tweak the dose, get him more comfortable, then there's no reason he shouldn't be back home.'

It was like somebody had let the air from Jen. She shrank, but looked relieved. When we got back to his room, Ben looked tired, but more comfortable. I left them to it and went in search of my budding authors.

I FOUND DAISY hard at work, dictating her story. She looked up as I got to her.

'How's Ben?'

'Sleeping. He gave us all a bit of a fright there.'

'Easy to pick up a bug. Could be anything.'

'Lucy's suggested he stay here for a few days.'

'How does he feel about that?'

'He seems OK with the idea. Just waiting to see how Gerry reacts. Jen's gone home to see her. Anyway, how's things over here?'

'Down on numbers today. Only three of us, all working away happily.' Daisy smiled.

'You mean nobody missed me? I should check in with the others.'

'They can wait five minutes. I've got something for you.'

She pointed to a corner of the room where a parcel sat propped against the wall.

'The paintings? Can I see?'

I retrieved the package and handed it to Daisy. She spread the three pictures on the table.

'I'm particularly pleased with that one.' She pointed at the third one. The familiar black figures crossing the road, moving towards a greengrocer's shop. The racks of fruit outside providing a splash of intense colour. 'That one's all Lucy. She's got a real eye for this kind of thing. I'm thinking of trying to get her to follow in my footsteps. She could make a lot of money in my old business. I suspect she's not quite finished helping people here, but one day…'

They all looked great. It was easy to believe they formed part of a group with the two my parents owned. All we had to do now was convince Docherty they were real. I told Daisy about my reservations.

'You'll be fine. Docherty's greedy and dishonest. He'll see what he wants to see. Demus knows all the tricks and Gabby knows her art. Between them, they'll have you believing the story, never mind Docherty. It's the small things you have to get right.'

'You sound like Ambrose,' I said.

'Cheers. Not sure how a girl's meant to react to that. Ambrose sounds like Idris Elba's voice just dropped.'

'I didn't mean…' Daisy was grinning. 'It's just something he said a few weeks ago. If I'd listened then, maybe me and Jen could've avoided a massive row.'

I obviously needed to talk, and the story spilled out. About the house, and me wanting to make a grand gesture. About keeping quiet about Robbie being released. Everything except the funny business. There were some things she didn't need to know.

'Ambrose is right. You're an idiot. Your heart's in the right place. Just not your brain. Forget the grand gestures. Like I said, it's the small things that make a story complete. Jen needs you now more than ever. She needs to know you've got her if she struggles. You need to be there with a tissue before she knows she needs it. Make sure Charley is OK. Be with her. Moving house is the most stressful thing you can do. No way does she have the capacity to cope with any thought of that now. Do the small things.'

I looked into Daisy's eyes.

'You're a wise old bird, aren't you?'

'Less of the old, you cheeky little bugger. I can still kick your arse in a straight fight. You'd have to help me in and out of the chair, granted. But I reckon I'd give you a good kicking.'

'I don't doubt it. And there's no need. I've got the message.'

'Good. Have you spoken to your parents about applying for an apartment at the complex? There're all kinds of strings I can pull. Having them there would be ideal. You might even visit a little old lady in her declining years.'

'Now who's taking the piss?'

'I'm allowed to call myself old, but I'll destroy anyone who agrees. Now, get your finger out, and get the application in.'

25

Thursday. No going back now. Well, there could be. I could just run away and pretend none of this had ever started. Then I thought again about what Ben had said last night.

'If it's the last thing I see on Earth, I want you to nail Docherty.'

Talk about piling the pressure on.

The week had settled into a familiar pattern. Jen dropped Charley at school, then picked up Gerry en route to the hospice. Gerry had adapted well to her crutches but less well to her husband spending his days in a hospice bed. On Tuesday, there'd been talk of him being well enough to go home by the end of the week. Then Wednesday's chemo session seemed to give him a good kicking. It was almost like he was back to square one.

Gerry and Jen spent their days chatting to Ben or reading to him. When he slept, which was often, they transferred to the lounge and tried to keep each other's spirits up. Ambrose was helping by picking Charley up from school. After dropping off a meal for Gerry at home, I'd spend an hour with Ben in the evening. To be fair, he often slept through my visits. I tried not to take offence.

203

My days, at everyone's insistence, felt like being back at school. Demus and Gabby tried to morph me into Alexander Defoe, an art historian and Lowry expert. Demus had suggested a full makeover, like he'd done last year when he became Parker. I remembered the problems he'd had with the beard and vetoed it. Besides, I was quite proud of my own fledgling growth. Admittedly, alarm bells clanged when half of it had grown through grey, but I thought I looked distinguished. My major concession to a disguise had been the addition of some oversized glasses. I'd been denying it for months, but I actually needed them for reading these days.

'The glasses are great,' said Demus. 'Cleaning them doesn't attract suspicion and can buy you time to think. We could do with you being a smoker, ideally. That gives you an excuse to go outside and spend time by yourself. Useful if you need to speak to one of us.'

'There's no way I'm starting smoking, much as I loved Roddy.'

'Thought you might say that. Here, try this.'

'A vape? Hideous things.'

'Yes. But a useful prop. Like I say, if it gets hairy, it gives you an excuse to get outside.'

'Hairy? You promised me this was safe.'

'It is. What's he going to do? Hit you with his cue cards? He's five foot four. Even you could take him out.'

'Cheers. I think.'

'Anyway, it's not going to come to that. You know your stuff. Today's about laying out the story. We do that right and Docherty will be hooked.'

I donned a brown corduroy jacket with leather elbow patches, the glasses, and clutched the vape. Staring back from the mirror was Alexander Defoe. He was shitting himself.

'Test me again, Gabby.'

'You don't need it. You're ready,' she said, placing her hands on my shoulders, and squeezing. 'Lowry's full name and date of birth?'

'November first, 1887. Laurence Stuart – No. Laurence Stephen Lowry. Born in Stretford. Died twenty-third Feb 1976 aged eighty-eight.'

'Well done. Time to go.'

I picked up a cheap mobile phone. It's what us undercover agents call a burner. I'd memorised the number. With luck, Docherty would call it by the end of the day. I was ready. Well, once I'd been to the toilet.

'BREAK A LEG,' said Demus as he waved us off.

If only I could. Having people running around making me cups of tea seemed infinitely more appealing than this.

'I could do with the loo.'

'You've just been,' said Gabby. 'It's just nerves. It'll help your performance.'

Gabby was coming with me to make sure I didn't bottle it, then she would bow out and leave me to it. She knew a coffee shop near the studio that we would use as a meeting point afterwards. At least driving on unfamiliar roads gave me something to take my mind off what was coming. Gabby knew the area well, and we soon pulled into the studio car park, in the heart of Salford's Media City. She pointed out the Lowry centre, just across the water, before leaving me at the door.

A receptionist showed me into a small room with three armchairs around a low table. She'd offered coffee, but I turned it down. I didn't want my hands to shake more than necessary. Five minutes later, the door opened, and Docherty oozed into the room.

'Mr Defoe?'

'Yes,' I said. 'Is Mr Docherty ready for me now?'

Docherty's spray-tan smile almost hit the floor. Demus was spot on. Pretend not to recognise him and wrong foot him from the off.

'Err,' said Docherty, before recovering. 'I'm Mr Docherty. Please, call me Johnny. Everybody else does.'

I shook his hand. It felt like it had just been somewhere horrible. Angel would say he was one of *those* people. You just knew his fingers would smell of something unpleasant. Docherty gestured to the seats, and we settled in.

'Gabby tells me you've known each other years.'

'Yes. We bonded over a love of Northern artists,' I said.

'And you specialise in one of my heroes, I believe.'

'Laurence Stephen Lowry, by any chance.'

Should that be Stuart? Had I blown it already? Apparently not.

'The very same,' said Docherty, as if this somehow made us besties. 'I asked you here today to see if you'd be a good fit as an art expert on my show, *Johnny Doc's Treasure Trove*. Are you a fan?'

'If I'm honest, when Gabby mentioned it, that was the first time I'd heard of it. Is it good?'

Docherty laughed, suddenly nervous.

'We picked up a BAFTA last year.' I did my best puzzled face. Now Docherty looked rattled. 'I suppose I can't expect distinguished academics like yourself to watch prime-time TV, unlike the other 4.5 million viewers a week, according to the latest figures.' His smile was just starting to struggle.

'Anyway, I thought we'd have a brief chat here, then I'll take you through to our studio. I'll ask you to review a couple of paintings and get you to value them, just like we would in the show. If the camera likes you, we can go from there.'

'Gabby suggested there would be an appearance fee?'

'I like a man who has an eye on the finances. Don't worry. For the right person, I can be very generous. I'd like to think we could do business together, too.' Little did he know, I would sooner punch him in the face than have a long-term relationship with this man. He stood up.

'Shall we?'

I wasn't sure what I expected. The studio was tiny and looked almost identical to the room we'd just left, including the furniture. Docherty explained it was just used for inserts in the show.

'The actual filming will be on location in a series of stately homes.'

An assistant came in and clipped a microphone to my lapel. I knew all about this. I'd been on *The One Show,* after all.

'Right, Mr Defoe. The camera's rolling. I wonder what you make of these?'

Docherty removed a black cover from two easels next to my seat. Even though I knew what to expect, it still came as a jolt to see the two paintings from Mum and Dad's loft. I had my spiel well-rehearsed. As Demus had taught me, I used the exact phrases, and the story soon flowed. My nerves actually ebbed away as I got into my stride. I talked about the compositions and the techniques involved, all thanks to Gabby. Docherty obviously wanted to cut to the chase.

'Mr Defoe, are they genuine Lowry's?'

'Without a doubt.'

'Could you put a value on them?'

'It's a very difficult area, as you doubtless know. The pictures date from a period in the late forties when Lowry was in reduced financial circumstances. He often sold paintings to pay the bills, just like the nineteenth century French painters in Paris. I would need to do some more checks, but I believe the pair would fetch maybe two, or three thousand each.'

Docherty seemed deflated. Gabby had warned me he would get more drama from the show if they were worth more.

'Cut,' shouted Docherty, turning to the technician behind a glass screen, shaking his head. Had I blown it? 'Thank you, Mr Defoe. If you'll wait in the meeting room, I'll review the footage.'

'Thank you. Of course, I didn't get to the most interesting part of the story. That's why I need to do more checking. If I'm correct, these are two of a series known as *The Five Doors*. It's a bit of a myth that's grown up around Lowry. You must've heard of them, an expert like yourself?'

Docherty seemed wrong footed again by the sudden praise of calling him an expert.

'Of course. Remind me of the details, if you would.'

'Well, Lowry never exhibited *The Five Doors* together. Indeed, some deny their existence altogether. Each painting apparently depicts a different shop doorway, hence *The Five Doors*.'

'So, if these two are here, where are the others?'

'A very important question. I believe I know the owner of one of them. If someone like yourself wanted to acquire the set, it's possible I could persuade him to sell in the right circumstances.'

'That could be interesting. Ms Wolf's estimate was in the same ballpark. She said that all five would be worth in the region of twenty thousand pounds.'

I held eye contact with Docherty, just as Demus had taught me.

'May I speak frankly, Mr Docherty?'

'Johnny, please.'

'Well, Johnny. I believe you spoke to Gabby Wolf about the pair of paintings and how they fit into the series. I fear Gabby is being a little naughty about her estimated valuation of the pentaptych. She often is where money's involved. Now, I trust that a sizeable finder's fee will be due to me if I join you in this project?'

Docherty mirrored my stance and moved closer. He dropped his voice.

'Of course. We have to trust each other.'

'Good. You see, if all five paintings were in one's possession, their combined value will rocket to around six million pounds.'

'Six fucking million?' The showbiz veneer had slipped, and the grubby fraudster shone through. He whispered, 'Six million? Are you sure?'

'I'd say that was a minimum. There are collectors in Japan, California, Russia. All you need is two of them going head-to-head at an auction…'

I held out my hands and looked at the ceiling.

'How would we go about locating the other paintings?'

'We'll talk. Now, I believe you mentioned a contract…'

Docherty was hooked.

26

I was still buzzing from my magnificent performance earlier. If there was an Oscar category for Best Scam Set Up, I reckon I'd be a certainty. Demus was happy but warned me there was still a long way to go. Even before I'd dropped Gabby at the gallery, Spud confirmed there was activity on the fake websites. Docherty was checking out the story. With luck, he would do a superficial check, then rely on his hand-picked expert. And that would be me.

Jen called as I queued at the traffic lights to get on the motorway.

'Don't want to distract you while you're driving. I'm at Mum's. Do you fancy picking me up here and we'll pop in for an hour with Dad?'

'OK. What about Charley?'

'She's here looking after her gran. She's currently on her seventh pretend cup of tea since we got here.'

'At least she'll only need a pretend wee after all that.'

'Trust you. Drive safely.'

'Will do. Got to go. Lights have changed. See you soon.'

My plans for a hot bath and a large drink would have to wait a while. I didn't mind. Jen was relying on me again, rather than banishing me to the sofa. I was determined to heed Daisy's advice and forget the grand gestures (even though it had bi-folding doors) and just be there for Jen. If she wanted to spend another hour at the hospice, it was my job to support her.

Traffic was busy. When was the motorway between Manchester and Leeds not busy? I'm sure they use it as a training ground for the people who put cones out. They're a constant feature and have been for as long as I remember.

Just two hours later, I'd covered the forty-two miles mostly in second gear. Had it always taken a while to stand upright after a long drive? A six-year-old in a nurse's uniform greeted me at the front door.

'Do you have an appointment?'

'Yes. I'm here to see Nurse Charley for a cup of tea at now o'clock.'

She checked the plastic watch hanging from her uniform.

'Come in and sit down. Keep your feet off the furniture.'

Was there any call for that?

Before the nurse could enforce any more rules, Jen appeared with a proper cup of tea, and I took my seat in the waiting room. Gerry had a foot elevated and appeared to be covered in a series of mismatched blankets. Most of them had sleeves. It looked like it had been a long afternoon. Jen sat opposite me, the afternoon sunshine lighting her face. She looked tired. Not that I would tell her, obviously. She was so beautiful. At that moment, I wanted to scoop her up, and protect her from anything bad that the world could throw at her. I settled for a chocolate biscuit.

Jen allowed me the luxury of ten minutes to drink my tea before being bundled back into the car for the drive to the hospice.

'Laters,' said Charley. She was busy making imaginary spaghetti hoops for her patient.

Jen rolled out the heavy artillery and suggested that Charley should watch the *Pig* on TV. Gerry insisted she was fine, and we left them to it. In the car, Jen was keen to hear all about the meeting with Docherty. I was as self-effacing as usual as I gave her every detail. I was still in full flow as we pulled into the car park without even asking what was in the carrier bag Jen was clutching. She handed it to me as we entered reception.

'Donuts. For the nurses – not you.'

'I'm sure they'd want to share them.'

We signed in and made our way down the now familiar corridor. We'd timed our arrival perfectly. There was a small gathering in the office. Tea break. I handed over the bag.

'Ooh, you shouldn't have.'

'Yes, he should.'

'What about my diet? Oh, sod the diet. Thanks, Frankie. Ben's awake. He's very popular tonight. Already got a visitor.'

We left the nurses to devour the donuts and headed to Ben's room. A mystery visitor? How intriguing. Jen pushed the door open.

'What are you doing here?' Jen sounded angry.

I stepped inside and immediately registered the neatly folded yellow raincoat over the back of the chair. Robbie stood and turned. Before she could say anything, Jen had pushed past me and was heading back down the corridor. Ben's voice was barely above a whisper.

'Please, Frankie. Bring her back. She needs to hear what Robbie has to say. Ask her to come back for me.'

I nodded and set off in pursuit. The door to the family room clicked shut. I knocked quietly. When there was no reply, I opened the door. Jen was still standing and turned to face me.

'Why is she here? Did you know she was coming? How dare she think she can just waltz back into my life as if nothing happened?'

I took Jen in my arms and held her through the sobs. I tried my best soothing voice.

'Where's this anger come from, Jen?'

Jen pushed her face in my chest. I could feel hot tears against my skin where my top shirt buttons were open.

'She was my best friend and just betrayed me. Cut me off completely. Have you any idea what that's like for a teenage girl? She wasn't just my best friend. She was my only friend. She ditched me, left me completely alone.'

'Ben thinks you should come through and hear what she's got to say.'

'But I don't want to see her. I've managed quite nicely for years. What can she possibly say that'll make a difference at this stage?'

'It would mean a lot to Ben.'

'Why? What do you know?'

'Just talk to her. I'll wait outside, give you all some privacy.'

'I don't understand.'

'Just come back. Let her explain.'

Jen meekly allowed me to lead her down the corridor. I opened the fifth door and Jen stepped inside. A few yards further down the corridor was a lounge. It was empty, and I took a seat with a view back towards Ben's room.

The room was softly lit and very peaceful. It was as if it had learnt to absorb the hurt of a thousand families over the years and help them find peace. I was suddenly exhausted. The adrenaline of the day combined with the sudden emotion. It would be all too easy to fall asleep. I pulled out my phone as a distraction. The first thing I saw was another email from the estate agent. Was I sure about not putting in an offer for the house? I sighed and typed a reply. Plans had changed. We were no longer searching for a new home, even one with bi-folding doors. I felt better immediately. This was proof that I was listening to Daisy. No grand gestures. Just do the small stuff. Support Jen and the rest of my family.

They'd had five minutes and there'd been no slamming of doors or worse. I figured it was safe to go back inside. There were only two chairs, so I sat on the floor with my back against the wall. Jen was silent, listening as her former best friend recounted the story.

Robbie told her everything. She told her about the attentions of Willis, the trip to Jen's house, the talk with Ben, and how he confronted Robbie's father. She told about the intimidation Ben had suffered at the hands of the police and how Robbie cut contact to protect them.

By the end of the story, all four of us were in floods of tears.

I became the official tissue monitor, handing a box around the others.

Without a word, the two women stood and embraced. All the years they'd spent avoiding and ignoring each other on their way to being forgotten. Jen reached out and grabbed my hand, squeezing hard. I thought of joining the hug but wasn't sure of the etiquette. Should I really hug my wife and ex-fiancée at such a moment? I settled for doing a slightly awkward shuffle before eventually releasing my hand and sitting on the edge of Ben's bed. It was obvious he wanted to say something.

'Jen,' I whispered. When she looked at me, I nodded towards Ben. Jen and Robbie sat down and leant towards him. Ben's voice was barely more than a croak.

'I'm so pleased you two got to speak and finally understand. I hope that means you'll get back to being friends. It means so much to me. I know I don't have much time left. You've made me extremely happy. Now,

I'm knackered. I want you all to bugger off and leave me to sleep.'

Ben closed his eyes. We all took the hint and buggered off.

27

By eight o'clock on Friday morning, I was alone in the office, pretending to work, when a phone rang, and startled me. My iPhone was on the desk and not the source of the ring. Did I have an intruder? It was only then I realised it was the burner phone. Docherty was calling.

'Hello. Fra—' Shit. Shit. Shit. Had I stopped just in time? 'Alexander Defoe speaking, how may I help?'

'Mr Defoe. This is Johnny Docherty. May I call you Alexander?'

'Yes. Yes, of course.' I was just glad he wasn't calling me "Frankie, you treacherous bastard". I tried to get my heart back in my chest.

'Or is it Alex?'

'No. Alexander. My mother is always insistent.'

'I apologise. Alexander, I'd like to offer you the role of on-screen expert. Your screen test was excellent, and you obviously know your subject. I'm just putting together a contract which I hope you'll find satisfactory. It pays a standard appearance fee for each show and, of course, all travel and accommodation expenses.'

'How exciting. I don't see that being a problem.'

'Good. That's wonderful. I'll get my assistant to send the details, but you need to attend a rehearsal, well more of a walkthrough at the venue on Wednesday. Bit short

216

notice, but I'm sure you understand. Now, if I may, I'd like to offer you some additional consultancy work.' Here we go. I crossed my fingers and clenched my eyes shut. 'Obviously, I need your utmost discretion in the matter, for which I'm willing to pay generously.'

'Of course. How can I help?'

'I'd like you to help me procure the three missing paintings.'

'But nobody's seen them together in more than half a century. It's a Herculean task,' I said.

'For which you will receive commensurate compensation. I'm in no doubt you're the man for the job.'

I paused, as if considering the offer. Inside, I was jumping on the spot like a forty-year-old Charlie Brown.

'May I ask about the old couple who currently own the pair?'

'They'll be more than happy with the two grand you suggested as a valuation. As you said, it's only by possessing all five that they become valuable. Don't worry, there's a sucker born every minute. They'll have their fifteen minutes of fame, then crawl back to whichever piss-infested retirement home they inhabit.' My knuckles had actually turned white. I was going to destroy this man if it was the last thing I did. 'So, do we have a deal?'

'Email me the figures. If it's satisfactory, we will proceed.'

'Excellent. How soon could you start?'

'I'm free this afternoon. Would that be soon enough? Actually, without pre-empting our agreement, I already know the whereabouts of one of the three. I believe a bid of five thousand should be enough to secure it.'

'That would be most acceptable.'

I looked at the painting on my desk and smiled. The asking price was to have been a grand, but I really didn't like this man. This could be fun.

AFTER THE CALL with Docherty, I had to hurry to the hospice. I'd fallen behind on feedback for my small group of diarists and wanted to catch-up. One by one, the daycare group arrived, quietly slipping in, or greeting me across the room. Daisy arrived with a fanfare of trumpets. Lucy was pushing the chair.

'Morning, Frankie. You wet the bed or something?'

'Just showing dedication to the team. We can't all sit around on our arse all day.'

I caught Daisy's eye as she searched for a comeback. Then it hit me. How could I make such a crass comment about somebody in a wheelchair? My brain hit apology mode, but Daisy howled with laughter.

'Fair play. You can have that one. Come on, I'll buy you a coffee.'

'You know full well it's free.'

'Not my fault. You can pour then.'

'Play nicely, you two. I'll pour,' said Lucy, parking the chair by a desk. In seconds, she was back with two steaming mugs, placing them both on the desk. 'Frankie, can I have a word?'

Something about the look on Lucy's face cut through the banter and I followed her across the room.

'What is it, Lucy? Is it Ben?'

Lucy nodded.

'Is Gerry coming this morning?'

'Yes. Jen's picking her up once she's dropped Charley at school. They should be here any minute.'

'Doctor Mahmoud, Ben's oncologist, is calling in this morning. He'd like to see Gerry at the same time.'

'That doesn't sound like good news.'

'Doctor Mahmoud called in last night on his way home from the hospital and spent time with Ben. I'm not breaking any confidences. Ben asked me to speak to you before Gerry goes in. The doc feels Ben isn't strong enough to continue with the treatment. I'm afraid chemotherapy now would do more harm than good. Ben's agreed to stop treatment.'

There was a ringing in my ears. I felt hot. Lucy gently took my arm and guided me to a seat. We all knew this moment would come, but to hear the news now just didn't seem right. Surely there was...Lucy broke the silence.

'I need you to help me. I'd like to take Gerry and Jen to the family room to speak to the doc before they see Ben.' She looked through to reception as a short, grey-haired man was signing in. 'That's him arriving now. I'll let him know I've spoken to you. Could you meet Gerry and Jen and steer them towards us?'

'Of course. I think that was Jen's car just pulling up by reception. She'll be dropping Gerry off, then parking up.'

Lucy seemed to glide across the room as she joined Doctor Mahmoud. I took a deep breath and walked slowly towards reception. I heard Gerry's laugh as I approached. She was sharing a joke with a nurse as she tried to prop one of her crutches on the counter, ready to sign in. Recounting the story to me set her off laughing again as Jen joined us. Even though I was standing with them, it was like they were in a separate room. Nothing quite seemed real. The easy laughter would soon be replaced by the kind of anguish I could only imagine. Losing Roddy was the hardest thing I'd ever lived through. Imagine being told you were about to lose your soul mate.

Gerry started down the corridor. Jen caught the look on my face.

'Is everything OK?'

In a quiet voice, I explained we were to go to the family room. She seemed to know what was coming. We caught up with Gerry as she tried to reverse through the fire doors. She, too, seemed to understand when I opened the door to the family room. She eased into a seat and started to sob as Doctor Mahmoud greeted her.

It took less than five minutes, then he left. The three of us sat in silence, each lost in thought. I didn't feel I should break the spell. Whatever sadness I felt could be nothing compared to Gerry and Jen. A soft knock on the door snapped all of us out of the trance. Lucy slid into a seat. Her sad smile was like a balm spreading over all of us.

'Ben's awake,' she said.

Gerry's voice disintegrated as she spoke.

'I can't go in looking like this.'

'Take a moment, but Ben knows what Doctor Mahmoud has told you. You'll find he's put a lot of thought into what happens now. Let's go through.' She touched Gerry's arm. Coupled with the smile, she seemed almost Jedi calm. *This is not the droid you seek.* It was remarkable. Gerry nodded, and we all trooped towards the fifth door.

Ben was sitting up in bed and was in danger of being suffocated by Gerry and Jen. Lucy quietly produced an extra chair from somewhere and I sat down. Eventually, Ben came up for air.

'Right. That's the last time we're doing the crying bit. Whatever time I've left, I want it to be happy. That's how I want to be remembered, so get it out of your systems now. I don't want to be surrounded by mardy arses.'

'Grumpy old bugger. Who says I'm coming again?'

Some of the old Gerry poked through the tears and the atmosphere changed. We spent the next hour being a family, chatting about who'd done what to whom. It reminded me of the night we spent at the pub on the big coast-to-coast walk last year. All too soon, Ben started to droop.

'Why don't you have a little sleep? We'll still be here when you wake up.'

'I will, but can you all bugger off, and do something useful? Seems weird if you're just watching me sleep.'

'Come on,' I said. 'You can help with the daycare groups.'

'Is it Friday?'

'Yes, Dad. All day,' said Jen.

'Get Daisy to call in before she goes home for the day. I've something to ask her.'

Jen kissed her dad, and we left Gerry to say goodbye in private.

JEN AND I spent the morning with the writing group. She welcomed the distraction and threw herself at the task with enthusiasm. I thought back to the first time we'd met. That night at the community centre, she'd been so patient when I was making no progress with my writing. Her encouragement was the start of everything, both professionally and personally.

Just before the lunch break, a pale and tired looking Gerry sat beside us.

'Ben's awake. He's asking to see you and Daisy,' she said.

'Of course,' I said. Daisy finished the paragraph she was dictating. 'Come on, trouble. We're going for a walk.'

'So long as we go straight there. None of your tricks to lure me into a tryst.'

'You're insatiable.'

'And all talk. The spirit's willing, but the body's knackered. Where are we going?'

'Ben wants to see you.'

'Best not hang about then,' she said. 'What? Too soon?'

I shook my head and smiled. I suppose the dark humour kept things going around here. As usual, everybody in the place wanted a quick word with Daisy as we made our way through the building. Buster the dog joined us, trotting happily down the corridor. As we reached the ward, the laughter faded. When we got to the fifth door, Daisy visibly tensed her shoulders. I paused my fingers touching the handle.

'You OK?'

Buster's nose nudged Daisy's hand. There was the briefest of pauses as she stroked the black dog before she spoke.

'Let's do it.'

I pushed open the door, and we reversed through. Ben appeared to have shrunk in the last couple of hours. He was adjusting a newly fitted nasal cannula.

'So, this is where you're skiving?'

Daisy had switched on the bright and cheerful.

'Just trying for a bit of peace and quiet, but it's like Salt's Mill on a Bank Holiday in here.'

'Good to see you, too,' she said.

'Now, behave, you two. Hi, Ben. We brought you a visitor.'

Buster sat on the floor and looked up at the pale-looking man. Ben patted the bed and Buster hopped up, settling immediately as Ben stroked his head.

'I'll give you some privacy for a natter,' I said.

Ben waved his hand.

'No. Stay. You need to hear this.' Ben took a couple of breaths. 'Daisy. You know more than anybody what I'm dealing with. I know if I ask you to do something, you'll do it.' I could see Daisy was fighting hard to stifle a smutty comment. Ben continued, 'It's quite simple. I know how much Roddy meant to this one and Jen. Docherty needs to pay for what he did. Never liked the smug bastard, anyway. What I'm saying is, don't use this as an excuse to go easy on him. I'm relying on you to keep Frankie focussed. He's got a job to do.' Ben closed his eyes. Just when I thought he'd nodded off, he spoke again. 'Kate Bush 1979…Saw her at Manchester Apollo that year. Aside from Gerry, the most beautiful woman I've ever seen…Anyway, it's my password for Netflix. When you end up in here, feel free to enjoy it on me.'

Ben closed his eyes and fell asleep. Daisy squeezed his hand as I wiped a tear from my face. I wheeled the chair in silence back to the dayroom, leaving Buster to look after Ben. As we got back to the desk, Daisy took my hand. I thought we were about to have a moment.

'Write that password down for me. I've always fancied watching *Orange Is the New Black*.'

28

Things were picking up pace. Docherty was keen to acquire the three missing paintings. It was a good job I knew the owner of one of them. At least, that's what I told Docherty. He checked again that I, or more accurately, Defoe, was the only person who knew of his search. While we were assuring discretion, I asked if Docherty had shared his knowledge with anyone else, including his assistant. He hadn't and had no intention of broadcasting his activities. With no chance of Yasmin Franklin being involved, it was time to introduce Docherty to the vendor.

I chose the venue carefully. It had secluded corners where deals could be done. It was too busy for the staff to remember every face. The in-house gym ensured most customers were wearing headphones rather than listening to conversations. The coffee shop at a hotel in Leeds was perfect for a little Saturday morning deception. I reckoned I could be a spy. If it wasn't for the long hours and the high risk of being shot or poisoned.

Demus had insisted on a code name. It was only when I spotted him in the corner that the name Blue Eyes made sense. He rose and formally shook my hand.

'You never know who's watching,' he said.

'The eyes are mesmerising.'

'That's the idea. While people are looking at the bright blue contact lenses, they're not clocking the bloke off the telly.' I picked up the menu for a second, then placed it carefully back in its little stand. 'Relax,' said Demus. 'All you have to do is remember to introduce me as Blue Eyes. I'll do the rest.'

'Here's looking at you, Blue Eyes.'

My Bogart impression earnt me a shake of the head. Out of the corner of his mouth, Demus said, 'He's here.'

Sure enough, Docherty was making his way towards us. Several pairs of eyes followed the TV star through the room. So much for keeping a low profile. It had the unexpected benefit of earning us table service and three coffees were duly ordered. I cleared my throat.

'Mr Docherty, this is Blue Eyes,' I said, relieved to have nailed it.

'Please, call me Johnny.'

'Blue. Pleased to meet you,' said Demus. The low growl almost made me do a double take.

'Interesting name. Were your parents always traditional?'

Docherty flashed the famous smile. I've never felt such a powerful urge to punch someone.

'I find in my line of work an alternative name is useful, at times,' said Demus.

'And what is your line of work, if I may ask?'

'You may ask.'

Docherty waited for an answer before realising he needed to actually ask his question. He seemed off balance.

'OK. What is your line of business, Blue?'

'This and that. I have a varied business portfolio. At heart, I suppose, I'm a trader. I buy and sell for a profit or earn a commission for locating rare objects.'

'Which brings us to the reason we're here.'

Demus paused as the young waiter unloaded a tray of drinks and complimentary shortbread. I didn't realise hanging about with celebs had so many bonuses. We assured the waiter we would have a good day, and he left us to it. Demus took a package from beside his chair and offered it to Docherty. He pointed at me. No point having a hired hand and opening your own parcel, I suppose. I extracted the painting and Demus cleared a space on the table.

'I assume you don't mind if Mr Defoe scrutinises it?'

'Be my guest,' said Demus with a shrug.

I leant over the table, running my expert eye over the painting of a florist's shop. The flowers adding the splash of bright colours to the drab monochrome of the cobbled street. I couldn't believe Daisy and Lucy created this in the last week. I was doing my best chin scratching while making interested noises. Just in time, I remembered the eyepiece that Gabby had loaned me. It was brass and probably worth more than we were going to ask for the picture. She'd provided me with a script and I launched into my part with gusto.

'The frame's cheap tat, probably added in the sixties.' I peered through the eyepiece, moving slowly for what seemed like ages. To my relief, I finally found the signature. I looked up and simply nodded to Docherty.

'Mr Defoe would appear to confirm the provenance. I'm led to believe a bid of £5000 will secure the picture. Is that true?'

'Alas, if only it were.' Docherty looked at me as if I'd misled him. This was the first I'd heard of any change of plan. 'Certain information has come to my attention in the last few hours, which will significantly inflate the item's value.'

'And what would that be?'

'Let's just say I know the estimated value of having all five paintings in the set. I also know the whereabouts of a second painting. The information and this painting together will now cost £25,000.'

If Docherty was flustered, he didn't show it.

'I understand your logic. However, I couldn't possibly go that high without access to all five pictures. Ten would be my limit.'

'That's a shame.' Demus downed his espresso. 'If you'll excuse me. My mother always taught me to go to the toilet before I leave somewhere like this. I have a long drive ahead.'

I packed the painting away again. Was pushing the asking price so high really worth the risk of Docherty walking away? When Demus was out of earshot, Docherty looked at me.

'What are the chances he actually knows where another of the paintings is?'

'He doesn't strike me as somebody who makes things up. I suspect he knows.'

'And what he doesn't know is we'd then have four of the five paintings…'

Was Docherty about to bite? I got braver.

'Are you prepared to up the bid?'

'Maybe. Let's see if he has any wriggle room.'

When Demus returned, Docherty turned on the smile again.

'Blue, let's not be hasty. Have a seat. We can at least enjoy the shortbread. It really is delicious.'

Demus resumed his seat but resisted the shortbread. He had incredible resolve. I had another piece.

'What would you say if I upped my offer to fifteen?'

'I'd say that's still not twenty-five.'

'You drive a hard bargain.' Was Docherty's demeanour was changing…

'Something I learnt to do very early in my career. That, and avoid the spotlight,' Demus said with a conviction even I believed.

'Interesting. In my experience, there are only two types of people who shun the spotlight – the chronically shy and those with something to hide. Could it be that *you* have something to hide?' Docherty almost sneered.

Demus smiled for the first time and pinned Docherty with those piercing blue eyes.

'Let's just say I don't invite scrutiny when it comes to my business.'

'I think we understand each other.' Docherty's tone was almost villainous with glee. 'Indeed, we may have the possibility of a mutually beneficial arrangement.'

Docherty took the silence as encouragement. This was better than anything I'd seen on the telly for ages. 'Over the years, I've made many contacts in many businesses. Some have availed themselves of a unique service I've developed.'

'Unless you can weave gold from this shortbread, I very much doubt it.'

Hang on, Demus. Don't shut him down now.

'Some would say it's just as impressive and profitable. Let's say a client has a sizeable sum of cash he'd like to keep under the radar, so to speak. That large sum, invested in my service could then return as a legitimate, tax-free lump sum. Shortbread to gold, as it were.'

'And does this service come free of charge?'

'There is a commission, naturally. A portion of that commission could be in the form of information or, say, a piece of art.'

'And, theoretically, how much of a lump sum are we talking about?'

'I have the capacity for a million, plus commission, of course, say fifteen per cent.'

'So, just so that I'm clear in my own mind…I give you £1.15 dirty millions. In return, I get a nice, clean million in return?'

'Tax free and legitimate.'

'How do I know you're not going to run off with my money? I don't suppose you can provide references?'

'I could make introductions to a selection of my satisfied clients. Maybe we could agree on a fee for the picture and the whereabouts of the others. Then we can allow Mr Defoe to get on with his day and we could have another coffee?'

'And maybe some shortbread?'

'Fifteen for the painting and ten for the information.'

'A pleasure doing business with you, Blue.'

The pair shook hands and dismissed me. I couldn't believe that Demus had pushed it to £25,000 and was about to get Docherty to confirm the money-laundering scheme. Not a bad Saturday morning.

That was as good as Saturday got.

29

tella and Ambrose volunteered to look after Charley for the rest of the day. She was more than excited to spend more time with her best friend, Issy. Jen had sounded upset, and I found her in the kitchen when I arrived at the hospice.

'How is he?'

Jen busied herself with making tea before blowing her nose.

'He's sleeping. Lucy explained that they've switched him to a drip feed of pain killers. He's likely to sleep a lot more as a…'

I held Jen close until the sobs subsided. We took our tea to a table as Gerry joined us. She was keen to know how the morning had gone. Anything to take our minds off what was coming, but none of us wanted to acknowledge.

The rest of the afternoon settled into a pattern. Three of us gathered around Ben's bed, trying to hold normal conversations. Buster appeared not to have left Ben's side all day. More tea. More chatter. At seven o'clock, Gerry was struggling to keep her eyes open.

'Why don't you go home for the evening? I'm sure Ben knows you've been here all day. You could go home, get some rest and come back in the morning,' I said.

'He's right, Mum. You need to look after that foot.'

Gerry seemed too tired to put up an argument.

'I'll take the cups back to the kitchen, then run you home.'

Gerry nodded, and I picked up the cups. Halfway to the kitchen, the familiar smile was coming towards me.

'Lucy, hi. Do you ever go home?'

'This becomes my home, to be honest. How're you all holding up?'

'Gerry's exhausted. I'm just going to run her home so she can rest, then back in the morning.' For the first time since I'd known her, Lucy's angelic face creased into a frown. She put a hand on my arm. 'You think we should stay?'

She nodded.

'Leave the cups here. I need your help with something.' I followed her to the lounge at the end of the corridor. She pointed to a large reclining armchair. 'Grab an arm.'

We dragged the chair into Ben's room. Gerry didn't acknowledge the change of plan and was soon asleep, foot elevated.

An hour later, we had to wake her. Jen noticed how shallow Ben's breathing had become. Buster whimpered. Then, with Jen and Gerry holding his hands, Ben took one last breath.

30

I awoke to the smell of fresh coffee and frying bacon. We were on the sofa at Gerry's, Jen fast asleep against my chest. We'd meant to go home when Gerry had finally gone to bed. Jen seemed to sense I was awake and sat upright.

'Time is it?'

I looked at my watch.

'Almost nine.'

'Can I smell bacon?'

'Your mum must be up.'

We made our way towards the kitchen, Jen pausing just long enough to open a window.

'Morning, you two. I wasn't expecting you to still be here, to be honest, but there's orange juice on the table. Your only decision is butties or on a plate with eggs?'

'Butties, please,' we said in unison.

'I'll do that, Mum. You sit down.'

'Nonsense. It's almost done now. Sit. Don't these smell lovely?' Gerry pointed to the vase of fresh flowers on the table. I had no idea what they were, but they did smell of flowers. Was Gerry being overly cheerful? I'm all in favour of fake it till you make it, but I hadn't expected this. 'What have you got planned for today? It's a beautiful morning.'

Jen tipped her head on one side.

'Mum…'

'Now, cut that out. No head on one side, thank you very much. Your father left very strict instructions not to mope around and cry all day. Been there. Done that. Now it's time to wake up and smell the roses. Or bacon. Speaking of which, this will be ready in five minutes if you need to wash your hands or anything.'

I took the hint and excused myself. Before I left the bathroom, I checked my phone. There were several text messages. Word had spread. There was one late last night from Ambrose to say that Charley was fast asleep. Another flashed on my screen now. Rather than reply, I decided to call.

'I'm really sorry, mate. If there's anything we can do, just shout.'

'Thanks, Ambrose. You've done more than enough keeping Charley overnight. I don't know what we'd have done without you two.'

'Don't worry. If it's OK with you, we were planning to take them to the park this morning.'

'That would be great. I could pick her up at lunchtime if that's OK. We need to tell her what's happened. Can't say I'm looking forward to that. They were so close.'

'Jen'll handle it perfectly, I'm sure. Not that you wouldn't, but…'

'I know what you mean. I just wish I could wave a magic wand and make all this go away.'

'Can't be done, mate. Remember me saying that it's the small things that make a relationship? Over the next few days, there'll be hundreds of small things. Make sure you remember that. Charley'll be quite happy with Issy for now. No rush to pick her up. Just call to make sure we're home.'

I hung up and headed back to the kitchen. Maybe Gerry had it right. We needed activity. Plenty of time for reflection later. Right now, I wanted to protect Jen, and

Gerry from an inhospitable world. If I was honest, I wanted safety too. What did I know about exposing master-criminal TV stars or impersonating art historians? Bollocks to all that. I wanted to sit in our cosy office with Jen and make stuff up. I wanted to pick Charley up from school and tell her daft bedtime stories. I needed familiarity, not to be some kind of hero.

After breakfast, it was as if Jen read my thoughts.

'What's your plan for the day? Once you've wiped the tomato sauce from your chin, of course.'

She reached out and used her index finger to wipe my chin. I took the hint and licked her finger clean.

'Well, I thought I'd help with the practical stuff. There must be a hundred things that need doing. Funeral director, picking stuff up from the hospice. I'm at your disposal.'

'Nice try,' said Jen.

'How do you mean?'

'Me and Mum can do all that.'

'But you both need to take it easy. Let me do the running around.'

'No chance,' said Gerry. 'I need to keep busy. Jen's right. Apart from attending a funeral at some point, your mission is to destroy that man.'

I looked at Jen for help.

'You made a promise to Dad yesterday. How are you going to bring down Docherty?'

So much for retreating to safety.

'I'll call Demus.'

FROM THE CONSERVATORY, I could hear the clink of the dishwasher being loaded. I took a seat opposite Ben's armchair, cushions still piled high. Strange to think of him sitting there just a few days ago, and now…

OK, Ben. I'm doing it.

Demus answered on the second ring.

'Frankie. I'm so sorry about Ben. Please give our love to Jen and Gerry. It goes without saying, if there's anything we can do, just shout.'

'Thanks, Demus. To be fair, the two of them are determined to organise everything to give Ben a good send-off. My specific instructions are to get Docherty.'

'And you're still up for that?'

'Without a doubt.'

'We all figured you'd need a few days to take a break.'

'No. Ben gave his instructions. We push on.'

'OK. Well, we've not been idle. I spoke to Gabby last night. She's been working with Angel and Spud to test the auction website. She's happy that it looks authentic and seems to work. The fake profiles are all set. I think we're ready to sell Docherty his second picture. I suggest we don't hang about. Could you get hold of him and set up the auction?'

'So, who are the profiles for?'

'Sorry. I forgot we'd had a meeting without you. Each bidder at the auction has a profile. Angel will logon as *Busker2*. Joe will be *Michelangelo*.'

'I take it he picked that?'

'Obviously. Gabby'll be *DW40*, and Docherty's been given *Whatsupdoc*. I shall be transformed into the auctioneer.'

'Isn't that risky? Surely Docherty will recognise you?'

'We have an avatar to represent me on screen. Don't ask me how they've done it, but the cartoon figure's mouth movements match the words I speak. It's remarkable.' The transformation in his voice threw me once again. In an instant, he'd become a fast-speaking auctioneer, complete with inflections to mimic changes in bids. 'I suggest that you're in the room with him during the auction. You'll be able to judge his reactions better.'

'What about the bids?'

'We start low and play it by ear. We can't give Docherty any reason to suspect it's not real. Angel and Joe will drop out early. Gabby will push as hard as she thinks she can get away with. The higher we push Docherty, the more invested he'll be when it comes to getting the others.'

'On that subject, what the hell was going on yesterday? You could've warned me you were going to raise the price so much.'

'I thought it best that you didn't know. Your reactions were genuine. Could you have acted that well if you'd known?' Demus had a point, but still…

'Look, this is just an improv exercise for me. The secret to good improvisation is to trust your other actors. Go with them. That's when the magic happens. It worked, didn't it?'

I sighed dramatically.

'Can this really work?'

'Of course it can. He's dishonest. That's the key we hold. We'd be useless without a key.' Demus couldn't hide the laughter. Angel had told them all. Of course she had. Bugger. 'Never underestimate that power of greed and obsession. Docherty has both in spades. Now, I've already cleared that everyone can free up their time over the next few days. Just down to you to schedule it.'

As soon as I ended the call, that's what I did. Docherty jumped at the chance. The auction was set for the following afternoon. While I was on a roll, I made a third call. I had to tell my parents about Ben.

'Hello.'

My mum's voice sounded tentative, as if she'd never answered the phone before.

'It's me. How are you?'

'Me?'

Had she really not recognised my voice?

'It's Frankie.'

There was a silence from the other end, followed by a muffled conversation. A male voice took over.

'Hello, Frankie.'

'Hi, Dad. Is everything OK?'

'Don't worry. Your mum doesn't usually answer the phone these days, but I was upstairs, and she beat me to it. She's just a little confused this morning. She'll be fine in a minute.'

'She didn't recognise my voice.'

'Like I say, just a bit confused. It happens sometimes. I'm glad you called. I've been looking at the website for the sheltered accommodation. It looks ideal. I've done a few sums, and I reckon we could manage, assuming we can sell this place.'

'What does Mum think?'

Dad hesitated before answering.

'It depends which version I get. When she's lucid, she sees the logic and is all for a move. When she's confused, she's terrified of leaving here.'

'I can't believe how quickly she's changing. It's not that long ago she was worried about you. How's your memory been? Sorry. Daft question.'

'No, it's not. I know my short-term memory's not what it was. The dementia group is a big help. They encourage me to make notes. Truth be told, I'm jotting this down as we speak. It helps me to keep track. I know it gets worse when I get annoyed with myself for forgetting stuff, so I try not to. Unless I forget.'

We both laughed, but this was heartbreaking.

'Dad. Do you really think she's up to going to this roadshow, being on telly?'

'It'll be a gamble on the day, but she's so excited. She talks about it every day. She's counting down the days on a calendar on the kitchen wall. Least we can do is let her have the day.'

He had a point. What was the worst that could happen? If she was very confused, I'm sure they would edit it sympathetically, even Docherty.

'OK. But don't worry about getting there or anything like that. Me and Jen will look after you both. Listen, I need to tell you some bad news. Ben died yesterday.'

'Oh no. Please pass on our condolences. We had such a good time at the wedding. I'll let your mother know later. Actually, she's here. She wants a word.'

I heard the phone being passed over.

'Frankie. Sorry I was upstairs when you rang. How's that granddaughter of mine?'

Just like that, the old Mum was back. I gave her a potted history of what Charley had been up to but avoided the subject of Ben. After Charley, Mum was most animated when she talked about the chance to be on telly. She went into a long, involved story of settling down as an eleven-year-old to watch the first episode of *Coronation Street*. She was still hooked to this day. I doubted some of the incredible detail she could recall. She knew what she'd been wearing, who sat where on the sofa. She even remembered having fish and chips for tea. It was only when I asked what they were having to eat this evening that she faltered. There was a pause, then my dad was back on the line.

'I think we've tired her out. She's gone to lie down.'

'How much of what she just told me was true?'

'Every word. That's how it is. She remembers every tiny detail from years ago but has no idea what she had for breakfast or even whether she's had anything.'

'I can't imagine how hard it must be for you. I'll get my finger out and get you on the list for the sheltered housing. It'll make it easier to help then.'

When Dad went off to check on Mum, I was left to reflect on the events of the last twenty-four hours. It was like a point where one generation was handing over to the next. One day, we'd be handing over to Charley. Maybe even a brother or sister, too.

31

I pulled up at the large, wrought-iron gates at just before three on Monday afternoon. I was about to lean out of the window to press the intercom when the gates opened. It all felt a bit creepy, but I pulled forward into the inner sanctum of Johnny Docherty. The wheels crunched on the deep gravel. I could see the house just ahead. All columns and curly finishes. He even had a pair of lions flanking the door. Course he did. *Prick.*

I parked next to a white Range Rover. The front door opened and there he was. The lord of the manor in pink chinos, Pringle sweater draped over his shoulders. Prick.

'Alexander, welcome to Ponderosa.'

'Hello, Johnny. Very impressive.' *Prick.*

'I thought it best to do this from here. Don't want any Tom, Dick, or Wayne listening in.'

He led the way along a polished wood corridor. On either side, at head height, were shelves of hideous porcelain dolls. The glassy stares followed every step. It felt like the start of a slasher film.

'You're obviously an avid collector,' I said. In my head, I added *Prick.*

'They're my babies and what got me into collecting fine art. These are just the overflow. Most of them are in the gallery upstairs. I'll take you up later, give you the full tour. First, though, we need to clinch the painting.'

'Indeed. I trust you have a decent internet connection for the auction?'

'Dog's bollocks, mate. Nothing but the best for Johnny Doc.'

You can guess what flashed through my mind. I thought it again when I saw a huge portrait hanging at the end of the corridor. Actually, this time it was "poser prick". He stood in the classic boxer stance, about to lamp the painter, no doubt.

'Is that you, Johnny?'

'In my younger days, yes. Quite a successful middleweight in my twenties. Had to give it up once TV called. Nobody wants a star presenter with a mashed nose. Not that they landed too many punches. Too quick for 'em.'

He did a little shimmy and pretended to hit me with a quick one-two. Even as a pacifist, I wanted so badly to dropkick him in the knackers. Instead, he opened a pair of double doors with a flourish.

'The library. Please, come through.'

I thought of Ben's library in the basement of his home. Cosy and peaceful, every book on the shelves read and reread, pages marked, covers tatty. This place looked like none of them had ever been opened. Rows of identical leather covers, words irrelevant, never read. Still, made a suitable backdrop for the photo ops. He pointed to a high-backed leather chair in front of a desk. I sat down and slid my laptop from its cover. Careful to log on as Defoe, I clicked on the auction site link.

What Spud and Angel had produced in such a short time was impressive.

'Do you have the password supplied by the auctioneer?'

'Yes. Hang on.'

Docherty fumbled with an iPhone, being careful to shield the screen from my eyes. If he only knew what I knew, he wouldn't bother. I slid the laptop across, and he tapped in the password. His attempts at secrecy would've been more effective had he not mouthed each character as he typed. *Prick*.

'Why don't I drive?'

He pushed the laptop back across the desk. I explained that today's sale was by invitation only and another three bidders would attend. The names of Gabby, Joe, and Angel, I kept to myself.

'We're still waiting for one to sign in, then I suspect we'll get started straight away,' I said.

Right on cue, the message appeared on the screen.

'Welcome to the sale, *Michelangelo*.'

Docherty snorted.

'What kind of idiot joins a serious art auction and names himself after a cartoon turtle?'

I was about to laugh until I realised, he was serious. To my relief, Demus began to speak in the singsong tones of the auctioneer. We were off.

'Ladies and gentlemen, welcome to today's private sale. You are all here by invitation only and financial sureties are in place. The sale will feature just one lot, namely *The Pub*, painted by LS Lowry. The work is believed to be number four in the pentaptych, *The Five Doors*. It shows the outside of a Victorian public house in Salford, with exquisite stained-glass windows, and the usual cast of characters in the street. A delightful piece, I think you'll agree. Who would like to start the bidding at, say, five thousand pounds?'

Docherty glanced at me. I shook my head. There was silence, and no on-screen response. Was this thing working? After what seemed like ages, Demus came back.

'No? How about three thousand? Come on, people. This is why we're here, after all. Thank you. The bid is with *Michelangelo* at three. Four. Five. That's more like it. Who'll give me more?'

I could picture Joe grinning and getting into character as he and Gabby pushed the bidding higher. Then Angel weighed in.

'We have a bid of ten. Thank you, *Busker2*.'

Docherty was looking nervous. As if in a trance, he whispered.

'Fifteen.'

I tapped the keyboard.

'Welcome to the auction, *Whatsupdoc*. The bid is with you at fifteen. Twenty? Thank you, *Busker2*.'

Docherty nodded.

'Twenty-five, thank you *Whatsupdoc*. Who'll give me thirty? We have thirty from *DW40*.'

Now it was my turn to be worried. Was Gabby pushing it too far? I looked at Docherty. He nodded.

I tapped in the bid.

'Thirty-five the—'

Silence.

'What's happening? Why can't we hear anything?'

'I'm sure it's nothing to worry about.' If only I felt as confident as I sounded. I tapped at the keyboard. Nothing. The connection seemed to have crashed.

'Here. Let me do it,' said Docherty. 'If you want a job doing properly, do it yourself.'

He grabbed the laptop and started hammering at the keys. That'll fix it. Prick. It did something. The error message had lots of numbers in it and was totally indecipherable, even to a former software engineer like me. I could feel my blood pressure rising. To my horror, the laptop decided now was the time to reboot.

'Why is it doing that?' screamed Docherty. 'What have you done?'

He pushed the laptop back at me.

'I'm sure the auctioneer will know we've had a problem and will suspend the sale. They'll wait, I'm sure.'

Would they even know we'd gone? It wasn't as if this was a proper site with professional support. It was all smoke and mirrors. An illusion. I somehow controlled my shaking hands enough to log on to the rebooted laptop and clicked on the icon for the auction site. At the third attempt, Docherty entered his top-secret password of 'JohnnyDoc'. My blood froze when I saw the message on the screen.

Today's sales have concluded. Thank you for your interest.

What the f…My thoughts were nothing compared to the torrent of invective that spewed from Docherty. The man seemed unhinged. At least I knew his commitment to owning all five pictures was genuine. Now somebody else had bought one of them.

Then I remembered that the auction was fake. It was three of my friends bidding against us. How the hell had one of them bought it? What did we do now? Judging by Docherty's purple face, a trip to a hospital was a real possibility for one of us, at least. By the sound of it, that could be me.

'This is your fuck up. I expect you to fix it. Use your contacts to secure that picture. Whatever it takes. Don't let me down again. I know people.'

A short arse in pink chinos had just threatened me. I'd never been more scared in my life.

At least, the tour of the evil-eyed dolls appeared to be off the table.

I picked up my laptop and Docherty almost frogmarched me back to my car.

BARELY HALF A mile from Docherty's temple of poor taste, I pulled into a lay-by. I was shaking.

What the hell was Demus up to now? Only one way to find out.

He answered on the first ring.

I resisted the urge to shout at him.

'I take it our friend wasn't happy to lose out?'

'You could say that. Given any encouragement, he'd have had me knee-capped already. I thought the plan was to draw him in even further by getting hold of another painting?'

'It still is. I thought this way may achieve more.'

'So, getting kicked out of the system was part of your new plan? The plan you never bothered to warn me about.'

'As I said before, the secret to good improvisation is to trust your partner. I take it your reaction was one of panic.'

'I almost shat myself.'

'Perfect. And could you have faked that if you'd known in advance?'

I had to concede he may have had a point, although any more of these surprises could finish me altogether.

'So, am I allowed to know the next phase of my plan?'

'Of course. Within reason.'

'Why do I not like the sound of that?'

'Trust me, Frankie. I'll have Docherty eating out of my hand and dropping himself in deep doo-doo in no time. Call him back. Tell him Blue Eyes has heard about his problem and would like to offer his services. He believes the purchaser now owns two paintings but could sell given the right kind of encouragement. Get him to meet us both at the art gallery in Leeds tomorrow morning at eleven.'

'Why the art gallery? Do they have a Lowry exhibition on?'

'No. They do really nice scones in the café. I'll see you there.'

32

As tea shops go, this is one of the more spectacular. I paused as I reached the top of the solid stone steps, glad to catch my breath. Once again, I promised myself I'd get more exercise. The walk from the station should not leave me like this. I looked to my left, just in time to see the familiar white Range Rover pull into a disabled parking space. Docherty got out and strolled towards the gallery. He ignored my outstretched hand. He was just as frosty and unpleasant as he had been yesterday. We stepped inside and turned left into the Tiled Hall Café.

Docherty may as well have been anywhere. The sheer beauty of the room had no impact. He didn't even register the magnificent, ornate ceiling and walls or the sheer scale of the room. He scowled and stomped to a seat by the window before grudgingly moving across to a table with more chairs.

'I'll get the teas then,' I muttered to myself.

As I joined the queue, I heard a voice behind me.

'Yes, please. And one of those scones.'

It was Blue Eyes. We shook hands formally. I pointed to where Docherty was slumped, scowling at nothing in particular. By the time I'd picked up the expertly piled tray and made my way across the room, the pair were laughing like old friends. Demus was obviously turning on the charm.

'You really must try these scones, Johnny. They're wonderful,' said Demus. I slid the tray onto the table, more than pleased that I hadn't spilled anything. 'Thanks, Alexander.'

Docherty was back to grunting. Demus poured teas and attacked a scone. I had to agree. They were very good.

Docherty just stared at his plate, as if he needed a servant to appear and spread jam and plonk a spoonful of cream on top.

Part of me wanted him to stomp off so I could have his scone.

Demus brought us back to why we were all here.

'Alexander tells me you had a technical mishap and your connection to the auction crashed. Such a shame.'

'Bloody websites. Never trusted 'em.'

'From what I've heard, the bidding got quite intense. I would never've guessed it would go for sixty-five grand.'

Bloody hell, Demus. Where did that number come from? Docherty had gone very pale. Had Demus pushed it too far?

'Shame. I wasn't prepared to go that high to get my hands on the second painting. Not if I need all five,' said Docherty.

'But it was my understanding you can get hold of two others shortly?' Docherty just shrugged like a sulky teenager. He sat up straight when Demus continued. 'What if I told you I could lay my hands on both the missing paintings? Naturally, there would be a fee involved.'

'Naturally. Are you saying you know who the anonymous buyer was?'

Demus smiled and picked at the crumbs from his plate.

'Not only that, but I happen to know they already owned one of the paintings. I've been working on this project for some time. Long before you came to me. Some of my enquiries are bearing fruit. The downside of gaining information is, even with my levels of discretion and secrecy, questions can attract attention. Eventually, certain people will join the dots, and you would have powerful competition in your search. But to have any chance of success we must move quickly. If I could obtain both pictures, you would have all five. You stand to make a huge profit.'

'If I were to sell, maybe. I'm a collector. Owning them would be my reward.'

'It must be nice to be wealthy enough to contemplate not cashing in. If only I were in that position. Alas, I have a minor problem with the authorities.'

Where the hell was he going now? Docherty got there before I did.

'Would that problem ease if certain funds you had were suddenly legitimised?'

Demus made a point of looking around the room. Three tables away, a baby wailed. Docherty scowled towards the table, then realised the mother had recognised him. The scowl instantly flicked to a warm smile. The woman blushed and fussed with the screaming child. I watched as the other two leant forward, heads almost touching across the table.

'I believe I can make your rival's desire for the paintings disappear,' said Demus, blue eyes catching the sunlight streaming through a window. 'In return, I expect my large lump sum to become…legitimate. The fee for your service, I believe, is £150,000. The fee for my services, therefore, is identical to yours. You only need to pay for the paintings. I believe a similar amount will persuade them to part with the items and clinch the purchase. Do we have a deal?'

'We do. Get me the two paintings. We have a new series of *Millionaire's Row* filming next month. Let me know who will represent you on the show.'

The two of them shook hands. I didn't merit a second glance as Docherty rose from his seat and headed for the door. Prick.

'More tea, Frankie? I feel a celebration is in order. I'll even throw in two pieces of shortbread.'

He picked up the tray and headed for the counter. I helped myself to Docherty's scone.

33

The last thing I needed today was another encounter with Docherty, but I couldn't avoid it. He never even mentioned it yesterday, but today was the rehearsal at Wetwang Hall. It had come around so quickly. Satnav wasn't needed today. The estate and gardens were just off the main road, barely twenty miles from Mum and Dad's house.

If the wrought-iron gates at Docherty's house were the entrance to a world of poor taste, this place was the opposite. It positively screamed old money and political influence. The gates were open. Just inside was a clipboard-wielding man in a high-vis jacket. I had to admit I got a buzz from announcing myself as an art historian. The man told me to follow the road towards the rear of the house where the production team was based.

The Yorkshire stone glowed in the morning sunshine. The hall was impressive. I'd looked it up last night. The original building was a simple, if sizeable, house on three floors. Four downstairs windows on either side of a double width oak door. In the nineteenth century, new wings added grandeur, tripling the width, and forming an impressive courtyard at the back. As I rounded the building, I could see the sheer scale of the space. Three enormous trucks were tucked into one corner beside a row of equally impressive motorhomes. Another high-vis jacket waved me towards a space in a row of cars and I was told to report to the first motor home. Docherty's PA, Yasmin, strode towards me. I couldn't help thinking life would've been easier if Demus was playing the role of expert, but his previous relationship with the woman in front of me had ruled this out.

At least she was efficient. In seconds, she'd whipped through the dos and don'ts for the time on-site, pointed out the access gate that I'd need to use on the day and waved at where the toilets were. When we got to the largest of the motorhomes, she leant closer, and spoke as if confiding in me.

'Johnny's waiting for you. He's in a foul mood. I think the extra pressure of this week's show going out live.'

'Does it always go out live?'

'Special edition for the hundredth show. The network felt it would add a certain frisson.'

'Frisson? It adds a whole new level of terror for me.'

'Don't worry about it. Just concentrate on your words and leave the worrying to me. Good luck.'

She smiled and gestured at the door. Inside, Docherty sat at a polished walnut desk. He barely registered I was there before standing and moving across to a pair of armchairs. He waved me towards one.

'What do you know about Blue Eyes?'

I sensed that was as close to being wished a good morning as I could hope for. What was going on? At least we'd rehearsed a back story.

'We met at a conference around ten years ago. A mutual acquaintance introduced us. He was looking for someone to broker a deal. We worked together many times after that.'

'Do you trust him?'

Where was this going? Demus had reminded me to give the impression of considering my answers and appearing relaxed. I was suddenly bricking it.

'He's never given me any reason not to trust him.'

'Is that the same thing?'

'I, err, think so. Look, Blue Eyes has his own business. I have mine. Would I do business with all the people he does? Maybe not. As I say, he's always been professional in our dealings. Is there a problem?'

'I'm not sure. Yasmin brought this to my attention this morning.'

He handed me an iPad. I read the article that was open and went cold.

Police are investigating the death of a Korean business owner. A dog walker discovered a body on a remote Yorkshire beach this morning. Police later confirmed it as Mr David Won, aged 40. They believe Mr Won was in the UK to negotiate the purchase of several valuable pieces of art. His family have been contacted…

'I don't follow,' I said, truthfully.

'David Won was 40. *DW40* was the name of the buyer at the auction. Yesterday, your mate offered to make the purchaser reconsider his desire to own the paintings.'

'You don't think…'

He obviously thought. Had Demus really killed *DW40*? I felt sick. Then it hit me. We'd made-up *DW40*. It was Gabby typing on a keyboard. Murdering his sister was definitely extreme. What the hell was going on?

'How did Yasmin know about *DW40*?'

'She knows everything. I trust her with every aspect of my life. Can I extend that same trust to you, Mr Defoe?'

'Me? What have I done?'

'You introduced me to him. If he's now done—'

'I'm sure there's a rational explanation. We don't know for sure this man is *DW40*, let alone that D—' I stopped just in time. 'That Blue Eyes had anything to do with this.'

'Seems like an awful coincidence, if you ask me. Any idea why he's not answering his phone this morning?'

'I've no idea. Let me try him.'

'No time now. We have a strict schedule today. I need to make sure the preparations are going smoothly. I should be ready for you in about an hour. You can wait in the trailer next door. Yasmin will be in touch.'

MY LEGS WERE like jelly as I made my way to the other trailer. I really had to find out what was going on. A laminated sign on the door of the trailer announced it as the Green Room. Luckily, it was unoccupied. I placed a pod in the machine and made myself a tiny coffee. Four of these might do the trick. Then again, I was already jittery. I texted Demus. It was short and to the point. Two minutes later, my phone vibrated. After checking that nobody was listening at the door, I almost hissed into the phone.

'What the hell is going on?'

'Morning, Mr Defoe. I take it he's seen the article?'

'He has. I suspect you were somehow responsible. How did you know he'd find it?'

'Ah, well. It turns out, Yasmin dislikes Docherty far more than she dislikes me. She's been helping for the last few days. Angel played a blinder, getting the story onto a certain website. From there, it was only a matter of time before lazy journalists and bots spread it as true.'

'Couldn't you have warned me?'

'Improv – remember? You've got to trust me.'

'So, you haven't really murdered anybody?'

'No. Of course not. Not yet, anyway.'

'Not funny.'

'It is a bit, surely?' I could almost hear him grinning. Grudgingly, I joined him.

'I suppose I should've known you wouldn't have killed *DW40*.'

'She's my sister. Would be awkward at Christmas, wouldn't it?'

He had a point.

'So, what happens next?'

'I gather from Yasmin that you're at Wetwang Hall?'

'Yes. Some kind of rehearsal.'

'Good. I'm on my way. Now that Yasmin's onside, I can pay you all a visit. Keep your chin up.'

The phone went dead. He was enjoying this far too much. My nerves were shredded, and it was only Wednesday.

I'D JUST USED a third coffee pod when Yasmin appeared at the door of the motorhome. Now that I knew she was a collaborator, should I have given her some kind of signal? Then again, she probably knew more about the plan than I did. Anyway, there was no time for all that, and she whisked me away across the estate.

It was like a small town was being built in the grounds of Wetwang Hall. Yasmin explained that Johnny's pieces to camera would be done by the lake, with the house in the background. Food trailers were being positioned already. Seeing them reminded me that Justin and Robbie would be here on the day selling ice creams to the hordes of Yorkshire pensioners.

In the near distance, I could see a substantial stage being erected.

'That's the set for the game show element,' said Yasmin. 'It's still classed as a building site at the moment, so I can't take you there.' She paused. 'And here is where we'll do your section.'

It was a tent. She must've seen the look of disappointment on my face.

'I thought I'd have the lake and house in the background.'

'Afraid not. We used to film these segments in the open, but there was always some idiot who thought it was funny to bare their arse or swear at the camera.'

'Bad pensioners.' We both laughed. Did my parents know what they were getting involved with? That reminded me. I still had to work out how to deal with my part in the show vis-à-vis my mother. Did I trust her to keep my identity a secret or did I try to deceive the woman who'd looked after me for the last forty years? That was a decision for this afternoon.

'Doing it this way means we can get a handful of invitees clustered around to look like a crowd and cut to shots from the grounds.'

Yasmin introduced me to a cameraman called Martin, then got me to take a seat behind a rickety-looking table.

'You'll sit here. The couple who own the pictures will sit here.' She gestured to the other two seats. It seemed fairly straightforward so far. 'The pictures will be on the easel. Obviously, these are just photocopies, but they're the correct size. We'll have the real ones on the day. You need to be comfortable with the position of them and the camera when you're talking. We used to just wing it, but the number of experts who proved to be incapable of doing five minutes on screen without knocking the easel over was incredible. So, I'll be a little old lady. You do your bit and Martin will film you. It'll give us approximate timings and spark any points that you need to cover. Any questions?'

My crucial question was, could I run away? The thought of having to speak about the paintings for five minutes and not make a tit of myself was terrifying. All too soon, Yasmin was counting me in. I remembered to ask her how she came to own the paintings, then launched into my spiel. By the time I finished, I was acutely aware of the droplets of sweat making their way down my spine and pooling in the back of my trousers. Classy. At least I got through my five minutes without knocking the easel over.

'Cut. Thanks, Mr Defoe.'

'How did I do? Not too long, I hope?'

Yasmin looked at her clipboard.

'Two minutes, seventeen seconds. Don't worry. We'll run through it again later. I've jotted down a few things you missed out. Slow down your delivery a bit. And you may like to take a breath every now and again. I don't want you passing out through oxygen deprivation. On the next run through, I'll play the part of the couple and throw in a few questions. That should help. Back in a minute.'

Yasmin patted my shoulder as she stood up. I looked at the notes. Apparently, I hadn't described which shops featured in the pictures, or where they were. Or who painted them. Or when. Or the tasty-looking bread at the bakery. Other than that, I was spot on. Martin confirmed I'd be OK to nip out for a few minutes. I made a beeline for a row of Portaloos. I was about to enter when it hit me. Were they in use yet? The last thing I needed was for them to be hitched to a truck and driven off to the other side of the estate. It was only when one of the crew emerged from the end one that I convinced myself it would be OK.

I survived both the Portaloo and the second rehearsal. Four minutes, twenty seconds and I quite enjoyed it (the rehearsal, not the Portaloo). Yasmin confirmed she was happy, then threw me completely with her next question.

'What are you planning to wear on the day?'

I'd not given it a thought. At least Jen had made sure I now had a respectable range of smart shirts rather than the music T-shirts I'd worn every day in the past. Yasmin took pity on me.

'Go for something nice and simple. No day glow swirls and stripes. They play havoc with the cameras.'

'I think I can manage that.'

Yasmin touched a finger to an ear. Was that the signal? Should I reciprocate? Turned out to be her earpiece. She touched it again.

'You have a visitor in the Green Room. Old Blue Eyes is back.'

She winked theatrically. I knew there'd be a secret signal.

Demus looked very much at home. I suppose he spent a lot of his life on a film or TV set. I accepted the offer of coffee without thinking of the effect it would have on my jitters.

'We're seeing his lordship in ten minutes,' said Demus.

'What? In the big house?'

'No, not that lordship. Calm down. I meant little Lord Megalomaniac out there. I have something for him.'

He tapped the package that was propped against his chair.

'Any little surprises I should know about?'

'Trust me.'

I didn't like the grin. He was up to something. As we drank our coffee, a familiar voice began barking out instructions to some poor junior assistant. Whatever manner of cockup the woman had perpetrated, Docherty deserved everything that was coming his way. The entire room reverberated to the slamming of the door just feet from where we sat. Yasmin's head appeared at the door.

'Mr Docherty will see you now.'

The smirk on her face suggested she hadn't quite forgiven Demus for his past behaviour. She was looking forward to this. I wasn't.

Demus checked his immaculate tie in the mirror, picked up the parcel, and turned to me.

'Shall we?'

Yasmin waved us through the door. Docherty was drinking hideous looking green sludge. That may account for his bad mood. The pair of them swapped pleasantries. My presence barely seemed to register with him. I was the hired hand. Blue Eyes was important. Docherty appeared wary and locked eyes with the man sitting opposite.

'I sense you're conflicted,' said Demus.

'Concerned.'

'Tell me your concerns, Mr Docherty. I may be able to help.'

I squirmed, the tension triggering a low rumble from deep inside my body. Docherty paused before reaching for the iPad. He passed it across without comment. Demus took his time, scanning the article twice before handing back the tablet.

'That didn't seem to come as a surprise to you,' said Docherty.

Demus smiled and leant forward, his face inches from Docherty's.

'Hardly. I'm not sure what you expected, Mr Docherty. We reached an agreement. I would remove your opponent and obtain the merchandise. In return, you would provide me with a service. Rather sizeable sums of money were part of the agreement. I hope we still have an agreement, Mr Docherty. My associates view breach of contract very…seriously.'

This time, the rumble within my stomach broke for cover. Both men glared at me.

'Sorry,' I said, squirming to prevent a recurrence. A switch flicked. Docherty was charming once again.

'Not at all. No need for any alarm. As you say, large sums are at stake here. I just prefer to know what I'm dealing with. I'm assuming, like me, you have an emergency exit plan in place. Just in case.'

'You mean a cosy hideout, a precaution. Somewhere well out of UK police jurisdiction?'

'Exactly. South America has several such attractions. My estancia is particularly attractive at this time of year. As you say, merely a precaution.' Docherty blessed us with his TV smile. He actually thought he was impervious to the law. 'I take it you have the merchandise?' He nodded at the package. 'May I?'

He was in. Pure greed swept away the suggestion that Blue Eyes could've killed a man. Demus opened the ribbon holding the package in place. Some of Docherty's poise evaporated as Demus handed over the two paintings. *The Pub* and *The Baker* joined *The Florist*, and he was like I was at Christmas as a child. All that stood between Docherty and six million pounds were the two remaining paintings. That, and the fact they were fakes. He was going to be well pissed off when he found out. Excellent.

'I'll have Yasmin transfer the balance immediately. A pleasure doing business with you, Blue Eyes. Mr Defoe, perhaps you could ask Yasmin to step inside.'

He'd dismissed me again. Yasmin was already on her way when I stepped outside. Demus followed, and we walked back to the car park together.

'That went rather well, I'd say, Frankie.'

'Remind me never to play cards with you. We have him hooked. How do we actually bring him down?'

'If only we had every word recorded. I'm sure the police would find the conversation fascinating.'

I stopped and gawped at Demus. He didn't even break stride, staring straight ahead until he reached his car.

'Every word, Frankie. Every word.' He tapped the badge on his lapel. It was then I noticed the tiny black circle on Buddy the Labrador's coat. He was wearing a wire. 'Right. The rest is on you and your parents if we're to totally humiliate him. Good luck. I'll see you soon.'

The two remaining paintings were less than twenty miles away at my parents' house. They were going to enjoy their day on telly. I needed to make sure they were ready. Half an hour later, my dad greeted me at their front door.

34

We sat at the kitchen table and drank tea. Mum had taken herself for a siesta.

'She been on the sherry?'

Dad laughed and shook his head.

'Nay, lad. She's always tired these days. A nap in the afternoon just livens her up a bit for watching telly later.'

'You look tired.'

'I am, son. There seems to be more and more to do every day.'

'How does that affect your memory?'

'When I get tired, I get a bit confused. This thing saves my life.'

He slid a spiral notebook across the table. It was full of reminders and lists. Items ticked off; others crossed out. Some repeated.

'It was certainly a good tip from the dementia group. Any progress on getting Mum there?'

'She won't have it. Says she's too tired. Gets annoyed when I push her. I don't know what we're going to do.'

'Well, the good news is that my friend Daisy has pulled a few strings and got you high up on the waiting list for the sheltered housing.'

He looked puzzled. Then I realised he didn't have a clue what I was talking about.

'My mistake. I thought I'd told you. I must've forgotten.' He seemed to believe me, and I explained again, from the beginning.

'Won't we need to sell this place before we could move?'

'Don't worry about that. I'll organise everything.'

I bought myself a moment by making a fresh pot of tea. If he'd forgotten something as big as moving house, how was he coping with Mum? She was even worse. I was losing both of them. Time was slipping away. As I got back to the table, Dad was scribbling another note. He saw me looking.

'I need to book a taxi for Saturday.' Before I could ask why, he pointed at the calendar on the wall. A series of neat crosses covered every day of the month so far. Today was clear. There was a big red circle around the twentieth. 'It's *Treasure Trove* at Wetwang on Saturday.'

The system of reminders seemed to work. Could Mum really handle her role in the deception? Could I? Before I could have the conversation, my secret phone burst into life.

'Sorry, work.'

'I'll get the pictures ready before I forget.'

As Dad set off to the living room, I answered the call.

'Johnny, how can I help?'

'I've been thinking about the two missing pictures. I want to conclude this as quickly as possible. You need to contact the old biddies and convince them to sell. No need to tell the world that the paintings have surfaced. You can go up to ten grand for the pair. Just make it happen. I want those paintings by tonight.'

'But what about the gap in the show?'

'Let me worry about that. There's plenty more suckers with tat to peddle.'

'Isn't that a bit unfai—'

'Do I have to remind you of the contact you signed? You work for me, not them. I'll compensate you for not appearing in the show. Yasmin will text you their details. Call them now, then let me know when I can expect delivery.'

I realised my next words went to dead air. He really was an unpleasant piece of work. Seconds later, I was looking at a text detailing my parents' names and contact details. I wanted nothing more than to tell him to stick his TV show where the sun would make his eyes water.

I had to admit, getting them to sell the pictures to Docherty now would solve a problem. How do I sit at a table with my parents and fool them into thinking I'm an art expert called Alexander Defoe? Do I let them in on the secret and trust them to pull off the deception? Do I somehow crank up the disguise and try to fool them? Who was I kidding? The best bet was to persuade them to sell. We could still bring down Docherty with what we had already. It just wouldn't involve the public humiliation he richly deserved.

'Hello, son. How long have you been here? You should've shouted. I was just getting these ready. I need to order a taxi for Saturday. Don't let me forget.'

'Hi, Dad. Sit down a minute. I've got something to ask you.'

'Sounds serious.'

'No. It should be good news. The TV people have been in touch with me. They want to offer to buy the paintings from you, rather than going to all the trouble of trekking to Wetwang and hanging around all day.'

'But what about being on telly? Your mum's set her heart on being on. She's got a new hat and everything.'

'But the trip to Wetwang and all the standing around. It would tire her out.'

'No. She's been looking forward to this for ages. I've not seen her so excited in years. It's the only thing she talks about. This isn't about the money. It's more important than that.'

I could see the pain in Dad's eyes at the thought of disappointing Mum. There was no way I could do it. I'd have to call Docherty back and tell him it was no deal.

'Don't worry about the taxi, Dad. Jen's going to come and pick you up. I've got some stuff to do for work so I can't make it. But she'll make sure you get there OK.'

'Hasn't she got loads to do? Organising a funeral's not easy.'

He'd remembered Ben had died and was thinking about others before himself. Typical.

'It's all arranged for next week, Dad. She's looking forward to a day out with you at the weekend. I'm hoping to get finished with work in time to join you for that afternoon tea you promised me. Look, Jen'll be wondering where I've got to. I'm going to have to get back. Give my love to Mum, and I'll see you on Saturday.'

Leaving abruptly was the only way I could cope with the emotions swirling through me. Back in the car, I took the easy option and called Yasmin. I explained they'd insisted they were going on the show. She told me not to worry, she'd deal with her boss. As I drove home, I had just one thing to worry about. How the hell was I going to pull this off?

I CALLED JEN as soon as I got on the road.

'You sound a bit down. Is everything OK?'

'Just worried about Mum and Dad. They're both struggling.'

I explained the events of the afternoon. She listened patiently as I unloaded.

'Get yourself home safely. I need to pick up Charley from Stella's. Ambrose has been so great getting her all week, I was going to call and buy them a bottle of wine as a thank you. How I about I get one for us and we order the takeaway of your choice?'

'That sounds nice. We need to get our thinking caps on, too. How am I going to fool Mum and Dad into thinking I'm an art historian on a TV show? I didn't risk telling them the plan.'

'I'm sure we can come up with something. I'll see you in an hour or so.'

The rest of the drive went in a blur. In the early days of driving, I would never have believed that it was possible to drive sixty miles with no recollection of any of it. It came as a surprise to be pulling up at home.

I announced my arrival from the front door, and Charley came hurtling towards me. She was excited about something.

'I did a picture of you.'

'That sounds lovely. Where is it?'

'Kitchen.'

I carried her through before she wriggled out of my arms.

'Careful,' called Jen as she came for a hug.

Charley was back. The picture looked like a scarecrow.

'I thought you said it was me?'

She collapsed in the familiar giggles.

'It is. You look like Worzel Gummidge.'

I tickled the artist, not something we art historians do very often.

'It's very good,' I said. 'Not sure how I feel being told I look like Worzel Gummidge, though.'

'She's got a point,' said Jen. 'It's the beard.'

'Actually, I was going to ask you to trim it later. Tidy me up for my TV appearance on Saturday.'

'Don't worry about that. I've got an idea.'

She returned to the hob.

'Something smells nice,' I said.

'I was making a batch of pasta sauce to keep madam here happy for a week or two. Tomato and fennel sausage. Life was simpler when beans on toast was the height of her culinary experience.'

'Don't suppose we could have some, too? I'm starving.'

'Of course. You sure you're not sickening for something?'

'How do you mean?'

'Turning down a takeaway of your choice.'

'There's a first time for everything. I can think of nothing I want more tonight than to eat pasta with my wife and daughter.'

'OK. Make yourself useful and open the wine.'

Charley took that as her cue to set the table. How come I got so lucky to marry into this wonderful family? Worzel took pride of place on the fridge door. Whatever happened at the weekend, Jen and Charley would make everything feel better.

It was good to all eat around the table together. The usual routine involved Charley eating early and being shipped off to bed before we settled down. Her capacity to eat olives was amazing for one so young. Jen had often said that our daughter would love to exist on a diet of pasta and olives.

Jen supervised Charley's bath before bed while I stacked the dishwasher. I was extremely pleased when Charley demanded that I read the bedtime story. By eight o'clock we'd settled on the sofa, Elbow providing the music. As usual, I spoke to the top of Jen's head as she snuggled under my arm. I loved the smell of her hair, much to her amusement.

35

Whoever said 'feel the fear and do it anyway' had never had to cope with my digestive system. The more I thought of what I had to do on Saturday, the more my brain (and stomach) turned to mush.

Yesterday had turned into nightmare of forgotten facts and botched rehearsals. Every time I ran through my valuation, I forgot something different. Demus called a halt when I was finally reduced to sitting on the floor and sobbing.

'Why did this have to be the live show?'

'Try to put that bit out of your mind,' said Demus. 'It's going to be you and your parents sitting at a desk.'

'With a cameraman beaming every word to millions of people.'

'But I can guarantee they'll all love the entertainment when Docherty gets his comeuppance. You don't have to be word perfect. Being live is actually a benefit. Whatever happens, they have to just keep going, at least until the ad break. Just visualise your triumph. That's all that matters. If all else fails, just throw up on lIve TV.'

That just brought back memories of my appearance on The One Show and started the whole cycle of worry again.

At least today was Friday. My day at the hospice. It was strange going back there without Ben, but helping the writing group took my mind off everything else. Besides, feeling sorry for yourself was banned by Daisy. Her pep talk was short and sweet.

'What's the nightmare scenario? You make a dick of yourself on primetime Saturday night national telly. Some people have made a career of doing just that. Besides, you should be used to it.'

It's having friends like this that keeps me going.

With Saturday looming, I was glad of another cosy night on the sofa with Jen.

'How're you feeling, you know…'

Jen took a sip of wine.

'I'm calm. I think that's the best way to describe it. So much of the last year was spent dashing around, worrying about my parents. Dad was very clever, the way he talked about what he wanted once he'd gone. He told me not to feel sad. Can you believe that? He also said not to feel guilty if it was all a bit of a relief when it was all over.'

'He talked to me about that, too.'

'I think, in the end, he was at peace. Ready to go. He'd had enough of being prodded and poked, poisoned, drugged, and operated on. Dad was tired and determined to have a good rest. He said if there was an afterlife it could bloody well wait until he was ready.'

I knew without looking that Jen was smiling and weeping at the same time. We sat for a while, comfortable with the silence.

'After the funeral, I want to get back to work straight away. That was another thing that Dad insisted on. No snivelling, as he put it.'

'Only if you're ready for it. Flic's not putting any pressure on us to finish the script. Demus seems to have designs on being a full-time undercover agent.'

'It's good that you get on so well with him.' She took another sip of wine. 'What time is it?'

I looked at my watch.

'Ten to nine.'

'Come on. I've got plans for you.'

'Wehey. Before nine on a weekday? Mrs Dale, you're insatiable.'

'Not that, plonker. We have a disguise to work on. Come on. Kitchen, now. And get your shirt off.'

'What the hell are you going to do to me?'

The answer came as an evil smelling bottle of hair dye. They say that blonds have more fun. It appeared I was about to find out if that was true.

I'd had bright red hair as a kid. It had gradually got darker over the years until the appearance of some grey at the temples. Blond had never been on the cards before. I sat at the kitchen table with an old towel around my shoulders. Jen took to her task with enthusiasm and was soon inspecting her handiwork from all angles.

'Are you sure this is a good idea? Shouldn't we have had a professional to do this?'

'Relax. This isn't my first rodeo. I did it to myself when I was still at school, so I know what I'm doing. Well, I do now.'

'How do you mean?'

'I got the mix wrong. My hair went green. Cost a fortune to get it sorted out. I was washing up for months to pay off the debt.' She put both hands on my shoulders to block my attempted escape. 'Sit. What's the worst that could happen?'

'I could be on telly tomorrow with green hair.'

'No. Don't worry. It would more likely just fall out. The big difference is that I've read the instructions this time. Now, look up. I need to do the beard to make it look right.'

When she was happy, I was handed a book and told to keep quiet for thirty minutes. She had stuff to do. That statement was even more chilling than the rest of it.

Eventually, it was back to the sink for rinsing. I began to towel my hair dry before the big verdict. I rubbed at the beard too, then opened my eyes.

'Shit. What the f—'

'Calm down. It's only a ponytail.'

'I thought it was some kind of rodent. I'm glad you think it's so funny.'

Jen was helpless and held up the furry creature I'd seen on the draining board.

'It's a hair extension. I've just dyed it the same colour. Tomorrow, Matthew, you'll have yourself a ponytail.' More laughter at my expense. 'Here, have a look.'

She handed me a mirror she'd brought from upstairs. It could've been worse. I wasn't sure about the addition of a ponytail, but I looked roguishly handsome in the mirror.

'Been ages since I had a Barbie.' Jen laughed. Maybe my new look wasn't a keeper. She took my hand. 'Come on. Let's see if blonds really have more fun.'

Maybe it was a keeper after all.

36

Despite the sunshine, there was a cool, early morning breeze. It didn't help. I was sweating already. One last check in the rear-view mirror. The ponytail was still in place. It felt as if Jen had welded it to my scalp. Charley's reaction had dented confidence in my new look. She mentioned My Little Pony. For a six-year-old, she had a powerful way with words.

I locked the car and strode towards the production trailer. Yasmin was waiting.

'Wow. Bit of a change of image.'

'Too much?'

'No. You look great. Very Brad Pitt. Sort of.' Did she really need to add *sort of* to that sentence? Yasmin paused as the roar of an engine drowned any possibility of conversation. She pointed behind me to where a helicopter was gently touching down.

'Is that Docherty?'

'His new toy,' said Yasmin. She didn't bother to hide a smirk. 'He can't possibly be expected to use roads full of pensioners. He's a star, don't you know?'

'Prick.'

I followed her into *the Green Room*. Any nerves I was feeling up to that point were nothing compared to a fresh horror. There were other people. Somehow, I'd never even thought that there were other experts on the show. Genuine experts, who knew their stuff. They also knew how it all worked, excusing them from the rehearsal day.

A couple of them I even recognised from watching previous episodes. Yasmin introduced me to everyone. As she left, an older man with untidy white hair shook my hand.

'I take it this is your first time? Welcome aboard, Mr Defoe.'

'Thanks. I'm a little nervous.'

'Nothing to worry about. Nothing at all. I've been at this for years. Surprised we haven't rubbed shoulders before. Where did you study?'

Thanks to the training from Demus and Gabby, I was ready for this. Picking somewhere obscure was all covered in the carefully prepared back story. No chance of anybody challenging the idea.

'I had a bit of wanderlust in my youth. Ended up at Massey University in Wellington, New Zealand.'

'How fascinating. How's Professor Priddy? Not seem him for years.'

What the actual f…? That is not possible.

'Oh, you know. Same as ever, old Priddy. Never changes.'

'Still up to his old tricks then, eh?'

He dug me in the ribs and winked. Not only had I picked somewhere on the other side of the world that this bloke knew, he even seemed to know secrets about the lecturer I thought I'd made-up. I had to get away before my I blew my cover completely. Then I remembered the vape. I held it up in triumph.

'Would you excuse me? Frightfully nervous and addicted to this.'

'Of course, old chap. At least you haven't followed Priddy's example.'

He let out a laugh that I can only describe as filthy. Old Priddy seemed like a character. I stumbled out of the door and away from the trailer. A familiar voice came from over my shoulder.

'Alexander, I'm glad I bumped into you.'

I turned and stared into those piercing blue eyes.

'What are you doing here?'

'I wouldn't miss this for the world. I convinced Docherty to invite me as his guest for the day. Even got an invitation to join him and his lordship in the big house for dinner later.'

'You're actually enjoying this, aren't you?'

'Immensely. Love what you've done with your hair, by the way. *Game of Thrones* awaits.'

'I knew it was a mistake. I look ridiculous.'

'I've looked worse many times, believe me. Besides, you want it to look slightly odd. If you're going to fool your parents into thinking you're Defoe, it has to be good. This way, they'll be looking at the glasses, beard, and ponytail rather than their little lad. Trust me. It's going to be fine.' Demus looked over my shoulder. 'Hello, Yasmin.'

'Mr Eyes. What a pleasant surprise.' There was a case for Yasmin being the better actor in this group. There was no hint of wanting to murder Demus. 'Mr Defoe, could I borrow you for a moment?'

'Of course.'

Demus bowed slightly and left us to it.

'I thought you should see the set for the game show element, now that it's constructed.'

We set off across the site, pausing only to allow two ice-cream vans to overtake us. I did a double take as I recognised the drivers. I'd almost forgotten that Justin and Robbie would be here.

A miniature village had sprung up within the grounds of the hall, complete with bunting strung from any available surface. Already, the smell of fried onions drifted across from one van.

'This looks like a lot of work for one show,' I said.

'It's not just us. We film today, then there's an eighties music festival tomorrow. You should come, bring your wife and daughter.'

'I'm not sure that fits with the picture we've painted of me for your boss.'

'Don't worry about him. He'll be long gone by then. The thought of spending an evening with the public would finish him.'

'Not his cup of tea?'

'No. He'll be sitting at home torturing kittens and counting his money.'

'You don't like him very much, do you?'

'Whatever gave you that idea? He's a stepping stone. If you pull this off today, I see a big step up in my career coming.'

We'd reached the small, natural amphitheatre.

Rows of seating were ready for later. On stage stood five doors, each bearing a large number.

We climbed a flight of stairs and stepped onto the stage.

'So, Docherty will be on the stage by that small blue cross on the floor, with your parents beside him.'

'I thought it was just the winners of the game bit that got through to this stage?'

'It is. They'll win, trust me. He'll call the experts on one by one from the wings.' She opened a curtain for me to see. 'When he introduces you, you'll come through the curtain, carrying the two paintings. Stand beside Docherty so he can make some feeble joke. You'll be the last to be introduced. There'll be two celebs and two other valuers on stage with you. He'll build up to inviting you all to go behind the curtain and choose a door. There's no choice. You go for the fifth door, the blue one. That's very important. Changes every week, but this time it's—'

'The fifth door,' I said, to be helpful and show I'd understood.

'Once you're all behind the doors, the curtain lifts, and Docherty drones on about something, or other. Then it's the big climax. They pick which door they want to be their prize.'

'So, if they correctly pick the fifth door, they win the big cash prize?'

'If only. Whichever door they pick, they win the cabbage – assuming I give you the correct envelope. It's all rigged, obviously. He really is an evil bastard.' I nodded, wondering if I could remember all this. Strange how the fifth door was a repeating pattern at the moment. I was also quite shocked that the game was a fix. Nothing about Docherty should surprise me now. 'I hope you manage to nail him.'

'Me too, Yasmin. Me too,' I said.

'Right. Let's get you back to the Green Room.'

'Is it OK if I don't? It's too stressful. Could I have a walk around the site?'

'OK, but I need you back there in half an hour. Otherwise, Napoleon'll be on the warpath.'

She strode off, already in animated phone conversation. I couldn't resist heading towards Justin's ice-cream van. Angel was busy attaching bunting to the top of the van and a neighbouring vegan juice bar.

'Fancy seeing you here,' I said.

Angel grinned at me but remembered just in time that I wasn't Frankie.

'How are you, Mr Defoe?'

'Bricking it.'

'Love the ponytail. Hang on.' She leant across the van and handed me a cone. I didn't understand why she was laughing quite so hysterically. Then she moved the cone to my forehead. 'Unicorn. Perfect,' she managed before losing all control.

'Everybody's a comedian today.'

Justin leant out of the serving hatch.

'Ignore her, mate. She's hyper at the prospect of working with me all day. Here, try this.'

I accepted the ice cream without thinking of the risk to my pristine shirt. The taste was not what I was expecting.

'Bloody hell. That's good. What? Hang on. I can taste mint and…lamb? Is this lamb and mint sauce ice cream?'

Justin beamed at me.

'I know it shouldn't work, but it's selling like crazy.'

'It's fantastic. Have you perfected the chicken tikka masala yet?'

'Back to the drawing board, I'm afraid.'

'Let's just say it had side effects,' said Angel, completing the bunting. 'Crushed nuts?'

'That's a very old joke.' Angel shrugged and offered me a plastic box, anyway. I dipped the ice cream in. 'Tastes even better, now.'

'Raspberry sauce?'

'I think not.'

'Have you seen Robbie yet?'

'Only as you drove past me earlier.'

'She's hired an assistant for the day. You should say hello.' She pointed to the other van on the opposite end of the site.

'It's on the way back to base. I'll pop by.'

'Good luck today,' said Angel. 'See you later for a few beers.'

I finished the ice cream with no spillage. Maybe it was going to be a good day. The gates were obviously open as the crowds, mainly pensioners, were strolling in the spring sunshine. I picked my way through the throng to Robbie's van to be greeted warmly. It was *who* greeted me that threw me. Gerry.

'I didn't expect to see my mother-in-law selling ice cream,' I said.

'Seemed like a good way to launch my new life. Ben wanted me out and about, trying new things. This is certainly new. And the two of us have a lot of catching up to do.'

She put an arm around Robbie. Today was getting more bizarre by the minute.

'Love what you've done with the hair,' said Robbie, handing me a cone.

'Too late. Angel's already done the unicorn gag.'

'Damn. Knew she was good.'

'Good to see you both. Need to go. My public awaits.'

37

There they were. Mum and Dad sitting in the tent awaiting a valuation expert. Mum's eyes were the size of dinner plates. The last time I'd seen anything like it was Joe at the club a couple of years ago. I was fairly sure it was for a different reason. She nudged Dad as I walked in. This was it. If she recognised me now, it was all over.

'Mr and Mrs Dale? Hello, I'm Alexander Defoe. I'll be valuing your lovely paintings today.'

Mum blushed, but no sign of recognition. She seemed to have lost her tongue and looked at Dad to respond. He, too, seemed oblivious to my true identity. Maybe I could get away with this. Mum's eyes swivelled again at the sound of another voice. It was Docherty. The on-camera persona switched on as he breezed in, cracking one-liners about the fashion choices of a select gathering allowed in the tent.

He shook Dad's hand.

'Mr Defoe. Nice to see your father's de-mob suit still fits.'

Mum actually giggled, then blushed as Docherty kissed her hand. I so wanted to smack him in the mouth, but Mum was loving every minute. Our host explained viewers at home were currently watching a piece he'd recorded earlier. In moment he would introduce this segment before handing over to me for the valuation. I was fumbling for a handkerchief to mop my brow, but a young make-up artist beat me to it. She used a wad of tissues to remove most of the terror-induced sweat from my face, before plastering me in some kind of powder. She looked at my face. I could've sworn she shrugged in a 'buggered if I could do more' way.

Now that Yasmin, the camera, and sound technician had joined the group in the tent, it was cosy, to say the least.

'Quiet, please,' called Yasmin.

She pointed at Docherty, and we were off. In my head, I ran through my opening lines as my nemesis went into full Johnny Doc mode. I had to hand it to him. He was good. Not my cup of tea, but his audience was lapping up every word. Far too quickly, he was saying my name, and stepping out of the shot. I was on.

Despite a croak, I remembered to ask about how long the paintings had been in my parents' possession.

'They were a wedding present just over forty years ago.' My dad spoke as if he was telling Alexa to perform calculus. He was more nervous than I was. As he spoke, I cleared my throat without incident. I nodded encouragement and launched into the next part of my speech. This time, I remembered to cover who'd painted them, when, and where. I made no mention of them being part of a set of five. Docherty had warned me not to risk setting expectations that they could be worth a fortune. Throughout all this, I kept my eyes glued on the paintings sitting on the easel next to my shoulder. I was almost there.

'I think, at auction, we'd be looking at around five to eight thousand for the pair,' I said, hoping I'd reached the finish line.

'Eh? What did he say?' The interruption was from a man who looked like he could've been Lowry's grandad.

'Shh,' hissed the tiny woman beside him. The ensuing silence was filled with one of the loudest farts I'd ever heard. The tent descended into nervous sniggers.

'Cut.' Yasmin tried to stifle her laughter as the woman berated her husband. Then she realised we were doing this live and frantically gestured for me to keep going. She waved at various crew members as if to give instructions while deftly using the clipboard to encourage oxygen into the tent.

A look that could've killed quietened the audience. She pointed at me. As she moved her hand from my eyeline, I could see Mum put her head on one side. Was she pleased at the valuation? It was impossible to tell. I took a breath and launched back into my speech.

'So, I'd estimate the value—'

'That's not right.' I looked in horror at my mother. She was pointing at me. Dad put a protective hand on her arm, but she wasn't about to be silenced. I looked in panic at Yasmin for help. She just shrugged. 'I remember my uncle telling me all about these paintings. He was in his studio, and we'd gone to visit. It was Whit Sunday, and I was showing him my new shoes. When I asked him what he was painting, he said cobblers. I remember my mother telling him not to be rude in front of me, but he explained that the shop window was going to be full of boots and shoes. I asked him what the shop was called, and he said I could name it. That's why the sign says *K. Blake, Cobblers*. Karen Blake was my best friend at school.' My jaw had long ago hit the floor. Docherty reappeared at the entrance to the tent, sensing that something was wrong. 'He told me they'd be worth something one day. Not because he was the artist. He'd painted them on top of some drawings that my aunty had done. Said she was going to be famous. One day, the paintings would be mine, and I had to get somebody to clean off the paint and the ink drawings would still be underneath. I'm surprised at you, Frankie, telling fibs like this. And what the Joe-buggery have you done with your hair? You look like Catweazle. Honestly, what will Jen think when she sees you on telly?'

'Is this true?' Docherty bellowed at me as he pushed through the astonished pensioners. All thoughts of his beloved four million viewers had evaporated in the crisis.

'Bugger me. She's right. Frankie, what are you doing here?' Dad had just caught up. Before I could think, Docherty was inches from my face. I think he'd just realised he'd spent a fortune on pictures that weren't worth millions.

'Do you know this lying scumbag?'

My mum picked up her handbag, ready to defend her son as Yasmin hissed at the cameraman to keep going.

'Don't you take that tone with me, young man.'

'You're right, madam. I apologise. He's the one I've got a problem with.'

With that, Docherty turned to me and connected with a punch to the ribs I never even saw coming. As all the air left my lungs, he hit me again, and my nose exploded. From my position on the ground, I could only see the feet involved in a scuffle. Somehow, I pulled myself to my knees in time to see Demus rush at Docherty. The former boxer's training kicked in and he landed a punch squarely on the famous actor's jaw. Demus fell to the ground beside me. Yasmin screamed and pushed Docherty out of the way. I tried hard to suck oxygen into my lungs. The sight of my friend on the ground and motionless changed everything. Get up, Demus. For God's sake, get up. Yasmin was shaking now. She placed two fingers on his neck and screamed again.

'There's no pulse. You've killed him, Johnny.' She scrabbled at Demus's shirt before launching into CPR. She shouted. 'Call an ambulance.'

Why on Earth had I got us into this? I felt helpless as Yasmin went to work. I wanted to sing 'Staying Alive' but wasn't quite sure why. It all happened so quickly. There was movement in the crowd as silence descended. Docherty didn't hesitate. He legged it. The hard of hearing old man with severe flatulence was pushed out of the way and Docherty took off across the estate. Jen was suddenly beside me. I got to my feet as she fussed over me. I'd got my breath back and looked at the prone body of my friend. For a dead person, he got straight to the point as he opened his eyes.

'Don't just stand there. Get after him.'

Strangely enough, the crowds parted as the blood covered former unicorn threw off his glasses and set off through the entrance of the tent. I could see Docherty ahead, making good ground. In my punch addled state, I reckoned I could catch him. Fifty yards later, my wobbly legs decided otherwise. I couldn't let him escape. Not now we'd come this far. If he reached the helicopter, he could be over the North Sea and out of the country in minutes.

'Frankie. Over here.'

It was Angel, hanging through the serving hatch of the ice-cream van. I summoned all my strength and sprinted for the van, launching myself at the open hatch. My ribs connected with the edge of the counter. For the second time in a few minutes, I was gasping for air. Angel grabbed the back of my trousers and hauled me in. I dropped to the floor of the van, breathing hard.

'For future reference, the door may have been easier,' she said. 'Justin. Step on it.'

There was a grinding of gears and a cloud of blueish smoke before we lurched forward. I tentatively checked for broken ribs and, to my horror, found how much blood there was. I felt faint.

'Come on, plonker. It's raspberry sauce. You landed on the bottle.'

She hoisted me to my feet. To add insult to injury, the box of chopped nuts flew from the shelf above my head and covered me. I was being turned into a dishevelled sundae. I leant out of the window. We were closing on Docherty, but he certainly could shift. We had to slow down to pick our way through the crowds.

'Hit the siren,' shouted Angel.

Justin understood, and the *Match of the Day* theme belted from the speakers. Startled pensioners turned to see the ice-cream van bearing down on them, forty yards of bunting flying behind. It was good to see their survival instincts were still strong. They scattered, and Justin hit the accelerator. The impact on our speed was almost nil. Speed was not top of the list of design features in an ice-cream van. It was no good. Docherty was barely fifty yards from his gleaming helicopter as we approached the car park.

'Stop,' yelled Angel. 'Come on.'

As the van screeched to a halt, she dived headfirst through the hatch and executed a perfect forward roll before sprinting to her motorbike. I tried to do the same and hit the ground like a dropped lasagne. I tried to gulp in air as the bike roared into life.

'Get on,' shouted Angel.

I threw my leg over the seat and held onto Angel as she roared away. We were closing as a trail of bewildered old people thinned out, but we were still fifty yards away. Docherty was slowing, but he was still ahead, ten yards to go. As he reached the door of the helicopter, he turned, and raised his middle finger at me. Angel hadn't given up. Almost there. She applied the brakes. My stomach lurched as I felt the back wheel slide.

'Shit. Hold on,' she screamed.

I closed my eyes as the ground came up to meet us, braced for yet another impact. Instead, Angel somehow controlled the roaring bike. We slid along the ground. That stung a bit, but I was past caring. We spun to a halt just short of the helicopter door as it slammed shut. Docherty grinned at us through the window and pointed towards the sky. He was about to escape.

Seconds later, my old friend, the newly anointed DC Newhouse, strolled around the silent chopper. In his hand, he held a shiny ignition key.

'Think he might need this,' he said. 'Useless without a key.' Tinkle opened the door and invited Docherty to slip into a nice pair of handcuffs. We'd got him.

Angel grinned at me.

'Just realised something. Justin took your key so you couldn't get a johnny. Smirky took the key, and we got a Johnny. Neat,' she said.

'YOU SILLY SOD.'

Jen had a way with words. She flung her arms around me. I winced. Once again, my all-action lifestyle had led to me damaging my ribs – the first such recorded incident of injury by raspberry sauce.

'I'm OK, love. Don't worry. Just banged my – ow.'

The slap in the ribs hurt more than the fall from the bike. I blocked the rest of the slaps as Jen beat out the rhythm as she spoke.

'Will (*slap*) you (*slap*) stop (*slap*) trying (*slap*) to (*slap*) be (*slap*) a hero?' (Pause – *slap*)

'Ow. Sorry. It won't happen again. But we got him.'

Angel had just secured the motorbike and came to join us.

'Hi, Jen.'

'And you're just as bad. Come here.'

'You're not going to start slapping me, are you?'

Instead, Jen threw her arms around Angel.

'I wish you wouldn't lead him astray. He's very impressionable, you know.'

'Here, you might want to give this a decent burial,' said Angel, picking up my estranged ponytail from the ground. Jen pushed it into her pocket.

'Let's not be too hasty.'

I did my best to raise an eyebrow, but the swelling from Docherty's punch made it impossible. Jen seemed to notice my battered eye for the first time and kissed it gently.

'That's nicer than the slapping,' I said, careful not to trigger another onslaught.

Over Jen's shoulder, I could see the blue flashing lights as police reinforcements arrived.

Smirky waved before joining Docherty in the back of the police car. Tinkle sprinted off towards the Portaloos. A familiar face emerged from the newly arrived car. Cagney strode over. For once, he was smiling.

'Well done, Frankie. You've done an excellent job.'

'Thanks.' I shook the outstretched hand. It was unusual for him not to be arresting me. 'How did you know to be here?'

'Your friend, Mr Wolf, has been in touch with us for a couple of weeks. It probably doesn't surprise you I was dubious at first, but he was extremely insistent. DC Newhouse and PC Smith were very persuasive. Your friends, Ambrose and Stella have prepared quite the dossier of evidence against Mr Docherty. Fraud, money laundering, intimidation. You name it, they've found evidence for it. When they told us about the helicopter on site and the possibility of him disappearing overseas, I instructed young Newhouse to take out insurance.' He waved an evidence bag containing the key again for emphasis. 'Useless without a key.' Was there anybody left in the world who didn't know the story? 'Docherty's assistant has been very helpful and has even more evidence from the footage of today's events. All in all, a good day. If you'll excuse us. We have a criminal to lock up.'

Cagney was very pleased with himself. Tinkle was back.

'That eye looks nasty, Frankie. You should get it checked out.' As she spoke, two representatives of St John's Ambulance arrived to do just that. Tinkle's radio squawked something unintelligible. 'Sorry. Paul wants to get off. I'll see you soon.'

After a bit of prodding and poking, the verdict of the medical experts was that I'd had a punch in the face but should be OK. They departed. Angel climbed onto her bike and headed back to the car park. Jen and I strolled, arms linked, in the same direction.

'By the way, what have you done with Charley?'

'She's in the ice-cream van with Mum. Strangely enough, she's been in charge of the raspberry sauce.' I started to laugh, but it hurt. Jen put a protective arm around my waist. 'I meant what I said, you know. No more action hero stuff. We need you now more than ever.'

'I promise to stay out of trouble in the future,' I said.

'Good, because I've got a proposition for you.'

'That sounds like a great idea. Just be careful of the ribs.' That got me another slap. 'Not that…I know I told you not to make grand gestures, but I've got one to make.'

'Oh, yes. What's that?'

'I think I've found us the perfect house.'

'But you said—'

'I know, but this really is perfect, now that we need more space.'

'Now that we've got Docherty, I can go to IKEA—'

'Stuff IKEA. Are you listening to what I'm trying to tell you?'

She grinned at me. Then the penny dropped.

'More space.? Are you preg—'

'Yes. I was planning to tell you tonight, but you wheedled it out of me with your rapier-like logic.'

I squeezed Jen in an enormous hug. Bugger the pain in the ribs. I held her face in my hands and looked into her eyes.

'I'm going to have a baby,' I said, grinning from ear to ear.

'Technically, I think it's me that'll actually have it. But yes, we are about to produce a brother or sister for Charley.'

We strode on for a moment as I mulled over the news.

'You said you'd found the perfect house. Can I see it?'

'You already have.'

'What? The one with the bi-folding doors?'

'No. Afraid not. It's my mum's house. It's perfect. You've said yourself what a terrific house it is for kids to grow up in. Mum's already talking about rattling around on her own. The beauty of it is, she wants our house. She's always loved it, and she wants to be somewhere that Dad knew. What do you think? Could we swap houses?'

'I think that'd be a great idea.'

'Good. Because we've already spoken to the solicitor. He's drawing up the contract.'

38

couple of weeks later, Jen and I arrived at the hospice. I carried a box of books into reception and Jen signed us both in. The small group that had become 'my writers' gathered at the far end of the dayroom. They seemed strangely subdued. I thought the box would've triggered more excitement. Editing the various stories committed to paper by the group had taken up the time while my injuries healed. I'd made each into a small book and had half a dozen copies printed to give to the group.

The journal produced by Ben had been quite substantial. I still had more to edit but had read Ben's own words at his funeral. They were perfect. The day itself had gone well, if funerals could go well. It did precisely what it was meant to do, a way to say goodbye to a much-loved husband, father, grandad, and friend. We all cried. A lot. But we also laughed a lot, particularly when it came to the reading about the coast-to-coast walk last year.

We did as Ben insisted we should and had a celebration of his life in the house that he loved, with the people he loved. Next week, it would be our house. Me, Jen, Charley, and the six centimetres of baby growing happily in his mum were moving in. I told everyone I met that by now the baby's kidneys would work and he could pass urine. He's taking after his dad already.

Just that morning, I received a postcard from Spain. Maya of Northumberland, thanks largely to my solicitor friend, was assured of a settlement with her husband. She was house hunting and planning to become Maya of Benidorm very soon.

The level of chatter increased as everyone picked out favourite bits of their books. There was still one pile on the table. Where was she? One of the young volunteers, Jack, made his way over.

'Message from Lucy. Could you meet her on the ward?'

'Yes. Of course.'

I looked at Jen, and my heart sank. She took my hand, and we walked together through the dayroom, and down the long corridor. The nurses' station was unusually quiet. We entered the ward and spotted Lucy at the far end of the corridor. She waved a hand and pointed at the door behind her.

'She couldn't wait to see you. She's in here,' said Lucy, giving us her full, beaming smile.

We reached the fifth door and went inside. Daisy was in her wheelchair.

'You took your time, didn't you? Hello, Jen. You're exempt from criticism. This big lump, however…fancy getting decked by that ponce from the telly. Come here and give us a hug. No handsy business, though. I get enough harassment from the staff without you starting. Besides, your wife's here. I know it's hard to resist but…' I gave her a hug just to shut her up. It didn't work. 'And you can wipe that sad look off your face as well. I know what you're thinking, but you're wrong. I came in for a bit of a rest. Picked up an infection from some bugger at the hospital. Going home today. Can't wait. Might get a proper cup of tea then.'

'Careful, you. You might end up wearing the next cuppa I make you.' Lucy laughed.

'You know I'm only messing. But a cuppa would go down nicely.'

'You can have it in the dayroom. We're ready to kick you out now. I need the room for somebody more deserving.'

Lucy smiled and left us to it. I squeezed Jen's hand. It couldn't be easy for her, being back in this room. Daisy realised it too.

'Sorry, Jen. I never thought…' she said.

'It's fine. I like what you've done with the place.' Several photos adorned to the wall to make it more like home. 'Besides, it's a very different outcome this time. You seem very well.'

'I am, love. They reckon the cancer's not getting any worse. That's a great result, at the moment. Now I can't wait to get home. Grab my bag and wheel me back to the dayroom. I've got work to do.'

'Oh yes. What are you up to?'

'Well, Frankie, just between us…' She looked around theatrically before dropping her voice. 'I'm coaching Lucy in the dark arts of forging pictures. She's got a genuine talent for it. With my expertise and connections, she has a bright future.'

'So, she's thinking of leaving here?' I said.

'No. Won't hear of it. Far too dedicated. As she put it, nobody likes a goody two shoes. She figures a bit of part-time dodgy dealing would balance the ledger a little. Nobody ever got rich doing the selfless stuff she does. This way, she'll be able to afford the odd treat now and again. Remember, Mum's the word.' She tapped the side of her nose and cackled again.

'By the way,' said Jen. 'Thanks again for getting Frankie's parents to the top of the waiting list. They moved in yesterday. They love it. How on Earth did you manage it?'

'All part of the ill-got gains, I'm afraid. Just as Lucy should be able to afford the odd treat, I've had a few over the years. One of them was the house. It's been my home for years. When I realised I needed more help, I set up the charity and built the extension. The charity gets free use of the building, and I get peace of mind and a nice warm feeling. Everybody wins. Come on, I'm parched.'

Jen took the case, and I reversed Daisy's chariot into the corridor.

'To the teapot,' called Daisy, pointing down the corridor.

Better result this time, I thought as I gently closed the fifth door.

ACKNOWLEDGEMENTS

It's fair to say that this book went through a longer gestation period than most in *The Fifth Series*. I sent an early version to trusted beta readers, as usual. The responses weren't as good as I'd hoped. My editor, as usual, put her finger on what had gone wrong.

A throwaway comment earlier in the series suggested Frankie had things too easy. In trying to give him more problems, I overshot and succeeded in taking away his Frankie-ness. We identified the changes that were needed.

Easy.

Nope!

Making one minor change in A meant that B no longer worked. By changing B, C no longer worked. You get the picture! As a result, I set about re-writing the first two-thirds of the story.

Just to make life interesting, while other people were reading the early draft, I got busy writing the second Carrie Tyler book. I learnt a valuable lesson. A certain mindset is required to write a darkish thriller like *The Price We Pay* or *Fair Play* (Carrie Book Two). There has to be a distinct style in order to chase serial killers or trace missing teenagers. To then switch to Frankie's crazy world was a gigantic leap.

I think I got there, but switching modes took time and energy.

As ever, special thanks to Keith, Linda, Jessica, and Emma. Without you, this book wouldn't exist.

Thanks to Pulp Studios for another great cover design.

I hope you enjoyed *The Fifth Door*. Please take a moment to leave a rating or review on Amazon / Goodreads. They make such a difference.

To make sure you don't miss any news, signup to my Newsletter by visiting royburgess.com

In return, I'll send you a link to download *The Fifth Lolly Stick*, a collection of short stories from the pen of Frankie Dale (sort of).

Frankie and the team will return in 2026.

www.ingramcontent.com/pod-product-compliance
Lightning Source LLC
Chambersburg PA
CBHW011032190726
48290CB00011B/2810